THE LION, THE LAMB, THE HUNTED

THE LION, THE LAMB, THE HUNTED

ANDREW E. KAUFMAN

THOMAS & MERCER

The characters and events portrayed in this book are fictitious. Any similarity to real persons, living or dead, is coincidental and not intended by the author.

Published by Thomas & Mercer

PO Box 400818
Las Vegas, NV 89140

ISBN-13: 9781611099744
ISBN-10: 1611099749
Library of Congress Control Number: 2012922578

To my readers

My blood runs reckless and untamed

CHAPTER ONE

Black Lake Cemetery was a study in contrasts. A velvety lawn, vibrant and lush, shrouded by people in dark attire with vacant expressions—all aimed toward the focal point, a slick mahogany casket perched over a shadowy hole.

I allowed my eyes to settle there for a moment, along with my thoughts, but nothing good came of it, just a grim and sobering realization.

There wasn't enough dirt on this earth to bury that much evil.

I forced my attention away from my mother's grave, fidgeted with my tie to loosen the knot. This place was hotter than the hinges of hell, an oppressive blanket of humidity and temperatures climbing to heights so ambitious that even my eyelids were sweating. Summertime in Georgia, just as I'd always remembered. I hadn't been back in years. I hadn't missed much. Listening to the preacher, I felt like I was attending a funeral for a stranger—and in a way, I was. Dedicated and loving? I must have missed that day.

I moved on to the crowd, recognized less than half of them. An outsider looking in—that's all I was—surrounded by sharp glares and astonished whispers: *What's he doing here?*

Welcome home.

So nobody expected me to show. I got that. Not sure *I* expected me to show. Don't know why, but I felt compelled to do it. I suppose some part of me needed to close the door on her once and for all, to see she was really gone.

Cancer of the spine. Apparently she'd complained of back pain for months but never bothered seeing a doctor. Typically stubborn, and she paid the price for it. Diagnosis to death: less than three weeks. I arrived just in time to see her go.

It had been at least fifteen years since I'd last seen my mother. I found a mere shadow of the woman I remembered: thin, frail, and conscious only long enough to hiss her parting words at me. All three of them.

"Fix your hair."

That was it. That was her. With all the pain and suffering, her venom still managed to find its way to the surface one last time.

Then she drifted off. Never opened those joyless eyes again.

The crowd began to disperse. I turned from her coffin and began walking to my car. Then I heard a faint, familiar voice behind me. I glanced back and saw Uncle Warren doubling his steps to catch up. Too late to pretend I didn't hear him.

"Doing okay, Patrick?" he asked, sidling up beside me, his tone a strange hybrid of disingenuous and awkward concern.

I forced a polite smile, kept walking. "Fine. You?"

"All right, I suppose." He let out a long, labored sigh, as if the moment required it. "You know…it's hard, all this."

I half smiled, half nodded. Half believed him. And kept walking with my gaze on the pavement.

"So," he said. The sudden bright tone in his voice startled me. "How're things at the magazine?"

"Great. You know…busy."

A seemingly endless pause stretched between us, and then he said abruptly, "Your momma was a good woman."

It sounded more like an argument than a fact. I gave no response. The comment didn't deserve one. I also wondered when senators started using words like *momma*.

He continued, "You're still coming by the house to take care of the paperwork, right?"

I nodded tentatively. Apparently, he'd set up a trust account for me years ago. I didn't need his money, didn't want it, and I planned on telling him so. I just figured his sister's gravesite wasn't the place to do it.

"And I hope you'll stay in town for a bit," he added.

"Leaving tomorrow," I replied, a little too quickly.

"Then maybe you can come by the house, see if there's anything you want. You know, sentimental items."

That stopped me in my tracks. I stared at him for a long moment, then said, "You just don't get it, Warren, do you?"

"Get what?"

I looked away, shook my head.

He started to say something, stopped, then let out a quiet, exasperated sigh.

I reached for my car keys, fumbled with them, then felt his hand on my shoulder. I don't know why, but something really bumps at my nerves when people do that, and Warren does it a lot. It wasn't the only reason I found him irritating, but it was one of them.

"Patrick," he said with a stern and level stare. The hand stayed on my shoulder. "I'd really like for us to have some quality time together."

I thumbed through my keys some more without looking at him, my discomfort swelling to colossal proportions.

"You know," he continued, his tone now bordering on preachy, "you *could* spare a little time for family."

Then he paused and stared at me as if waiting for a response.

I gave none.

Instead, I got in my car, drove away.

~

I pulled up the winding drive that led to Warren's mansion, a garish, white monstrosity on the edge of Lake Hathaway. Think modern-day Tara surrounded by water and screaming new money. I'd spent a good part of my childhood here. My mother had liked to drop me off under the pretense of giving me a week-end with Warren—male-bonding time, I guess—but really it was more a dumping ground than anything else, a way to get me out of her hair. Not that I'd minded. I came from a less-than-modest cookie-cutter bungalow, and Warren's spread was like a trip to Disneyland. I'd swim, boat on the lake, and play on the twelve-plus acres. Warren was usually away on business, and it had been like having the place all to myself, along with a staff of ten waiting on my every need.

Now I walked into the living room, and, swear to God, it was as if time stood still: every conversation killed, every head turned, and every eye trained on me. Awkward doesn't come close to describing what I felt as I moved through the crowd, disapproval hovering over me like a menacing cloud. I pretended that I didn't care, but inside I knew this was a big mistake.

What the hell was I thinking?

Actually, that was the problem; I hadn't been.

Realizing it was too late to turn around, that I'd look even more foolish if I did, I got the hell out of there and headed toward the one place where I knew I could find refuge: the library.

I descended the steps, walked inside, and breathed in its dis-tinctive scent, the one I loved: paper and binding glue, seasoned by time. The combination had a calming effect on me as a kid and was doing the same now. I felt my nerves untangle.

I loved it here, loved everything about it—the way it looked with the endless array of books stacked across all four walls, the feeling of running my fingers across the leather-bound spines. I'd often sit in the corner, sometimes for hours, lost in imaginary exploration. For me, reading was adventure, but most of all, reading was escape—escape from a life I never understood. Opening a book felt like taking a trip someplace else. Someplace better. Tom Sawyer, Huck Finn, the Hardy Boys—these were my friends. It didn't matter that they weren't real; they were there, always, whenever I needed them. And the best part: *she* couldn't go with me.

I walked across the mirror-slick wood floors, then reached up to a shelf for *Oliver Twist*. Running my fingers over the words, I smiled and remembered.

"Patrick?"

I swung around to find Tracy Gallagher grinning at me. The sight of her made my heart speed up, but I wasn't sure if it was the hormones or the nerves—probably both. She was older now, but man, she still looked great.

I guess you could say Tracy was my first love; the only problem was, she never knew it. She had lived three houses down from me, and I would have moved heaven, earth, and everything in between to be with her. A classic case of unrequited love. We were good friends while we were young—that is, until adolescence set in. Then the social pecking order kicked into gear, and away she went, straight to the top, with me falling somewhere near the bottom. I don't think she ever meant it to be that way—just one of those things, I guess. We drifted apart, but I never forgot her.

"It's been a *long* time," she said, walking toward me. Her smile was warm. "How've you been?"

"I'm well, Tracy. You?"

She moved past me, and for a split second, I caught her scent. Something linen mixed with something floral, and in that instant, it was high school all over again.

Gazing up at a shelf, she shrugged. "I'm okay, I guess. You know...husband, two kids, living out in the burbs. Never got out of this place. Smart move on your part that you did."

Not like I had a choice, I thought as I put Oliver back on his shelf. "Doesn't look like much's changed around here."

"Nope," she said through a restless sigh, "it never does."

"Hot and muggy, with a chance of showers by afternoon?"

She grinned, still studying the rows of books. "You got it." Then she turned to me. "So...a famous writer now. Pretty impressive."

I shrugged. "Just a news magazine."

"Modest. You always were."

"Was I?"

"About as unassuming as they came."

I returned my gaze to the shelf, nodded.

"I have to say, though, I was kind of surprised to see you came back."

"You and everyone else," I said through a forced laugh. "I'm not exactly the town's Favorite Son."

She dismissed the comment with a wave of her hand. "Screw 'em."

"Right," I said and grinned. "Screw 'em."

"But you look good, Pat. You really do. I'm glad things got better for you after the..."

"The overdose," I said quickly, as if by doing so it might take away her discomfort.

"Yeah." She fell silent for a moment and pushed her hair behind one ear. It was a nervous habit she'd had since childhood. "Sorry. I didn't mean to..."

"No. It's okay. I'm fine with it. Really."

She offered a thin smile.

"Can I ask you something, though? Was I the only one who thought she was evil?"

An unsettled expression crossed Tracy's face, and then she turned her head away, shaking it. "Everyone thought she was kind of crazy, I guess. The ones who wanted to see it."

"Did you?"

"Want to see it?"

"Did you know?"

6

She turned back toward me, but this time her expression was easy to read. "I should have done something that day, Patrick. I should have stayed and listened."

That day. My stomach twisted into a knot. I struggled against my thoughts, pushed the words out slowly. "But you had no way of knowing…"

"I knew," she said, nodding, and then, softer, "I knew. I was just…afraid."

"Afraid?"

"Of the other kids. Of her. Of…everything, I guess." She looked down, hair behind the ear again. "I just left you there. Alone. It was all my fault."

I lost Tracy's voice and quite possibly my mind. The knot pulled tighter in my gut, and suddenly everything came rushing back to me. I was there again, living the nightmare. White light. White noise.

"Patrick?"

I snapped back to the present, stared at her with what I knew was a dazed expression. The lump in my throat made it damned near impossible to speak, my voice coming out gritty and tight. "I'm fine."

"You sure?"

"Yeah…look, I'd better go back upstairs."

"Patrick…"

"Fine, really." I attempted a smile, then pushed past her. Headed up the staircase, quickly, and straight for the bathroom.

I locked the door behind me. My back against the wall, eyes closed, I took in a long, steadying breath. A thousand thoughts rushed through my head. A thousand memories.

Then I pulled the pad from my pocket and, with shaky hands, wrote the word *vicious* fifty times.

CHAPTER TWO

In *The Count of Monte Cristo*, Alexandre Dumas wrote that houses have souls and faces like men, and their exteriors carry the imprint of their characters. To me, our house always looked dark and ominous, a shadowy projection of the horrors inside its silent, secretive walls. As a kid, I remember staring out through those dreary windows and wondering whether the world outside was as awful as the one within. Bad memories lived there. Horrible ones.

I decided to take Warren's advice and go back anyway—not for sentiment, as he'd suggested, but to rid myself of those memories. I needed to go through the place, chase away my ghosts, and then walk out that front door one last time.

But going in was another story.

I stood in the doorway and felt my nerves jangle with slow-burning apprehension. Bad vibes seemed to rock this place from its foundation. I stepped in, stopped, then looked around.

She'd done most of her dying here before moving on to hospice, but as I walked in, I could still feel a sense of approaching death hanging heavy in the air. Stillness, but not the kind that lent itself to peace or tranquility—no, this was something different, a

life waiting to end and a peculiar numbness that seemed to reso-
nate throughout.

The kind that gnaws at your insides.

Warren had obviously hired a cleaning crew to wipe away the
postmortem effects, everything in its place, not a speck of dirt anywhere. An oxygen tank covered in plastic stood in one corner; in
another, an empty trash container sat on the counter. I gazed at the
bed: neatly made. *A sanitized version of hell*, I thought, then moved on.

I peered into my former bedroom and shook my head. She'd
wasted little time converting it into her sewing room once I'd left
for college.

"I put your things in the garage," she'd said matter-of-factly
at Thanksgiving break. "Take what you want. The rest goes to
Goodwill."

Great to see you, son.

Moving on to the living room, I gave it a quick scan and then
a drawn-out sigh; nothing ever seemed to change here. Those tat-
tered drapes. The outdated television. I thought about that damned
music box, and a sharp pang of anger flickered, then fizzled. The
thing meant more to her than I did.

As filthy rich as my uncle was, I never understood why my
mother insisted we live in such lower-middle-class squalor. Was
it to elicit sympathy? Because she never thought she deserved better? Warren had offered repeatedly to get us out of here.

"Camilla," he'd plead, "let me help you. You don't have to live
this way."

"Don't need any charity," she'd say in her typically dismissive
tone. "I can manage on my own."

So we existed on a meager income, inside a two-bedroom box
in a part of town that people kindly referred to as "undesirable."
Our threadbare secondhand furniture had the smell of other people's lives—ones I was sure had been much better than mine—
and I wore clothes to school that had outlived their usefulness on
someone else's back before landing on mine.

"You don't need fancy new clothes," she'd tell me in her sing-song voice. "What you have is just fine."

God, I hated that woman.

Warren did his best to help, gifting me with what she wouldn't provide, but I always sensed it was more because he felt sorry for me than anything else. He never really succeeded in being the stand-in male figure in my life, seemed he always radiated more pity than love. I knew the difference—most kids do—so I grew up resenting his misplaced, halfhearted attempts.

And I resented even more that he could have put an end to my mother's abuse but didn't. Instead, he chose to look the other way, always immersed in his political career, running here, running there to God-knows-where.

My real dad died when I was barely a year old, and I knew only three things about him. His name was Richard, he had a bad heart—which eventually killed him—and he worked in the textile business. When I was a kid, it took me a while to figure out what that actually meant. For the longest time, I thought he remodeled bathrooms.

Oh, make that four things. He left my mother with the burden of raising me alone, as she reminded me constantly.

When I turned eighteen, I put as much distance between her and me as I could. Warren offered to foot the bill for college, and I ran with it, seeing it as my one-way ticket out of hell. I moved as far away as I could. Odd, though, how distance doesn't always separate us from the bad memories and associations as much as we'd like. Even now that she was dead, her effects still lingered.

I opened the basement door and turned on the light—or tried. A naked yellow bulb dangling from the ceiling flickered a few times before going dark. I flipped the switch up and down, hoping to give it life, but had no luck: blown.

Found an old flashlight in the kitchen junk drawer, but, true to form, she'd let the batteries die. It seemed as if nothing here was meant to survive.

The clock radio on the kitchen windowsill stole my attention, and I froze. Bad memories everywhere. I couldn't believe she still had the damned thing. I reached for it, pulled the batteries out, then slammed it into the sink. Felt a note of satisfaction hearing it crack.

Got the flashlight working and headed for the basement steps.

It looked as if nobody had been here in years. Old sewing equipment hugged one wall: an antiquated machine, three tailor's dummies, and enough spools of thread to mend a small nation. Her sewing hobby never really got off the ground, despite all the supplies she'd picked up at garage sales. The floor was strewn with boxes covered in dust, cobwebs stretched between them, some labeled with marker, some not at all.

I pulled the lids up on a few but found nothing other than a whole lot of junk inside. Dozens of dusty colored bottles in one; another was filled to the brim with packages of crackers, expiration date: October 1983.

What on earth was she planning on doing with them?

Finding anything useful here was an exercise in futility. But then, as I headed back toward the steps, the flashlight beam connected with an open box, and I could see an old book that looked vaguely familiar. I pulled it out. *Gulliver's Travels*, one of my favorites. Curiosity got the best of me, so I examined the rest of the contents. More books from high school, a jumble of papers, and small objects that I couldn't see clearly in the dim light. I tucked the box under my arm, then headed upstairs.

As I reached the top of the steps, Warren moved into the doorway. I jumped. He stood, staring at me.

"Scared the hell out of me," I said, feeling my heart thump a few beats ahead.

"Find anything?" he asked, eyeing the box under my arm.

I felt an odd twinge of defensiveness. "Just some old books."

He nodded slowly as if measuring my words. I broke eye contact by glancing down at the box I was holding, keeping my attention on it as I spoke. "Not much down there except a whole lot of clutter, really."

"Quite a pack rat, your mother was. She never liked to throw anything away. It drove me crazy when we were kids. I think she got it from our mother. She was like that, too, you know."

Small talk. I offered a dim smile.

"You know," he continued, staring off into the kitchen, his voice tempered with cautious diplomacy, "I was just thinking I could drive you to the airport if you'd like. Maybe get a bite to eat or something on the way."

"Appreciate it," I said, glancing at my watch, "but I don't have much time. My flight leaves in an hour and a half, and I've got a rental car to return."

He mouthed—but did not say—*oh*, while nodding, as if suddenly getting the point. "No worries, then," he said, a little too brightly. "I just thought maybe—"

"Some other time," I answered back quickly, realizing I was squeezing the box tightly against my thigh. I caught myself eyeing the door, the one I wanted to walk out of for the last time, the one Warren was now blocking.

He stared at the floor and pursed his lips. I knew the move all too well—a mannerism he'd perfected throughout his political career, one he often used to give the impression he was thinking things over. "There's this matter of the house," he finally said. "I'm putting it up for sale. I'd like you to have the proceeds."

I shook my head quickly. "That won't be necessary, Warren, I—"

"No, really," he interrupted, "I'd like for you to have the money."

"No, *really*," I said, feeling my anger swell. "I *really* don't want it. Give the money to charity. It'll be the one good deed that ever came out of her."

He looked at the floor again, pushed out a heavy sigh. "You know, Patrick…"

You know, Patrick always meant trouble coming.

"I realize you and your mother didn't always see eye to eye."

"Never," I replied.

"What?"

"I said never. We never did."

"But she was my sister, and she's dead now," he said, his tone climbing the ladder of edginess, "and I'd appreciate it if you'd try and show some respect for her when you're around me."

"*Respect?*" That was it. I'd had enough. Enough of Warren, enough of her and this house, enough of everything. All I wanted now was out. "You see, here's the thing, Warren: you have to give respect to get it, and *she* never gave one ounce of it. Not one."

"But she was your mother."

"Barely," I said. "Now, if you'll excuse me." I pushed past him and headed for the door.

"Patrick!" he shouted. "Don't leave this way. I don't want bad feelings."

"You're about thirty years too late for that, Warren." As I jerked the door open, the box slipped from under my arm to the floor, and everything inside scattered. I got down on my hands and knees, started hastily shoving items back inside.

Warren hurried over. "Let me help you with that."

"I don't need your help!" I said. "I don't need it at all! You've done enough!"

He knelt beside me anyway, and we both grabbed for *Gulliver's Travels* at the same time. I gritted my teeth and yanked the book away with force, startling him. He held my gaze for a moment in total silence.

I scrambled to my feet, stood, rubbing my wrist.

"Are you hurt?" Warren asked.

"A scratch. It's nothing."

Warren stood up. "Let me take a look."

"It's fine."

He reached for my hand. "Seriously, Patrick, let me—"

I pulled it away. "I *said* it's fine. I'm not going to bleed to death. Okay?"

"But you could…you know you could."

"It's not that deep," I said, turning toward the door, anxious to get out of this house and away from Warren.

"Patrick!" he shouted to me. "Wait a minute!"

"No, Warren."

"But…"

"I said *no*. It's over."

He started to say something else, but I didn't hear it; I was already out the door. Walking away. Done.

Finally. Once and for all.

~

Inside the car, I immediately reached into my shirt pocket, then panicked. I'd left my pen and pad at the hotel.

Breathing heavily now, sweat crawling down the back of my neck, I began rifling through the glove compartment like a madman looking for a fix. Found an old map and a broken pencil, the point flattened. With shaky hands I scrawled *fragile* three times, barely readable, before the pencil tip broke off. I hurled it against the windshield as hard as I could, then felt tears rolling down my cheeks.

I closed my eyes and dropped my head onto the steering wheel, keeping it there for a long time.

If I never saw Black Lake again, it would be too soon.

Unlovable
Unlovable
Unlovable

CHAPTER THREE

Lies, my Mother Told me

From my earliest memories, my mother's moments of affection were as fleeting as they were inconsistent. Not many encouraging smiles or gentle touches, and the ones she gave often felt flat and shallow. She carried herself as if to discourage human contact, if not block it entirely. When I was young, I'd often grab for her hand as we walked, but she'd quickly pull it out of reach; the reaction seemed almost instinctual, like flinching from a blow or pulling a finger from a hot flame. Even as we moved through stores or crowded streets, I'd often find myself several feet behind, chasing after her, trying to keep up.

Once before bedtime, in a half-knee-jerk, half-desperate bid for affection, I threw my arms around her, but I might as well have been reaching around a giant boulder, hard and cold. Her entire body grew stiff and unyielding, and she turned her head away.

Feeling rejected and confused, I pulled back and gazed at her.

"I have a cold," she said, rising and moving quickly toward the door, cool and detached. Then she turned off the light and left my room.

I don't think I understood her rejection or its impact on me at the time. I thought all mothers kept their affection under lock and key. In my world, it was normal to want love and not get it, no different from wanting a toy in a store and being told we couldn't afford it. My mother didn't indulge in affection because emotionally, she was bankrupt.

But as I grew older and watched other kids and their parents, I began realizing my world was terribly out of whack. Of course, knowing this, I did what any kid would do: I blamed myself, often wondering what it was about me she found so appalling.

Then, one day, I got my answer.

We were driving home from church. Something had gotten under her skin—as was often the case—and for most of the day, her mood veered between silent sulking one moment and angry ranting the next.

"I hate it when you comb your hair like that," she said with a snarl, alternating her glance between the road and me. "That part in the middle. *God*, Patrick!"

"What's wrong with it?" I asked, now studying my reflection in the side-view mirror.

She gave a flip laugh that pushed my question into the category of preposterous. "You look like a horse's ass, that's what's wrong with it."

The comment stung, and tears filled my eyes. I know she saw them, but she didn't appear the least bit concerned.

We drove on in silence for a while, the tears streaming down my face. And then I had to know. "Why don't you love me?" I practically blurted the words out through my sobs.

"What?"

"Love me," I said. "How come you can't?"

She fell silent for a moment, keeping her attention on the road, then let out an exasperated sigh.

"Because, Patrick…quite simply, you can be rather unlovable."

CHAPTER FOUR

On the plane trip home, my mind kept drifting back to the fight with Warren. I was pissed at myself for letting him get to me. I shouldn't have. I mean, I'd hoped to make a clean break, but cutting off my nose wasn't part of the plan. Still, all bets were off the moment he started singing my mother's praises. She was my hot button, and he'd pushed it.

If I didn't know it then, I certainly did now: returning to Black Lake was a huge mistake.

But what the hell did I expect?

Luckily for me, I lived several thousand miles away. And my mother was dead. She couldn't hurt me anymore. Maybe now I could finally bury the past with her and move on, let Warren go as well.

~

After taking a cab from the Oakland airport to my apartment in Hayward, I let my suitcase drop to the floor and took in my surroundings. Desolation greeted me, followed by wretched despair— my two closest companions these days. There's something about returning home from a trip that draws one's innermost feelings of isolation and loneliness to the surface, makes an empty apartment seem emptier.

I'd been single for a couple of years now but was still reeling from the effects. I suppose it takes time. Samantha and I were together for nearly three years, and while I wouldn't consider it a nasty breakup, it wasn't the friendliest, either. I blame myself for that. I was neglectful, took her for granted, gave more attention to crime reporting than to her. I've been working for *News World* magazine, West Coast bureau, for seven years now. It's a nice gig. I get to do what I love, work my own hours from home, and as long as I file my stories on time, they pretty much leave me alone. Dead bodies and horror stories over a loving relationship: hardly a fair trade-off, but I took it anyway, foolishly. And lost out big-time. Don't think I'll ever meet anyone like her again.

It all came to a head on New Year's Eve. I'd promised Sam a long-overdue evening out; we'd ring in the new year at Bella, her favorite restaurant. She'd been looking forward to it for weeks, bought a new dress, got her hair done.

Then that afternoon I got a break on a story I'd been working. Unfortunately, the news hardly ever waits for a convenient moment to happen.

A woman on her morning jog along Half Moon Bay had come across a body—or rather, what was left of one. What she had actually seen first was a Manolo Blahnik pump sticking up between two boulders. It belonged to Sherrie Jensen, wife of Concord cop Rick Jensen. She'd been missing for almost two weeks. Authorities suspected he'd killed her but had nothing to prove it, and this was their big break. Mine, too.

I got the call at noon and arrived on scene within a half hour; of course, so did every other major news outlet. This was a big story, and everyone wanted a piece of it, so we camped out, knowing it was going to be a long day.

Which stretched out into a longer evening. I'd figured it would take some time to extricate the body; I just hadn't expected it to take *that* long. But it did. I phoned Samantha all afternoon with updates. Each time, I could hear the disappointment in her voice rising to more detectable levels. She knew what was coming; I did, too.

I called her at 11:00 p.m. to tell her we were still waiting on a body.

And she promptly hung up on me.

Finally, the very moment the ball dropped, as if on cue, the rest of Sherrie Jensen's body came up for air. I'd waited twelve hours for a rib cage with some flesh attached to it.

Happy New Year.

I rushed home covered in sweat and grime but still determined to salvage my relationship with Samantha.

No such luck. She was gone, and, taped to my laptop, a note: *Hope she was worth it. Goodbye.*

Jenson went to death row, and I took several press awards, along with an abrupt and unceremonious leap into bachelorhood.

It takes a certain kind of person to put up with a journalist, but I'm not even sure if one actually exists. Most people I know in the business are either born-again-single or stuck in dysfunctional relationships. It's a double-edged sword, I suppose. We love our work, and we long for love, but neither seems conducive to the other.

Since losing Samantha, I've resigned myself to singledom and all that it entails. My sink is always piled with dirty dishes, my floor a virtual bed of filthy socks and underwear. I relish bachelorhood, pound my chest fitfully, then burp into an empty beer glass, telling myself that this is The Life, that being free and single is a blessing.

Then I ask myself who the hell I'm kidding. Being lonely sucks—everyone knows that, me included.

I glanced at my answering machine on the kitchen counter. An unblinking zero stared back, mocking me, calling me a loser. What followed was a feeling of unqualified emptiness. I consoled myself by pretending it was okay, that that's what cell phones are for. Then I chased the thought away.

After fixing a sandwich, I dragged my suitcase into the bedroom and started unpacking. The book immediately caught my attention; it was inside a plastic bag along with the other items I'd taken from the house.

I spilled everything onto the bed and only then realized that many of these things weren't mine. They were my mother's.

I cringed: an old change purse I remembered her having, a letter opener I recognized, too, along with an ugly scarf I had always hated. Good Lord, I'd just purged the woman from my life. The last thing I needed was reminders of her. I tossed them into the trash.

Next up, a bundle of photos. Pictures of Mother—I pitched them, too—then one of me at age five, standing in front of Warren's 1968 Corvette. I was pretty sure his purpose for taking it was more to show off the car than to capture me. I remembered feeling incidental.

Flipped to the next one, of me at age seven, a dorky school photo: gold ribbed turtleneck pullover, Hair by Pillow, and a bucktooth. I laughed. If there had been a poster child for awkwardness, I was it, hands down.

Looking through the others, I couldn't help but notice the unifying theme: as the years moved on, my smile seemed to fade. By sixteen, I was practically scowling at the camera—angry, dark, sullen.

I was getting sicker, and it showed.

The joy was gone, too. No surprise there. I'd made my full tour of duty through hell by then and had the battle scars to prove it.

I stuffed the photos away in a sock drawer, then brought my attention back to the other items, most of which I vaguely recognized: a red plastic squirt gun, a few comic books, an old pack of gum with only two sticks remaining. Why she had saved any of these was beyond me. She'd tossed plenty of things far more valuable after I'd left for college without once bothering to ask if I wanted them.

But there was something I definitely did *not* recognize.

A gold chain and pendant. Upon closer inspection, I realized it was a Saint Christopher medal, and although the length was short enough to belong to a woman, I knew I'd never seen my mother wearing it. Turning it over confirmed it: the initials were *NAK*. I tried to think whether we knew anyone with a name that matched but came up with nothing.

I placed it on the bed, stared at it, then looked back at the pile and discovered something else: an old, yellowed envelope addressed to my mother, postmarked July 3, 1976, from Stover, Illinois. The letter inside was written on stationery from the Greensmith Hotel:

C–

I won't have access to a telephone for the next few days. Most of the lines are down due to the damage here. About your call during my stay in Chicago. Stop worrying. Trust me, that's one body they'll never find. Everything is taken care of.

–W

I swallowed hard. No name from the sender, but there didn't need to be. I recognized the handwriting: Warren's.

CHAPTER FIVE

The hairs on the back of my neck stood straight up.

It was as if I'd accidentally stumbled across a conversation between two strangers. Evil ones.

What the hell do I have here?

And where was this body hidden that no one would ever find?

The necklace. I laid it across my palm and studied it. Where did it come from? Was I misunderstanding? Overreacting?

But they were talking about a damned body, for Christ's sake.

Whose body? I had initials on a necklace, a date, and a location. I also had Sully. It might not have been connected...or it might be. He could help me find out.

I found the phone and dialed his number.

Jack Sullenfeld was my best friend in college and probably the smartest guy I know. He works as an intel analyst for the FBI, and he's my go-to guy when I'm on the hunt for sensitive data, information normally unavailable to the public.

Sully answered on the second ring. "Well, if it isn't—"

"I need your help," I interrupted, mindlessly rolling the necklace between my fingers.

"You sound funny."

"I'm under a little stress."

He paused, then spoke his words slowly. "Okay. What do you have?"

"Need you to look at missing persons or murder cases around 1976. Possible victim's initials: NAK. The location might be in or near Stover, Illinois."

"Male or female?"

"Don't know. Maybe female. Just whatever you can find, okay?"

He paused a beat. "You all right?"

"Yeah," I said, trying my best for a more casual tone. "Just working some leads on a story and feeling the pressure."

I hung up the phone and decided to do some searching myself. Fired up my Mac and logged on to Infoquest, the magazine's newspaper-archiving subscription service. Warren was a congressman back then. If he had been in Stover, chances were the press might have been there, too. A search for *Stover, Illinois, Warren Strademeyer, 1976* netted me a direct hit with a story from the *Black Lake Courier*, dated July 5, 1976. Apparently, Warren was in Stover studying emergency response systems after a tornado leveled the town. The story showed a photo of him walking through the rubble and talking to authorities. That would explain why the phone lines were down. Did another search, this time for *murder, Stover, Illinois, missing, body, St. Christopher Medal, 1976.* Came up with a string of stories from the *Stover Journal*, but one in particular caught my interest: a nineteen-year-old woman named Jackie Newberry, reported missing two weeks before the tornado hit. Last seen walking to the community college but never arrived there. A search of the neighborhood and outlying area proved futile. Authorities suspected foul play.

But her initials didn't match those on the Saint Christopher medal, and no mention of a necklace.

I toyed with the idea that maybe the necklace had nothing to do with this, but if that were true, where did it come from? Again, nobody I knew with those initials. A dead end, and I was dead tired. It was after midnight. I'd been up for hours, was suffering from jet lag, and was quickly losing steam. Exhausted, frustrated, and troubled, I decided to call it a night, hoping some rest might help bring new answers.

I fell asleep with a pad and pen on my chest after writing *defiance* fifty-seven times.

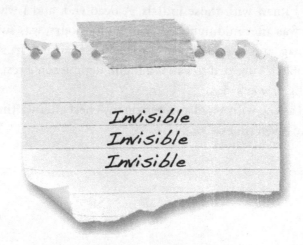

Invisible
Invisible
Invisible

CHAPTER SIX

You don't matter

I sometimes felt like a ghost walking through that house, my needs so often going ignored that it was as if they barely existed. As if *I* barely existed. And the saddest part, the most tragic, was that I bought into the neglect. I thought it was normal, that all mothers put their own needs before those of their children. I had no way of knowing otherwise. Ours was a world ruled by contradictions and inconsistencies, painted only in shades of gray. I wouldn't have known black or white if I'd seen them.

Then one day, a glimmer of hope.

She came running into the living room, shrieking with excitement. "You won't believe it! You just won't!" she said, clutching a handful of pamphlets against her chest, her face lighting up with delight. "The raffle! The one at church for the vacation! In the Cayman Islands! I won!"

"No way!" I bolted from my chair, leaving my book behind. "Really?"

"Really!" She tossed the pamphlets onto the coffee table, threw her arms around me, lifting me straight up in the air. "We're going to the Cayman Islands! Can you believe it?"

I couldn't believe she was hugging me so hard.

She grabbed one of the pamphlets and held it out in front of her, admiring the photos, practically out of breath from all her excitement. "I just never imagined I could…and with so many people entering and all…I just…this is the dream of a lifetime! We're going to the Cayman Islands! Seven nights, all expenses paid! It's so exciting!"

It was beyond exciting. It was wonderful.

"We'll be staying at a resort," she said and spread a brochure open to show me the photos. "Four swimming pools! *Four!* And the food, oh, the food! Buffets every night!" She let out a deep sigh of satisfaction. "It'll be the perfect family vacation. Just the two of us!"

The two of us. Family.

"Now, we have several choices when we can go," she said, her voice now taking on a practical tone. "What do you think? Next month? It'll be December. We'll be there during Christmas and come back with *gorgeous* suntans. How great would it be to have a suntan over the holidays! They'll be so jealous! They'll just be seething! I love it!"

"That would be great! Let's do it, Mom!"

Suddenly she froze, staring at me oddly, lowering her brows. A peculiar smile slid across her face, and then she began laughing.

I laughed a little, too. "What?"

She was still laughing, catching her breath. "Oh, that's so funny."

"What is?"

"You are, silly! What gave you the idea *you* were going?"

"But you said…that it was the perfect family vacation, just the two of us…and…"

"Don't be ridiculous!" Giggling now, she said, "I wasn't talking about you. I was talking about your uncle Warren and me. Why in the world would I take you?"

CHAPTER SEVEN

I woke the next morning clawing at my covers, sweat dripping down my face, heart pounding like a hammer inside my chest.

The dream again. The boy in the woods.

The nightstand clock said 9:02 a.m. Next to it was my notebook. I found comfort seeing it there, knowing I might need it.

I have a problem that I keep secret from the world. I make lists, the same word repeated over and over. I've been doing it for as long as I could write. On average, they take up about a page, but they can be longer than that. Much longer. I once wrote *havoc* more than 1,600 times. Filled about thirty pages. I was having a bad day.

I don't know why I do it, but I usually feel better after…at least for a while. It's kind of like having an itch—when the urge hits, I've got to scratch or it'll drive me crazy until I do. Well, actually, it's like a mosquito bite: the more I scratch, the more I have to *keep* scratching. That's why I need to be careful; otherwise, it can become, well…obsessive.

Of course, I haven't missed the irony: a writer trapped by his own words. Sounds like a cruel joke. It's like I'm straddling two parallel worlds, one I love and another I hate. I work like hell to hide it, but it keeps popping up at the most inopportune times. And I detest that I do it; I'm embarrassed as hell that I can't stop. But I've *got* to do it, have trouble functioning if I don't.

So I do.

That's not to say I always hide it well. There have been close calls. I've accidentally left my lists out for someone to find—Samantha being one of them—but I've developed strategies, have learned to shift into damage control when that happens. I tell people it's something I do to deal with writer's block, and that seems to end all speculation. After all, a neurotic writer isn't too far a stretch.

9:03 a.m. Time to stop obsessing about the dream and my lists and get moving. I jumped in the shower, shaved, then dragged a comb through my hair. I was halfway down the steps when I heard the phone ringing.

"Not feeling the love, Sully," I said.

"And a good morning to you, too, Mr. Sunshine."

"Sorry. Rough night."

"I've got two NAKs for you. Both around 1976, but nothing from Stover, and no females."

I grabbed a pen and an envelope to write on. "Give it to me."

"A forty-six-year-old male from Lester, Missouri, by the name of Neil Adam Kershaw. Found strangled in his car outside a hog farm in the wee hours. You can do a search and get all the info."

I wrote it down. "What else?"

"A three-year-old boy from Corvine, Texas, by the name of Nathan Allan Kingsley. Went missing from home. Never found."

I was already reaching across the counter for my laptop. "Thanks, Sully. Call you later."

"That's all I get?"

"Thanks, Sully. You're the best. Call you later."

I heard a groan before he hung up.

I logged in on Infoquest, started searching for *Lester, Missouri, Neil Adam Kershaw, strangled*. Several articles came up. I clicked on the first, dated August 6, 1976, from the *Lester Star Tribune*.

Authorities Identify Man Found Strangled Outside Hog Farm
by Reggie Adamson

The county coroner has released the name of a man found dead in his car on Tuesday. Authorities say 46-year-old Neil Adam Kershaw was strangled. His body was found inside his vehicle parked in front of Sampson's Hog Farm on the 200 block of Dunbar Lane around 3 a.m.

Authorities have no suspect but are asking for any information that could lead to an arrest.

And it looked like they got some. Apparently, Kershaw was quite the ladies' man. Had a wife, plus a girlfriend on the side. Unfortunately, the girlfriend had a husband, and *he* was none too thrilled when he found out they'd been carrying on. He killed her, then went after Kershaw. Authorities were able to link both crimes and make an arrest.

Case closed.

Next, on to Nathan Allan Kingsley. Infoquest brought me a story dated October 10, 1977, from the *Observer* in Corvine, Texas.

Arrest Made in Case of Murdered Toddler
by Frank D'Alessandro

Corvine authorities took 23-year-old Ronald Lee Lucas into custody last night, charging him with the kidnapping and murder of three-year-old Nathan Allan Kingsley. Detectives say they discovered evidence in Lucas's apartment linking him to the crime, which occurred more than a year ago. An anonymous tip led them to the suspect.

Nathan Kingsley disappeared from his home in June of last year, leaving parents Jean and Dennis Kingsley devastated and officials bewildered. Mrs. Kingsley had just returned home from the grocery store with Nathan when she stepped outside to check the mail. When she returned to the house moments later, the boy was gone.

Lucas is being held without bail in the county jail pending arraignment.

I narrowed my focus on the photo and felt my gut tighten. The boy was wearing a necklace—*the* necklace. I was pretty sure of it.

I pulled up a few more articles. Authorities believed Lucas had buried the body in the desert. As large an area as that was, chances were slim they'd ever find it.

Stop worrying. Everything is taken care of. Trust me, that's one body they'll never find.

Words from Warren to my mother—words that were now haunting me.

According to the story, they'd found plenty in Lucas's apartment linking him to the crime, evidence that sealed his fate: a sneaker and underwear belonging to Nathan and a knife—all with the boy's blood on them. Genetic testing wasn't a reality yet, but blood typing was, and they'd scored a match.

I shivered.

If all that hadn't been enough, Lucas was a paroled sex offender, and if *that* wasn't enough, a witness later surfaced, a mailman, who reported seeing Lucas in the neighborhood at the time of the kidnapping. With no viable alibi, Lucas didn't stand a snowball's chance in hell of escaping conviction. He spent several years on death row in Huntsville, Texas, then died in the electric chair in December 1983.

And there was more tragedy. Shortly after the murder, Jean Kingsley began spiraling into a series of mental breakdowns that took her in and out of a psychiatric hospital. During her final stay there, she hanged herself.

I thought about Dennis Kingsley losing his only son and then his wife—grief piled upon grief, everything that mattered to him gone in an instant. Left alone with nothing but his sadness.

I pushed on and found an interview and photo of the parents. From what I could see, an all-American family: Jean Kingsley, attractive and petite, and Dennis, large, with short-cropped hair, a thick neck, and arms like oversize rolling pins. He worked at the local cannery. Both appeared young, probably in their early to mid twenties. And desperate. "I only left him in his playpen for a minute," Jean was quoted as saying. "Only a minute!"

Just like that. Vanished.

No word anywhere about the necklace.

I held it up to the light and let it dangle: criminal evidence in my hand and, even worse, from a kidnapping and murder.

Next came more questions. Should I turn the necklace over to authorities? I considered it, but there was a risk. The possibility my own mother might have had a hand in it certainly raised the stakes. Not that it mattered; she was dead. But Warren wasn't, and it looked as though he was just as involved as she. A man who wielded considerable power. No way I should go traipsing off to authorities, necklace in hand, until I at least knew more.

Time to apply some of the basic principles from journalism school. I had the *what*, *where*, and *when*. What I didn't have was the *who*. But I knew where I might find it: Corvine, Texas.

I went back online for airline tickets, then once again packed my bags. The revolving door to my apartment was about to take yet another spin. I looked around, realizing I'd actually been here only a few days this month. Then I frowned.

I hadn't missed it one bit.

CHAPTER EIGHT

I arrived in Corvine later that evening and found a room at the Surfside Motel in the middle of town. No surf, just an empty old swimming pool that looked as though it hadn't held water in a number of years.

The next day, I went out to familiarize myself with the place. Although it had probably changed some through the years, I got the impression that Corvine hadn't grown much since the kidnapping. A smallish-looking desert town, about as nondescript as they come. Desolate, too. The downtown area consisted of nothing more than a series of outdated strip malls filled with shoestring operations: an AMVETS store, a five-and-dime, and a hat shop that looked as though it hadn't seen a living head for quite some time.

Who lives in places like this?

CJ Norris was a reporter for the *Corvine Observer* who had written a number of stories about the *Kingsley* case through the years. The press likes to do that; follow-ups, we call them. We'd revisit the birth of Christ if we could squeeze a new angle out of it. I called the main switchboard. After several rounds of "punch the number to get the department you want," I got a female voice that sounded rushed.

"Norris."

I heard keyboards clicking in the background. Glancing at my watch, I understood why: it was 4:47 p.m., crunch time in the newspaper biz. Even small towns have one. I hadn't thought about that. I should have.

"Patrick Bannister here," I said, "and I've just realized what a lousy time it is to be calling. You're probably chasing a deadline."

"You sound like you've got some firsthand knowledge there," she said, still clicking away.

"Guilty."

"Reporter?"

"*News World*."

"Ah," she said, "nice."

"If it's a bad time…"

"Sweetie, it's never a *good* time, you know that, but I can always spare a moment for a comrade. What can I do for you?"

"Well…I'm actually in town."

That made her stop typing. "In Corvine?"

"Yeah."

"On purpose?"

"Far as I can tell."

"Can't be for pleasure, so it has to be business."

"It is…"

"Yeah, well, we don't have much of that around here, either."

"I'm working on the *Kingsley* case."

"Nathan Kingsley?" A pause. "You know you're about thirty years too late, unless there's something new going on there?"

"Not that I know of."

"Hmm."

"What?"

"Just hmm, is all…"

"Can you expand on that?"

"Oh, nothing…just seems a little odd. You being from a national news magazine, calling me out of the blue about a kid who's been dead for a long time."

"Is there some rule against doing stories about dead people?"

"Well, no, I just—"

"And you do follow-ups on it yourself from time to time, don't you?"

"Yeah, but I'm local. I *have* to do them. You, on the other hand, well, you're from somewhere out in the real world."

"Define *real world*."

"Anyplace but here."

I laughed a little. Funny gal, this Norris.

She went on, "And last I checked, you folks in the real world have plenty of missing and murdered kids to chase after. So what gives? Talk to me."

I thought about how to answer that, searching my mind for a logical response, knowing full well what a horrible liar I am.

She cleared her throat. "Still with me there, Pat?"

"Still here, yeah."

"So…the *Kingsley* case. Why him?"

"I'm actually doing a story about missing and exploited kids, and we're looking at several cases. *Kingsley* just happens to be one of them."

"I see," she said, sounding less suspicious but not completely convinced, either.

"So I was hoping maybe we could meet and you could get me up to speed on the case."

"I can do that, sure."

"How about after work? Got some time?"

She paused, and then, "You sure seem in a hurry."

"Just to get out of here is all."

"I'm feeling you there, Pat. I've been trying to do that for years. Okay, there's a bar, The Sports Page, right across the street from our offices. Order me a Tom Collins. I'll probably need one."

Shattered
Shattered
Shattered

CHAPTER NINE

You shouldn't be here

My older brother, Benjamin, died when I was two. I don't remember him, but my mother told me he passed away at the age of four from the same kind of heart abnormality my father had.

She never recovered from his death; I expect no parent ever does, but they do usually move on. Not her. She talked about him constantly, and the theme was always the same: Benjamin could do no wrong. Sometimes it felt as though he ruled my life from the grave because I spent my childhood competing against him for my mother's affection. It was hard going up against a ghost, so naturally I lost.

I came to realize her grief wasn't normal, that it wasn't really even about Benjamin—it was about her. She used him as a tool to draw attention to herself, as a weapon to make me feel less-than. Whenever she became angry or upset with me, what usually followed was, "Your poor brother would turn in his grave if he saw the way you treated me. God rest his soul."

My poor brother. I don't know...sometimes I thought he got off easy; after all, he didn't have to live with her for very long. I was the one who ended up doing hard time.

I started blaming my brother just like my mother blamed me, grew resentful, privately referring to him as Saint Benjamin. Condemnation always rolled downhill in our house, and because Benjamin couldn't defend himself, he was an easy target.

Then one day, the inevitable happened; I'd always figured it would, I just didn't know how, or that it would hurt so much.

My mother had a music box that she loved. Her father had given it to her. It was a porcelain figurine of a young girl sitting Indian-style, facing a corner, with tears rolling down her cheeks. When my mother wound it up, the music played and the girl would slowly spin around. "There's my Little Sad Girl," she would often say. Personally, the thing gave me the creeps. Sometimes I'd walk into the living room and find her holding it lovingly against her cheek, her own tearful eyes closed as the music played softly. She'd look up at me, startled, then try to act unaffected, as if doing so might somehow negate her moment of vulnerability.

I arrived home to an empty house after school one day. Nothing unusual there. Mother always seemed to be running around, although I never understood where. I tossed my books on the counter, then searched the fridge for something to eat. Hardly anything there—also not unusual—just a single apple somewhere on the outer edges of its life span and a can of soda. The phone rang as I was pulling them out. I put the soda down so I could answer; it was a call from the dentist, reminding Mother of her appointment the next day. After writing down the information, I headed for the living room.

I had just turned on the TV when I realized I'd forgotten my soda in the kitchen, so I tossed the apple onto the side table, then headed back. A few steps later, I heard the smashing noise.

Little Sad Girl was on the floor in pieces.

Then I heard Mother pull up in the driveway.

She walked in, took one look, and froze in her tracks.

"It was an accident!" I said, shaking my head, stepping away from the broken pieces as if doing so might somehow separate me from my catastrophic mistake. "I'm sorry! I didn't mean to!"

"*No!*" She leaped forward, dropping to her hands and knees. Then came the tears as she scrambled around on the floor, frantically trying to gather up the pieces. I knelt beside her to help. That was when she shot me the death glare and, with her voice filled with venom and anger, screamed, "Get away! Don't you touch her! Don't you *dare!*"

I stood, then backed away slowly as she continued picking up the pieces, examining each one, and sobbing uncontrollably. I knew there was nothing I could say, nothing I could do except stand and watch.

Finally, she looked up and caught my gaze. With tearful, bloodshot eyes and in a tone low and angry, my mother said, "You...ruin...everything."

"I'm sorry!" I said, crying. "I didn't mean to—"

"Get out of my sight."

I turned away, headed for my room. And then behind me I heard her say those words, the kind you can never take back.

"I wish you were the one who died."

CHAPTER TEN

The Sports Page didn't seem very sporty. The theme, more than anything, was dark. Dark ceilings, dark walls, dark floors. Just your typical hole-in-the-wall bar. They did have a baseball game playing on the big screen, but that was about as athletic as it got. A kid who barely looked old enough to drink, let alone serve one, took my order. About a half hour later, CJ walked in.

"Sorry," she with a smile that matched her apology. "Got hung up at work. You know how that goes."

"I do. And don't worry about it. I've kept my share of people waiting. More times than I can count."

"We do make horrible dates, don't we? One of the many downfalls of being in this business, I guess."

She had that right.

A few moments later, Waiter Boy came back with a Tom Collins for her and another beer for me. CJ smiled her thank-you.

"So...," she said while settling into her seat. "Nathan Kingsley."

"Yeah. What can you tell me about him?"

"It was the biggest story this town's ever seen, but like I said, kid's been dead for a long time. Lucas, too..." She shrugged, took a sip. "We do a follow-up every now and then—you know, on the anniversary if nothing else is going on—but really, it ends up being more of a recap than anything else. Same old stuff, recycled."

"They never found him," I confirmed.

"Nope." She lifted her glass, swirled it around, stared into it. "And they were still able to convict without?"

"A classic no-body murder trial. No question the kid was murdered. Evidence was rock-solid. Lucas was dumb enough to leave some pretty incriminating stuff in his apartment."

"I read about that. The boy's clothing and the knife."

"With Nathan's blood on them, it left little doubt."

"And blood typing was enough?"

"It was all they had at the time, but they *were* able to confirm that the clothes belonged to Nathan. The parents verified. You put one and one together—"

"And you get two."

"Hopefully. If you do it right. Plus, there was Lucas's history. It tore at his defense that he was a convicted sex offender, but even worse was the eyewitness who placed him in the neighborhood at the time of the kidnapping."

"The mailman."

"Exactly."

"Pretty compelling."

"About as slam-dunk as they get," she said. "Only took three hours to come back with a verdict. Guilty on both counts. Then they went for the death penalty. Not much sympathy in Texas for child-killers."

"Or anywhere else, for that matter."

She took another sip, nodded. "True."

"So what about the body?"

"He buried it out in the desert somewhere. They're pretty sure of it. You could get more on that from Jerry Lindsay."

"Jerry Lindsay," I repeated.

She nodded. "The sheriff at the time. Retired now but still local. It probably wouldn't be a bad idea to hook up with him

41

anyway. He's an irascible old bastard but good for a quote or two. I usually drag him out whenever I do a follow-up."

"How about the boy's parents? What were they like?"

"Salt of the earth, decent, but very young at the time. Father worked. Mom stayed home. Dennis is still in town, lives up in the hills north of here. Keeps to himself. Can't say I blame him." She placed her drink firmly on the table and frowned at it, shaking her head. "Their lives really fell apart after Nathan died."

"The suicide."

"Yeah. Talk about tragic."

I nodded, thinking again of Dennis Kingsley and what he must have gone through.

"I guess it was too much for her to handle." CJ's smile was sad. "The guilt."

"How'd she let him out of her sight long enough for someone to grab him anyway? In her own home, no less."

"Well, according to the prosecutor, it all went down fast—real fast. They walked home from the corner store. Probably Lucas followed them and hid behind the house, waiting for the right time to make his move…which came when Jean stepped out to get the mail."

"How'd he get in?"

"Climbed through the bedroom window. The screen was tampered with."

"So the window was open," I confirmed.

She nodded. "It was June."

I thought about the physical logistics for a moment. "But how did he climb back out with a three-year-old in tow?"

"It was pretty easy, actually. The window was low enough to the ground where he could practically step right through it. They demonstrated it in court with an exact replica of the window and a life-size doll of Nathan."

I raised an eyebrow.

"Yeah," she said. "Very dramatic, very effective."

"And no one saw him leave with Nathan?"

"Nope. Just the mailman beforehand, but the timeline seemed to fit."

I wrote a few notes, then looked up to find her gazing pensively at me.

"Something wrong?"

She tipped her empty glass toward her and stared into it. "It may not be my place to say this…or maybe it is. I'm not sure. But I'm going to anyway."

I shook my head.

"The *Kingsley* case left a bad taste around here for a long time."

"Understandably."

"And someone like you, an outsider, asking questions, digging up the past—it's likely to rub a few people the wrong way."

"What exactly are you telling me?"

"Don't get me wrong. I completely understand what you're doing, where you're coming from. But the locals may not be so understanding."

"Is this some sort of warning?"

"Not so much a warning." A compassionate smile. "More a friendly word of caution from one professional to another."

"And that would be…"

"To tread lightly—that's all. Corvine's come a long way. They're nowhere near as backwoods as they once were—trust me on that one—but hell, even I still run into a tense situation or two while covering the story. And I'm local. People in this town are super hypersensitive about the case. I've learned to ask the right questions and when to back off. Do that, and you'll be fine. Don't do it, and you might be headed for some trouble."

CHAPTER ELEVEN

CJ's talk about unfriendly territory left me feeling a little uneasy. I got her point, and I understood it. Through the years, I'd run into my share of hostile subjects. But understanding didn't mean I had to like it.

Like it or not, she was right, as I quickly found out when I tried to visit the old Kingsley house. Bill and Norma Bansch now owned it and had been living there for the past fifteen years. When I called to request a look inside, Bill gave me a definitive no—then promptly hung up on me.

So much for southern hospitality.

But I wasn't going to let it deter me from stopping by and checking out the neighborhood. I needed to see where Nathan had lived and where his life had come to its tragic end.

~

It was a small place on the south side of town, just past the railroad tracks. Starter homes, I think they call them: tiny houses with even tinier yards. It was probably a quaint little neighborhood back in the day, but the years had chipped away at its charm;

pride of ownership no longer seemed to be a priority here. More than a few of the houses had paint peeling, driveways cracked, and no landscaping to speak of—unless, of course, you counted the brown, weed-infested grass.

I parked a good fifty yards from the Kingsley house, figuring I could make a quick getaway if someone became disagreeable. Then I took a good look at the place; it was in better shape than some of its neighbors, but something about it made me vaguely uneasy, as if there were a need for spiritual repairs. I didn't believe in ghosts, but…well, a young boy had been kidnapped from here, sexually abused, and murdered. That would creep anyone out.

I pulled a baseball cap down low on my forehead, then picked up a stack of flyers I'd grabbed off the counter at the local coffee shop: *Carpet stains getting you down? Clean one room, get the other free! 100% satisfaction guaranteed! Call The Carpet Doctor today for your no-obligation estimate!*

I crossed to the opposite side of the street and went to work stuffing flyers in doors.

The first thing that pinged my radar was how close together all the houses were, separated only by narrow driveways and thin slices of lawn. That would have made it more of a challenge to grab a kid in broad daylight. Also odd, I thought, was that only one person had seen Lucas that day—the mailman—and that was before Nathan disappeared.

Nothing during, nothing after.

Nabbing a toddler is noisy business; they tend to scream a lot when a stranger pulls them from the comforts of home and their mother. Someone should have heard something. I watched a few cars drive past from different directions, then looked up and down the street: open on both ends.

Very odd, indeed.

What's more, the newspaper said that Jean had gone to the curb to check the mail. But the mailbox was less than fifty feet from the front door. Unless she'd stopped to read a letter, it shouldn't have taken her more than twenty-five seconds to make it back to the house.

Lots of obstacles, and yet Lucas seemed to sail through them all with no trouble at all.

Closer to the Kingsley house now, I slowed my steps. I needed to see that back window. I peered up the driveway and saw the garage door was open and the inside empty. A good sign. I came to the front, shoved a flyer in the door, then moved quickly to the rear. Stood by the window. CJ was right: the ledge was only a few feet off the ground. Easy in, easy out. Kid didn't stand a chance.

But then I gazed out at the mailbox. Just as I'd thought; it was a straight line of sight. This meant Lucas had had a very small margin of error if he wanted to avoid being seen, and with a toddler under his arm, no less. Yet another obstacle.

What the hell did she do—hand the baby over to him?

Doubtful, but too many unanswered questions lingered in my mind.

Then I realized where I was standing and stepped back. Quickly. This was the exact spot where a toddler had been pulled away from his loving family and straight into hell. Sexually abused. Murdered. Tossed in the dirt somewhere out in the remote Texas desert like so much trash.

A three-year-old boy, for Christ's sake.

I couldn't stay there any longer, not by that window, not even in that neighborhood. I hurried down the driveway, crossed the street, then went straight for my car. Got in and sped off down the road without so much as a backward glance.

I may not have seen the Ghost of Nathan, but I'd seen enough.

CHAPTER TWELVE

My mind was speeding faster than my car after I left the Kingsley house. I shouldn't have let it get to me. I'm a reporter. I'm supposed to separate my feelings, keep them out of my way; it bothers me when I can't. I'll admit I've got a soft spot for kids, maybe because my own childhood was so lousy. My experience paled in comparison with what Nathan Kingsley suffered, but on some level, in some way, it still resonated. I felt for him. Death was too good for this Lucas guy.

Then I reminded myself that my mother and Warren also had a hand in this, and my stomach did another flip. *How the hell could they?*

I drew in a deep, shaky breath, tried to find balance in my perspective. Drove on.

I wanted to stop by the grocery store where Nathan and his mother had shopped that day, but I soon found that it no longer existed. Now standing in its place was the town's very first McDonald's.

There's progress for you.

I walked around the area for a bit instead, trying to grab hold of my emotions and maybe a better understanding of how

47

things had gone down that long-ago day. Tried speaking to a few merchants, but nobody seemed remotely interested in talking to me.

I was starting to get the message.

∼

Jerry Lindsay lived in a 1950s colonial-style house on the north side of town. His wife, Beatrice, answered the front door and led me to their sunroom, where the retired sheriff was drinking coffee and reading the paper.

At sixty-three years old, he was still rock-solid: six-foot-plus frame; broad shoulders; and large, rough hands that had clearly done their share of work over the years. He looked every bit the retired cop with his thick, silvery hair and matching mustache and an intense, unyielding stare that I imagined had proved useful in the interrogation room.

He stood and shook my hand—nearly squeezing the life out of it—then pointed at the chair across from him. It felt more like an order than an act of hospitality.

I slipped my pad and pen from my pocket as I took my seat.

"The *Kingsley* case," Lindsay said, filtering his words through mild laughter. "What on earth made you wanna pick up and come all the way out here for that?"

"It fits with a story I'm doing on missing children."

He grunted. "Huh. No missing kids over there in California?"

"We're a national magazine, Sheriff. I cover crimes all over the country."

He held my gaze, arched a brow, went silent.

I said, "Did you ever figure out what Lucas did with the body?"

"No, and I doubt we ever will."

"Why's that?"

"I'm guessing it's because he did a damn good job of hiding it." The tone was smug, the look on his face even more so.

48

I ignored both and kept pushing. "How far did your search go?"

"From county line to county line." He ran a hand through his hair, gazed out the window. "That little boy is buried in the desert somewhere. I'm sure of it."

"What makes you so sure? Was the conclusion based on any evidence?"

He shot his head back toward me. "No, it was based on common sense."

"Not sure I follow."

"As in, it's the perfect place to get rid of a body. Following me now?"

I nodded tentatively, forced a tolerant smile. "So…he never alluded in any way to how he actually disposed of it…"

"Nope."

"Refused?"

"I wouldn't say refused."

"What, then?"

"Claimed he was innocent, said he had nothing for us."

"Was there a plea bargain offered in exchange for the information?"

"Of course."

I could almost hear the unvoiced "you idiot" at the end of that sentence. I kept my eyes on my notes. "What about the items found in his apartment?"

"What about 'em?"

I looked back up at him. "Did it seem odd that he left incriminating evidence lying around?"

"Well, first of all, it wasn't *lying around.*"

"Where was it?"

He paused, shot me a blank stare. "And second, predators keep mementos from their crimes all the time."

"But a knife? And shoes and underwear with the victim's blood on them? Seems pretty risky."

In an impressively patronizing voice, he said, "Mr. Bannister, do you know anything about crime investigations?"

I hesitated, gave him my most civilized smile. "Only what I've covered in my twenty-some years of writing about them. Why?"

"I see," he said, appearing amused. "Well, there were only traces of blood on the knife. Same goes for the underwear and shoe. I doubt he ever noticed."

"Okay, but still a risk, right?"

A condescending laugh. "Nobody said the guy was a rocket scientist."

I glanced down at my notes. *Irascible?* CJ was being kind. Getting information from this guy was like trying to eat soup with a knitting needle. I circled back around to the question he'd ignored the first time. "And where did you say the items were hidden?"

"I didn't."

"So where were they, exactly?"

"I don't recall, *exactly*."

I pretended to take some notes but instead wrote the word *asshole* repeatedly. Then I took a breath and reloaded for another round. "Newspaper said the tip was anonymous."

"Okay..."

"Did you ever find out who it was?"

"Nope, and didn't much care because it led us right to our suspect. Everything added up. Can't ask for more than that."

"Was the tipster male or female?"

He eyed me but said nothing.

"Sheriff?"

Hesitation, and then, "Think it was a male."

"You don't know?"

"No, I don't *recall*. There's a difference."

I reached into my pocket for the copy of the Kingsley article I'd printed. Handed it over to him. He lifted his reading glasses from the side table, put them on, studied it.

I said, "See the necklace Nathan's wearing in the photo?"

He peered over the tops of his glasses at me. "The Saint Christopher medal."

"Was he wearing it when he was kidnapped?"

"According to the parents, he was."

"Did you ever find it?"

"Nope."

"Any idea where it might have gone?"

"We never saw it."

"So you don't know," I confirmed.

"We never *saw* it," he repeated.

This game had grown tiresome. I should have been gracious, should have walked away, especially after CJ's warning, but that just wasn't me. I decided it was time to turn up the heat on Jerry Lindsay.

Pretending to carefully weigh my words, I said, "You know, Sheriff, there's one thing I still can't figure out, and that's how Lucas managed to take the boy without anyone seeing or hearing him."

"There was the mailman."

"No, I'm talking about during the incident. Or even shortly thereafter."

"Made a clean getaway behind the house." He shrugged. "Nobody saw him."

I nodded. "Yeah, I get that, but what I don't get is this: you've got houses that are close together—very close—and Mrs. Kingsley only went out to the mailbox, which was, what, maybe fifty feet away?" I didn't wait for an answer. "And the area near the back window is in the line of sight of the street."

He said with a fixed expression, "Not sure what you're getting at."

"How could it be that Mrs. Kingsley didn't see or hear Lucas taking the boy?"

He shrugged. "She said she didn't see anything."

"And the fact she probably should have didn't bother you?"

"*Should have* is a matter of opinion, Mr. Bannister, and mine was that she was telling the truth."

"What about the neighbors? Or commuters in the area?"

He threw his hands up. "It's not my job to manufacture witnesses if there aren't any."

"I wasn't asking you to manufacture them, just finding it odd that no one saw a three-year-old boy taken from his home in broad daylight, on a through street, in a neighborhood packed tighter than a box of matches."

Lindsay squeezed his lips into a straight line and stood. "I think we're finished here, Mr. Bannister."

"Just like that?"

"I'll walk you to the door."

He did; in fact, I barely made it through before I heard it slam behind me.

Getting into my car, I shook my head and sighed. CJ had warned me, and now I was seeing it firsthand. Not many people wanted to talk about the *Kingsley* case around here, especially Jerry Lindsay.

Then I wondered what exactly he was hiding behind all that arrogance…and why.

Wickedevil
Wickedevil
Wickedevil

CHAPTER THIRTEEN

You have no Redeeming Qualities

My mother hated my love of the written word. Most parents would be thrilled to see their kid sitting down with a good book, but nothing seemed to irritate her more. She made a point of letting me know it, too, with her condescending glances, her eye rolling, her cutting remarks. Having a book in my hand meant leaving myself wide open to attacks; sometimes I'd feel anxious just picking one up.

"You know…," she said on one occasion, "kids who read too much never have any friends."

I stared at her, bewildered by the comment.

"Seriously." Her tone was matter-of-fact. "People don't like people who are too smart."

I didn't know what to say. I bit my lip and looked at my book.

She shrugged it off. "Have it your way. I'm just saying, if you want people to like you, you're going to have to dummy it down some. You're scaring them away in droves."

It was so easy. She could blame the books for almost everything: I was lazy and never got things done because of the books. The books were warping my mind, making me disrespectful. My grades were slipping because I spent too much time with my nose in my books instead of studying.

It just went on and on.

But her cruel words paled when compared with her wicked acts.

Sometimes while reading I'd suddenly realize the story wasn't making sense. Then I'd look at the page numbers and find that several had been torn out. It was always toward the end of the book, after I'd already invested a significant amount of time and imagination. Her way of twisting the knife, I suppose. She even did it to my library books. It seemed nothing was sacred.

Other times, I'd leave a book in one spot only to find it missing several hours later. When I'd ask where it was, she'd act as if she hadn't a clue. Often, I'd find it later tucked away in a cabinet with the pots and pans, at the bottom of a laundry basket filled with dirty clothes, or in some drawer we hardly ever used. I even found one under the porch once, covered in mud.

Some I never found at all.

But probably the most evil thing she did was to turn my own books against me.

The Book Game wasn't a game at all; it was a form of punishment. She'd force me to stand in a corner, face the wall, and hold two books up to my chest, elbows out.

And remain completely still.

Then she'd sit in her recliner, splitting her attention between the television and me. If I moved an inch, she'd add another book to the pile.

I remember standing with sweat tickling my forehead, elbows shaking, while she sat stuffing peanuts in her mouth and laughing—both at me and at whatever was on TV.

Her goal was to make me hate those books, but there wasn't a stack tall enough or heavy enough to make that happen.

Instead, I just ended up hating her more.

CHAPTER FOURTEEN

I stopped at the Copper Kettle on Third and Cedar to grab a quick bite, regroup, and recover from Jerry Lindsay. I needed the downtime anyway; I was feeling tired and low on energy. Travel does that to you—finding clues from a kidnapping and murder hidden among your deceased mother's belongings, even more so.

I pushed a pile of dry mashed potatoes around my plate and returned to my thoughts about Lindsay. The guy was an ass—no question about that. I just wasn't sure if he was born that way or hiding something. Either way, I hadn't bought any of it. The houses in the Kingsley neighborhood were practically piled on top of each other. Someone should have seen or heard something. *Jean* should have, even with her back to the house. By instinct, most mothers are hyperaware of their surroundings, especially when their kids are out of their immediate view. Why wasn't she?

Despite Lindsay's arrogant attitude and willfulness, the interview hadn't been a total loss. He'd given me one critical piece of information—probably the most important—even if he didn't mean to. Nathan was wearing the Saint Christopher medal the day he disappeared. That told me my mother could have been the last one to see the boy alive, or at the very least she was involved with, or knew, whoever had been. For years she'd been sitting on what was probably the most damning piece of evidence in the case.

What the hell was she doing with it?

My thoughts jumped to Jean Kingsley, a woman as mysterious as the mystery itself. I still didn't know much about her, but there was one person around who did: her husband and Nathan's father, Dennis Kingsley.

I called his number three or four times but got his answering machine. Time was at a premium; I had little of it to waste, so I decided to pay him a visit.

~

CJ wasn't kidding when she said Kingsley lived up on the hill. A mountaintop was more like it and, to make matters worse, with a long, unpaved road leading to it. I worked my way up, bumping and grinding along every inch, wondering at times if my tires would hold up—and wondering even more if I would.

To my surprise, it was a nice-looking place. Nothing huge or extravagant, but clearly he'd put a lot of work into it. Deep clay-colored walls; a terra-cotta roof; and huge, custom-built doors made of knotty alder. All that and a view of the valley that was nothing short of breathtaking.

I put the giant brass front-door knocker to use, giving it three hard raps. A moment later I saw a large, shadowy figure through the frosted glass.

My immediate impression was that time had not been good to Dennis Kingsley. He looked about fifty pounds heavier and many more than thirty years older. An unkempt, grizzled beard covered his face but couldn't hide the deep-set creases around the eyes. His expression told me he wasn't used to company, nor was he happy about having it. I'd figured as much, judging by the visitor-prohibitive location. The man liked being alone.

"I'm sorry to bother you, Mr. Kingsley," I said. "My name's Patrick Bannister, and I work for *News World*. I left a message on your machine."

He shook his head and pressed his lips together, an indication the conversation was going south before it ever started. But not if I could help it.

I continued, "I'd like to speak with you for a moment, if I could, about your son's kidnapping."

He narrowed his eyes; more creases gathered around them. Then he rested his palm against the door as if preparing to close it.

This town had more cold shoulders than a butcher's freezer. I was getting used to that but couldn't afford this one. *Think fast, Patrick.*

"I spoke to Jerry Lindsay just a short while ago," I offered quickly, hoping to prevent the inevitable door slam. "He told me to come see you."

A lie, but desperation knows no boundaries...or morals.

He loosened his hand a little, allowing it to slide a few inches down along the doorframe, but then he shook his head, frowned, and said, "I don't think I want to talk about my—"

"CJ Norris also suggested we speak," I interrupted. That part was actually true, and he must have liked it better, because I saw his face soften a bit.

He thought it over—or at least that's what he appeared to be doing—looked both ways outside his door, then opened it wider, grudgingly motioning me inside.

I followed him down a long, narrow hallway that led to his living room. Inside, the house was every bit as nice as the exterior. Wood beams crisscrossed the ceiling; the honey-colored floors matched them almost perfectly. Skylights spread a warm glow into and throughout the room. It had a comfortable and welcoming feel—a sharp contrast with the less-than-warm attitude he'd displayed when I first arrived. Clearly, there was more to this man.

I settled into the sofa, and he took the recliner. Still studying my surroundings, I focused on a string of family photos lining the fireplace mantel: Dennis, Jean, and Nathan. Big smiles during much happier times and the start of a new, exciting life—one that came crashing down too soon and without warning.

I pushed the thought aside and turned my gaze to Dennis. He was staring at me. Apparently, I'd not been alone during my visual exploration of his home. I tried to minimize the effect.

"Nice place you have here, Mr. Kingsley. Very nice."

He nodded slowly. Said nothing.

"And I really appreciate you taking the time."

"I have to tell you," he said, now sounding more troubled than annoyed, "I haven't spoken to anyone about my son in years. I'm a little uncomfortable."

"I understand, sir, and I can appreciate your hesitancy. I'll try to make this as easy as possible."

That seemed to disarm him a little. He studied me some, then said, "So what is it you need, Mr. Bannister?"

"I'd like to get some background on your family, if you don't mind." I removed the pad and pen from my shirt pocket. Knowing he wasn't quite feeling me yet, I decided to wait on Nathan, start with Jean. "Mr. Kingsley, I know your wife was very ill, but had there been any indication she was suicidal?"

He sighed long and slow. "There was very little that surprised me at that point. Things had gone from bad to worse in a hurry, and I guess by then I already knew it wasn't going to end well."

"Getting worse how?"

"She'd go from one extreme to the other. Hostile and abusive one day, withdrawn and depressed the next. Then it went from hour to hour and eventually minute to minute as the symptoms got worse."

"How so?"

He threw his hands up. "She stopped making sense. Talked about all kinds of crazy stuff. To be honest, it was difficult going to see her. Like visiting a different person each time. I never knew who the hell to expect. It just wasn't my Jeanie anymore."

"When you say 'crazy stuff,' what do you mean?"

"I don't know...pure nonsense. It went in one ear and out the other most of the time."

I nodded and offered a sympathetic smile. "Mr. Kingsley, would you have a problem with me speaking to the people at Glenview about her? Can I have your permission?"

He looked down at his hands. "Yeah, that's fine."

"What about the day your son disappeared? Can you tell me what happened?"

He gazed at me for a long moment, drew a deep breath, let it out quickly. "I came home and found my wife sitting on the living room floor, tears running down her cheeks, a dazed look on her face. And potatoes. Lots of potatoes all over the place." He looked off into the dining room, and his voice seemed to trail along with it. "For some reason, that still sticks in my mind. And her lip was busted."

"How'd that happen?"

He shook his head. "Said she'd hit it on the kitchen door while she was looking for Nathan."

I made a note of it, flipped the page. "Then what?"

"I asked her what was going on, but she wouldn't answer. Wouldn't even look up at me. So I asked again. Finally, she said, 'I've lost Nathan.' Just like that: 'I've lost Nathan.'"

"Then what?"

He brought his gaze back to me. "I asked her what she meant."

"And?"

"She just stared at me—I'll never forget the empty look in her eyes...and the tears...and the trembling. She was trembling something awful. It scared me. Just kept saying that somebody had taken our son. Over and over..."

I leaned forward. "And what did *you* say?"

"Not sure I really remember. I just...I didn't understand...I mean, there she was, on the floor, falling apart right in front of me and telling me she'd lost our son." He gazed down at the floor. "I kept hoping it was all some misunderstanding, that Nathan was in the other room fast asleep, safe, that he was fine, that…anything other than this."

"What happened next?"

"I panicked is what happened. Started running from room to room, yelling his name. Even ran down to the cellar but couldn't find him." His voice became a whisper. "I suppose that's when it hit me…that Nathan really was gone."

He was back in that horrible moment all over again. I could see it on his face, hear it in his voice. Feel it in my bones. The sheer panic of realizing his child had vanished. It was palpable and chilling. Tears began filling his eyes, and all at once, the large man with the rough exterior was transformed into a tightly wound bundle of raw emotion: sadness with a grip so tight there seemed to be no escape for him. He covered his face with his hands and began to sob, trying to conceal the tears seeping out between his fingers.

I took a deep breath, tried to maintain my reporter's demeanor, stay impartial, compartmentalize—all that stuff. But the human side of me hurt for him, truly ached. I could never in my life know what he must have gone through, never, because it was unimaginable. I didn't know what to say, what to do, so instead I began writing *monster* repeatedly in my notepad. Then I looked up and said softly, "Mr. Kingsley, would you like to stop?"

He wiped his face with his sleeve, shook his head, and then, still sobbing, said, "I called the sheriff, and within a very short time the neighborhood was flooded with deputies; they were everywhere, all looking for Nathan, but they never found him." His voice caught. "They never found my son…"

I worked through a lump in my throat, barely managing a whisper when I asked, "Mr. Kingsley, was there any chance you'd made some sort of contact with Ronald Lucas before all this happened? Or maybe your wife might've met him?"

"No," he said, shaking his head. "We were new in town, had only lived here a few months, barely knew anyone." He shook his head again. "No, definitely not."

"Where did you move from?" I asked.

"Georgia."

I could see my own shock registering on his face. "Whereabouts in Georgia?"

"A place called Black Lake."

I stared at him, my body motionless, my mind taking off.

"Something wrong?"

"No," I managed to say, hearing weakness in my voice despite my attempt to hide it. I cleared my throat, straightened my posture, did my best to look unaffected, and then, "The necklace your son was wearing the day he went missing. Can you tell me about it?"

"The Saint Christopher medal? That was a gift from his godfather."

"And his name?"

"Warren Strademeyer."

My heart gave a single, heavy thud, one that went straight up into my throat.

"Mr. Bannister?" I heard him say.

"Fine," I replied, but really, I was far from it. I forced myself to say, "So...this Warren Strademeyer. How did you and your wife know him?"

"He and Jean were friends since they were kids. In elementary school. A little town called Rose Park, in Georgia."

I nodded slowly.

"It was a different world there," he continued. "Warren was lucky enough to break away from it. He's a state senator now."

Boy, did I know that.

I said, "Do you have any contact with him these days?"

He shook his head with regret. "Not in years. Heard less and less from him after Nathan disappeared. Finally lost touch after a while."

"Why, do you think?"

"Warren was on his way up. Everyone knew it. He changed after he graduated from law school. Wasn't the same person anymore. He started moving in different circles. We weren't good enough to fit into them."

I nodded. "And all this happened right after Nathan disappeared?"

"Well…" He stopped, gave me a wary look. "Why all the interest in Warren?"

I leaned back, crossed my leg, tried to force casual. "The necklace was never found. Just trying to understand its history."

He nodded and seemed okay with that.

"So when did he give it to your son?"

"Right after he was born. He wanted Nathan to have it at his baptism."

"And do we know for sure Nathan was wearing it when he went missing?"

"He always wore it. Jean insisted."

"Did this Warren attend Nathan's memorial service?"

"No." He looked away, shook his head. "Claimed he had to travel on some kind of business."

I thought about the letter from Stover, Illinois, and those haunting words about a body.

Dennis continued. "Of course, that tore Jean up the most. Lousy of him, business or not, don't you think?"

I nodded, but inside, I wanted to scream.

CHAPTER FIFTEEN

The Kingsleys were from Black Lake. Warren was Nathan's godfather.

How the hell did I miss that?

I'd found the missing thread—or at least one of them—but it seemed to only raise more questions, the biggest one being, how did Warren and my mother get tangled up in the kidnapping and murder of a three-year-old boy? Maybe even worse, how could I not have known? I'd lived around the two of them my whole life.

There was no doubt my mother was evil. I'd seen it firsthand, lived it, knew she was capable of horrendous abuse. But was she capable of kidnapping and murdering a child?

As for Warren, the risks would have been astronomical, the implications nothing short of staggering. He was on his way up the ladder at the time, a congressman with even bigger political aspirations. What could be important enough to risk losing that? I came up with only one answer: money. It was all he ever seemed to care about, apart from his career. Could that have been enough to lure him to the dark side?

Then there was Ronald Lee Lucas. I still hadn't figured out his role in all this or how Warren and my mother would have even associated with the likes of him. It didn't make a damn bit of sense.

Or did it?

I allowed my mind to run free. A hired thug? A sexual predator who got carried away, then had to kill the boy to keep him quiet? But why would my mother and Warren hire him to take Nathan in the first place? What were they planning on doing with him?

Talking to Dennis seemed to only widen the mystery surrounding Jean, the relationship with Warren putting her in my crosshairs. Might she be the final link I needed to complete the picture? I couldn't ask her, but I could go where she spent her final days and took her last breath.

~

Glenview Psychiatric Hospital looked like it could drive a person insane if she weren't already. Chain link and razor wire surrounded the perimeter, and beyond that, ivy snaked its way up dirty red-brick walls. I let my gaze follow it to a bar-covered window where an elderly woman looked down on me, her face as white as the long, stringy hair that framed it. She nodded with a vacant, fish-eyed expression, then flashed a menacing, toothless grin that sent chills up my spine. I turned my attention away quickly, headed for the front door.

Glenview had once been a private facility, but the state had taken it over several years before. From the looks of things, they hadn't done much to improve it. I moved down a dimly lit, claustrophobic hallway so narrow that I doubted two people could walk it side by side. The asylum-green walls were cracked and chipped, the floors covered in nondescript, skid-infested tile. The overall theme: dismal and cold.

I came to the gatekeeper for this palace of darkness: a receptionist behind a Plexiglas partition blurred with fingerprints, grime, and other slimy things I was afraid to think about. Her expression told me she was sick of her job. Couldn't say I blamed her. Then I heard static and a speaker going live.

"Can I help you," she said. It sounded more like a statement than a question.

I leaned in toward a metal-covered hole in the glass. "Patrick Bannister for Doctor Faraday."

No verbal response, just a loud buzzer and a simultaneous *click* as the lock disengaged; I pulled the door open and found her waiting on the other side behind a service counter.

After signing in with my ID, I handed over my cell phone. Then a security guard arrived to escort me through a sally port that looked more like a cave. Smelled like one, too. Next stop, a service elevator: high stink factor there as well, like a nasty old gym locker.

Stepping off onto the fifth floor, I fell into sensory overload. The stench was so wicked and fierce that it burned through my sinuses—excrement, sweat, and cleaning agents all blended into one nasty funk that kicked my gag reflex into action. Then came the sounds: a woman's hysterical laughter echoing down the hall, clearly not inspired by anything funny, along with lots of cursing and other peculiar, vaguely human cries I could hardly identify. As we moved past the metal-grated security doors, patients peered at me with flat, vacant expressions; creepy smiles; and wild eyes that made my skin crawl.

Finally, we came to a port in the storm: a nursing station. The guard nodded to the woman behind the counter. She nodded back, and he left me there.

In her early fifties, she was a striking brunette, one of those women whose beauty seems to improve with age: high cheekbones; dark-lashed, pale blue eyes; and a pair of legs that could give a twenty-year-old a run for her money. The nametag said she was Aurora Penfield, Nursing Supervisor. I eyed a photo on the desk; it was her, much younger, with a small boy on her lap, both smiling big for the camera. Then I looked up and saw her staring, waiting for me to speak.

I cleared my throat. "Patrick Bannister for Doctor Faraday."

In a dutiful, mechanical manner, she reached for the telephone and punched a few buttons, giving me the once-over while waiting for an answer.

I smiled.

She didn't.

Then I felt a tug on my leg. Startled, I looked down into a pair of dark, cavernous eyes staring up at me: a woman squatting on the floor, probably in her sixties but with a distinctly childlike quality. Tangled, grizzled hair surrounded a hopeless, miserable face. She barked at me, then snarled, baring her teeth.

"Gretchen!" Penfield said, leaning over the counter, her tone cross and unwavering. "Move away *immediately!*"

The woman looked at Penfield, looked at me, then frowned. I glanced down and spotted a yellowish puddle forming between her feet, but before I could react, two orderlies stepped quickly toward us; they each grabbed an arm and pulled her up, then guided her away.

Nurse Ratched went back to her work as if nothing had happened and said, "Doctor's on his way. Please take a seat."

I did.

A few moments later, a side door opened and Doctor Faraday appeared. He was somewhere in his sixties, tall and slender, with a head of thick, silvery hair and wire-rimmed glasses that missed the fashion curve by a good twenty years. His face registered zero on the expression scale, as blank as the wall behind him. As we shook hands, I noticed his were rough-skinned and ice-cold.

He led me down a corridor and past a door with a glass observation window. Inside, a patient sat in the corner, hands under his gown, giving himself pleasure. He made direct eye contact with me and started jerking himself with more enthusiasm and fervor. Then he stopped, and a shit-eating grin slowly spread across his face. I looked away, feeling my nausea return for a second round.

When we reached Faraday's office, he took a seat behind his desk and I sat across from him.

"Jean Kingsley," he said, removing his glasses and rubbing his eyes. "Haven't heard that name in years."

"I'm doing a story about her son's kidnapping and murder."

He put his glasses back on, looked down at some paperwork. "I've reviewed her records. What exactly would you like to know?"

"We can start with the basics: her condition, how many times she was admitted, and for how long."

He puffed his cheeks full of air, then let it out slowly. "Mrs. Kingsley was a very sick woman. She suffered a series of breakdowns—three, to be exact—rather significant ones. She was admitted here after each of them. The duration increased with each visit, as did the severity of her condition."

"How long was her last stay?"

"About a month."

"Any indication why she killed herself? I mean, other than the obvious. Anything unusual happen that day?"

"Not at all. Mrs. Kingsley was dealing with enormous guilt over her son's murder. She blamed herself. As time went on, her memories and perceptions about the kidnapping seemed to become more distorted, as did her impression of reality as a whole."

"Distorted in what way?"

"Her recollection about what actually happened, the circumstances leading to it—none of it made any sense, and most of it seemed to lack truth. After a while, it started sounding like she was talking about someone else's life rather than her own. She was a different person."

"What kinds of things did she say?"

He gazed down at his notes, threw his hands up, shaking his head. "I honestly wouldn't know where to begin. Purely illogical thinking."

I leaned forward to glance at the notes. "Can I have a look?"

He dropped his arms down to shield them and stared at me as if I'd asked the unthinkable. "Absolutely not."

"But Mrs. Kingsley's no longer alive, and her husband gave me permission."

"That's not the point, Mr. Bannister. It's at my discretion whether or not to release them, and I choose not to."

I shot him a long, curious gaze. He broke eye contact by picking up the phone, hastily punching a few buttons, and then saying, "Ms. Penfield, please come to my office immediately."

"Doctor Faraday, you should understand my intentions here. I'm not trying to—"

"I understand your intentions just fine. You have a job to do. So do I."

Penfield walked in, spared me a quick glance, then gave the doctor her attention. He said, "Please put these records back where they belong."

She nodded, moved toward his desk.

I tried again. "Doctor, I don't want to put Mrs. Kingsley or this hospital in a bad light. I just want to tell her story so people can understand the hell she went through. Not seeing those records would be missing the biggest part."

Penfield suddenly looked at me with an expression that was hard to read. I couldn't tell whether it was animosity or...well, I just couldn't tell.

The doctor said, "The answer is still no, Mr. Bannister. The records are confidential. End of discussion."

Penfield grabbed the last of the papers, closed the folder. "Will there be anything else, Doctor?"

Faraday shook his head, and she threw me another quick glance before going on her way.

He said, "Now, where were we?"

I nodded toward the door. "We were discussing those records you just had whisked out of here."

"Look," he said, exhaling his frustration and shaking his head, "I'm sorry if it came out wrong. It's not that I'm afraid you'll put us in a bad light or anything like that."

"Then what is it? Because quite honestly, I'm a little confused about what just happened here."

His stare lingered a moment. "Let me put it to you this way: some things are better left alone. Trust me, this is one of them."

"I'm not following you."

"What I'm saying is that the picture you'd see of Mrs. Kingsley would not be a flattering one. And it wouldn't serve any purpose other than to make her look bad."

"Doctor, with all due respect, good or bad, it's reality, and it's my job to write about it, not hide it."

With eyes locked on mine, lips pursed, he shook his head.

I tried another option. "Then if you won't let me see the records, can you at least tell me more about what happened while she was here?"

He paused for a long moment, seemed to be evaluating my words, and then with reluctance in his voice said, "With each visit, she became more disturbed, more agitated…and more lost in her own mind. We couldn't help her. No one could. Things were becoming extremely tense. And unpleasant."

"Unpleasant how?"

"We were concerned about the safety of others."

"Why?"

He hesitated again. "There were threats."

"What kind?"

"Death threats. To the staff and other patients—actually, to anyone who came within shouting distance of Mrs. Kingsley. Quite honestly, she frightened people. We'd made the decision to move her to the maximum-security unit, and her husband was in the process of committing her. Permanently."

"Do you know what brought this on?"

He pressed his hands together, looked down at them for a moment, then back up at me. "When I said Mrs. Kingsley was a different person, I meant it."

"I'm sorry?"

"She was experiencing what we call a major depression with psychotic features."

"Which means…"

"She was severely delusional, seeing and hearing things that didn't exist, and…" He let out a labored sigh. "And she began assuming an identity other than her own."

"What identity?"

"She called herself Bill Williams."

"She thought she was a man?"

He nodded.

Glancing down at my notes, I raked my fingers through my hair, then looked back up at him. "Was she in this state all the time?"

"No. She'd slip in and out."

"When did it start?"

"Toward the end of her last stay."

"So, close to the time she died," I confirmed.

"Yes."

"And who was this Bill Williams?"

"Nobody, I'm sure. But in her mind, she *was* him. Her vocal tone became deeper, her mannerisms, even her facial expressions… all convincingly masculine. It was a startling transformation."

"Did she give any details about him? Who he was?"

"Just that he was a murderer."

"She took on the role of a killer…"

"Yes, and according to her, one of the most dangerous killers of our time, maybe ever."

"What did he do?"

"Question should be, what didn't he do? She reported that he began murdering when he was nine years old. Lured his best friend

71

into a shed behind his house, then beat him to death with a claw hammer to the point where the child's face was unrecognizable."

I cringed at the thought, said nothing.

"She talked about it frequently—as Bill Williams, that is. She—I mean, *he*—took great delight in the feeling in his hands when the hammer made powerful impact with flesh and bone... the release, the euphoric pleasure. And it doesn't end there. He just kept going. Several years later, after his mother remarried, he climbed into their bed while she and the stepfather were asleep and began spooning the husband. Then he shoved the man's face into his pillow...and a kitchen knife up his rectum. The mother woke in the middle of the night drenched in blood. Bill had wrapped the man's arms around her, then went off to his room and peacefully back to sleep."

"Good *Lord*," I said. "All this created from her mind?"

"I'm afraid so. A very disturbed one, I remind you, one that had lost contact with any form of reality."

"Did this Bill—or Mrs. Kingsley—talk about anything else?"

"Plenty. In her final days, she spent a good part of her time bragging about the other murders he'd committed."

"What did she say?"

"Horrible things. Gruesome things. Some of the most disturbing I've ever heard—and trust me, I've experienced a lot here."

"Details?"

"I've actually tried to forget them...but with a few, I've had a hard time doing that."

"You can't tell me?"

Doctor Faraday gazed out the window and shook his head very slowly. A tree branch shifted in the wind and threw an odd shadow across his face. "I'd rather not."

I drew in some air, blew it out quickly. "Can you at least tell me why she'd dream up someone so horrible, let alone want to assume his identity? Who was this guy?"

He turned back and caught my gaze, held it for a moment. "According to her, Bill Williams was the man who kidnapped and murdered her son."

The hair on my arms stood straight up—on the back of my neck, too—and suddenly the room felt frigid. I didn't say anything for a long moment, and then, "She assumed the identity of the man who killed her son…"

"Correction: the one she manufactured as the killer."

"Why would she do that?"

"With the mentally ill, there really isn't any rhyme or reason, Mr. Bannister."

"She ever say why she thought he did it?"

"No, and it hardly much mattered since it was all made up anyway."

"I appreciate you taking the time, Doctor." I stood up, gathered my things.

"Welcome," he replied with an expression that revealed absolutely nothing.

I reached over to shake his hand—it was still ice-cold—then, handing him my business card, I said, "My cell number's there if you remember anything else."

He led me back down the hallway and out toward the reception area, where a guard escorted me to the elevator. Penfield was standing there, staring at me. Once again.

"I'm going downstairs, Samuel," she said, her eyes locked on mine, her expression bare. "I can see him out, save you the trouble."

Penfield watched him move down the hall and then under her breath said, "I was here when Mrs. Kingsley died."

I felt my heart clap twice inside my chest. *Pay dirt.*

She went on, "And I *don't* believe she killed herself. Never did."

"What are you telling me? That she was murdered?"

"*Nurse Penfield!*"

Doctor Faraday's voice, coming from around the corner.

She glanced quickly in that direction, then shoved the folder into my hands. "Take this, then get lost. And I mean it! *Fast!*"

I dropped the folder down to my side, could see Faraday coming around the bend.

The elevator door opened, and I stepped inside quickly, the door closing just in time, barely revealing a nervous Penfield as she turned around to face Faraday.

CHAPTER SIXTEEN

They say angels come in the most unexpected disguises, but who knew mine would look like Aurora Penfield? The lesson, I suppose, was never underestimate the value of a bitter and disgruntled employee.

In my motel room, I opened the folder. Inside were the notes—pages and pages of them—Faraday had written during Jean Kingsley's stays at Glenview. I spread them on the bed, wondering which might hold the answers I needed.

The doctor's messy shorthand was hard to decipher but still clear enough to show Jean Kingsley's downward spiral growing more pronounced during her final stay:

June 15, 1977
Pt. in catatonic state. Unresp. @ external stimuli. No talk. Ref. to eat.

Then:

June 23, 1977
Pt. more respons. but disconnected @ external stimuli/reality. Aware of surroundings w/min. resp. Nurses report pt. sitting

by window, rocking an imaginary baby, singing to it. Words slurred/indistinguishable. Pt. claims she's holding her deceased son Nathan.

Disturbing but mild when compared with what followed next:

Jul. 5, 1977
Pt. more alert/respons. but anxiety sig. increased. Agitated. Complaining intruder in her bed hides under sheets, touches her inappropriately. Screaming all night.

Jul. 9, 1977
Pt. suffering from trichotillomania w/noticeable hair loss and trichophagia. Nurses rpt. pt. pulling hair out, eating it. Also found clumps around bed.

Jul. 14, 1977
Pt. engaging in self-injurious scratching behavior @ forearms and legs. Skin broken, bleeding. Sent to infirmary @ evaluation and treatment.

Then, toward the end of her stay:

Jul. 29, 1977
Pt. anxiety increase signif. Paranoid delusional. Claims someone "after her" but refus. to reveal said perp. or details because this will "turn up the heat." Pt. speech/manner agitated.

And around the same time, something even more interesting:

Jul. 31, 1977
Abrasion @ pt.'s right cheek of unknown origin. Asked about it=no response. Sent infirmary @ evaluation and treatment.

No infirmary report in the file; nothing about the outcome there.

I also found a few notes about Jean's delusional state in which she assumed her new identity as Bill Williams. Although the general information reflected what Faraday had told me, there were no specifics on her rants regarding Bill's murders. That seemed odd; surely the information would have been relevant to her treatment. Faraday had refused to discuss the particulars, and now they were missing from the notes. I wondered if it was more than a coincidence.

And there was something else he hadn't told me:

Aug. 3, 1977
Pt. talking @ someone she calls "Sam I Am." Highly agitated/ hysterical in ref. to him. When asked who person is, pt. offers no explan. Only that she fears him.

Aurora had been kind enough to include the visitation logs for Jean's stays at Glenview. I looked them over. Dennis Kingsley came to see his wife religiously, usually twice daily. He often arrived around 7:30 a.m., probably before work, then returned around 6:00 p.m., most likely after finishing his day. I saw some other names sprinkled throughout the logs, but not many, and none stayed for more than a few minutes. Few returned. She'd probably scared the hell out of them.

Except, that is, for one.

Michael Samuels. Three visits. Always late at night.

Sam I Am?

I searched for the guest log on the day Jean died: missing. Every date accounted for except that one.

Flipped back to the night before the abrasion was discovered on Jean's cheek. That log was still there: Samuels had paid her a visit around 11:30 p.m.

What did he do...whack her?

Looked back at the doctor's notes a few days after the abrasion appeared:

Aug. 1, 1977
Pt. woke screaming approx. 12:35 a.m., suffering @ night terrors. Nurses rpt. diff. time calming her. Admin. 150 mg @ Thorazine. No further incident.

Bad night, indeed. The woman was terrified. It was also around the same time she began talking about Sam I Am.

What the hell was the guy doing to her?

Apparently, he'd had the presence of mind to dispose of the records documenting his final visit the night Jean Kingsley died but not enough to cover all his tracks.

I dialed Glenview and asked for Aurora Penfield.

"What is it?" she said, her voice edgy and tight.

"I need to see you."

"No."

"Why not?"

"No," she said again, this time with more annoyance.

"But I need more information."

In a hasty whisper, "You're going to have to get it without me. I gave you what I could. Now leave me out of it!"

"Too late for that. I need to talk to—"

She hung up.

I stared at my phone for a long moment. The woman was scared; it seemed obvious.

I began gathering up the notes. A sheet slid from the loose pile to the floor. As I leaned over to pick it up, I saw an envelope halfway under the door.

I looked through the peephole. Nobody there. Opened the door, glanced both ways. Picked up the letter, flipped it over: standard business size, white, plain, nothing written on it.

I tore it open, pulled out the sheet of paper, unfolded it.

And nearly lost my breath.

Scrawled across the page in large letters, barely legible handwriting:

the snoop spies the snoop dies

My mouth went dry, my body numb. I placed the note on the nightstand and stared at it for a long time. A sick joke? Nothing remotely funny about this. Someone trying to rattle me? Then I remembered CJ's warning: *You might be headed for some trouble.*

Next question: Who wanted me out of town? Pretty much everyone, so far. But to go to this length? It had to be someone desperate enough. I considered the people I'd spoken to so far: CJ Norris, Dennis Kingsley, Jerry Lindsay, and Doctor Faraday. Norris was fine. Kingsley was standoffish in the beginning but warmed up once the conversation started. The guy seemed genuine; I liked him. Doctor Faraday, not so much, and Lindsay, not at all. I still couldn't decide if he was hiding something or just your standard macho shithead—either way, I didn't trust the old bastard. And if he had sent me this warning, I had to wonder why he'd want to keep me from digging, and, even more, what exactly he didn't want me to find out.

I walked over to the window and pulled the curtains closer together.

Thought about calling someone—but who? That would draw even more attention to me, something I could hardly afford right now. Nope, wasn't going to do that.

I wiped my sweaty palms on my pant legs, went to the desk, found some motel stationery and a pen.

Wrote *miscreant* fifty times.

Noticed my handwriting looked uncharacteristically shaky.

Decided to lie down for just a few minutes…

Cancel
Cancel
Cancel

CHAPTER SEVENTEEN

Sensitivity not spoken here

Things weren't all bad all the time. I had glimpses of what happiness might have felt like. I called them "almost moments." Times in my life when I almost got what I needed, almost made a connection, almost figured things out.

Autumn in Black Lake, a time of year I loved, the sweltering summer heat making its downward slide from miserable to mild, the leaves showing the latest in fall color, the winter months riding just above the horizon. School had just started, and I was busy at work on my first project for the year: constructing a family tree using photographs that went as far back as I could find. Warren brought a boxful over for me to pick through. He placed them on the counter, then silently migrated into the living room to watch the football game on TV.

I remember sitting at the kitchen table and sorting through photos, surrounded by the delicious smell of pumpkin pie. It was my mother's only indulgence of the holidays. Warren loved her pies, and what Warren wanted, he usually got.

Maybe it was a combination of the photos, of us all being together, the smell of fresh pies baking in the oven. Maybe it was because my mother appeared to be relaxed and in a decent mood for a change. I don't know—maybe it was all of those things. Whatever the reason, for a brief moment we almost felt like a real family. And that *almost* feeling was wonderful.

Sorting through photos, I came across one that made me curious. Mother was standing right behind me, and I held it up so she could see it. "Is this you?"

She leaned in for a better look, then smiled and nodded. "With my father."

"My grandfather?" I asked, now more interested. I'd never had the chance to know him; he'd died before I was born. I raised the photo for a better look, barely recognizing the girl in the picture as the woman I knew. Young, happy, and beautiful—it was such a sharp contrast. I wondered where along the way she'd left that girl, whether she ever missed her, if she'd even noticed—and what might have turned her so angry at life.

She took the photo from my hand and gazed at it. With the slightest hint of a smile and with an unaccustomed softness to her voice, she said, "I'd almost forgotten about that day…"

"Where were you?"

She lowered herself into the chair next to me, still lost in the photo. I edged in closer and looked on with her. "At the state fair. We went for my birthday. I'd just turned sixteen…"

She placed the photo flat on the table, began gently running her fingers over it.

Then the smile turned sad and tears filled her eyes. She sniffled, wiped them away quickly, as if to erase any trace of sorrow. It was a side of her I'd seldom seen, and suddenly I felt sorry for her. Unsure what to say, I instinctively put my hand on her arm.

She yanked it away, her sudden refusal making me flinch.

"The pies are baking," she said, then stood and rushed back toward the stove. "You're making a mess with those photos. Get them out of my kitchen."

And so I did, not knowing why that picture had allowed us to connect and, at the same time, not knowing why it had ended so quickly.

But I never forgot how good it felt.

CHAPTER EIGHTEEN

5:36 a.m.

My moment of rest had turned into hours; I woke up with my clothes still on, still thinking about the nasty-gram on the nightstand. There was no going back to sleep after that. Message received. I wasn't welcome here. But here I was, and I needed to stay focused.

I thought about Penfield. She'd said Jean's death wasn't a suicide, and although the files may have pointed to Michael Samuels as a possible suspect in some kind of abuse, I saw nothing that proved murder. I needed to talk to her, find out why she was so convinced. I glanced at the clock again. She'd be coming off her shift in about an hour.

～

A driving rain battered the windshield, and suddenly, negotiating the interstate felt more like a challenge than a chore.

I took the off-ramp to Glenview, then, about five minutes later, pulled into the lot. Somehow, the rain made the monster of a building look even more ugly.

I dialed Sully.

"I need your help, buddy."

"You know," he said, "you really need to work on that phone etiquette. It's standard practice in this country to say hello before you start asking for stuff."

"Sorry, I'm stressed."

"You said that last time."

"It still applies. Look, I need you to run a name and DL number for me."

"Hang on." I heard the rustling of paper. "Okay, shoot."

"Michael Samuels." I gave him the license number and state from my notes.

"Date of birth?"

"Don't have one, but I'm guessing he'd be somewhere in his fifties now. The license was active in the seventies—not sure if it still is. Find out anything you can about him...as *soon* as you can. It's important, Sully."

"I'm on it."

I clicked the phone off and looked out my window. The rain was coming down harder now. I glanced at my watch: five till seven. I got out of the car, moved beneath an overhang fifteen feet from the employee exit.

And waited.

About ten minutes later, a slew of employees began filing out the door, umbrellas raised, making it difficult to see if Penfield was among them. I narrowed my focus as they moved past, searching faces while trying to appear inconspicuous. One woman glanced over at me. I smiled. She smiled back. No sign of Aurora Penfield.

I waited another fifteen minutes in vain.

Where the hell is she?

I knew she'd been working this shift—I'd spoken to her last night. I also knew there was only one door employees were allowed to use as an exit. Had she gone home early? Stayed to work a double? I didn't have time to wait through another eight hours but desperately needed to speak with her.

I made my way back toward the parking lot, rain stinging my cheeks like tiny pebbles. When I got to my car, I heard two people talking. I looked up toward the employee door.

And there she was, speaking with another person as she made her way out.

Then she rushed toward the parking lot, long, shapely legs moving quickly beneath an umbrella. I jockeyed my position to move into her path. At about ten feet away, she spotted me, and her expression suddenly changed. So did her direction. She did an about-face and hurried back toward the building.

Fat chance.

I quickened my pace and chased after her. She was no match for a desperate reporter wearing sneakers. Moving beside her now, I said, "I have to talk to you."

She kept walking, steady in her gait, eyes focused straight ahead. "I told you I've got nothing to say."

"It's important."

"I don't care," she said, increasing her pace, still refusing to look at me. "Get away from me or I'll call security."

I stopped moving and stood. "What the hell's your problem? You give me the damn records, then you want nothing to do with me?"

She stopped too and turned back toward me, her lips tight around her words. "There are security cameras all over this parking lot. I risked my job giving you those records. Do you want me to get fired? I can't be seen with you. Now go...*away!*"

She skirted me and headed back toward the parking lot. I followed, raising my voice over the pouring rain. "Then you shouldn't have given them to me in the first place!"

"Don't make me sorry I did." She closed the umbrella, got into her car.

"But you did. So I'm not going anywhere until you—"

Slam.

Right in my face.

She started the ignition.

She wasn't getting away, not if I could help it. I began pounding on the window. "Aurora! Open up! Tell me why you're so sure Jean was murdered. Aurora!"

She looked past me, and panic washed across her face. I swung around and spotted a security guard moving in my direction with angry eyes on me. I turned back to the window just in time to find Penfield reaching for the lever, preparing to shift into reverse. In an act of desperation, I pulled the newspaper photo of Nathan Kingsley and the Saint Christopher medal from my pocket, held them against the glass.

Her eyes opened wide in astonishment, then slowly she moved her gaze up and met mine.

With rain dripping down my face and desperation in my heart, I mouthed the word *please*.

Penfield slammed the car into park, hit the unlock button, then closed her eyes and leaned her head back. I rushed around to the passenger door and got inside.

CHAPTER NINETEEN

She pulled out of the parking lot and onto the main road traveling north. Neither of us spoke. After a few miles, she drove into a rest area and parked.

With hands gripping the wheel, elbows locked, she turned to me and said, "This isn't just about a magazine story."

I shook my head.

"Want to tell me what you're doing with his necklace?"

"I can't."

She stared at me. I went on, "But please trust me when I say I'm one of the good guys, and I need you to tell me what happened to Jean Kingsley that night."

She gazed at me for a moment as if measuring my words, then looked straight ahead, bit her bottom lip. "She was murdered."

"Give me something to back it up."

She looked back at me quickly. "You read the records, right?"

"I did. But there's nothing that points to a murder."

"But it points to a suspect."

"You mean Michael Samuels," I said. "Sam I Am."

She raised her eyebrows, nodded.

"Who was he?"

"Claimed to be her nephew."

I looked out my window at nothing, scratched my head. "You know, being afraid of someone is one thing. Getting killed by them is completely another. If that's all you've got—"

"There's more." She dug into her purse and pulled out a cigarette, lit it, took a greedy drag, then opened the window a crack as she exhaled. "Her nightgown."

"What about it?"

"Supposedly, she hung herself from the door with it."

"Okay…"

"That wasn't the gown she went to bed in that night."

"How do you know?"

"She was agitated that evening. Spilled food all over herself. I should have changed her into a clean one, but I was dog tired, so I just sponged it. That's why I remember, because I was breaking a rule. And it left a stain."

"But why would someone switch her gown?"

"Because hers got torn. Kind of hard to make it look like she hung herself with it that way."

I waited.

Another drag, a quick exhale, then she tossed the half-smoked cigarette through the crack in her window. "When I went outside for my break, I saw Samuels in the shadows of the parking lot. He stuffed something into a trash can and walked away really fast. So I went over and looked, found a nightgown all bunched up and torn. With the stain."

"Okay. So, this Samuels guy. Did you see where he went after that?"

"No. The alarm went off, and everything went to hell real fast. I had to rush inside. That's when they found Mrs. Kingsley hanging in her room."

"And that's when you put two and two together."

"Yeah. Exactly."

"Did you tell anyone?"

A scornful smile. "I tried to. Told the sheriff and Faraday about it. I even took them outside to show them the gown, but when we got there, it was gone."

"What do you think happened to it?"

She threw her hands up and shook her head. "He came back to get it? I don't know. But I saw it, and then it was gone."

"So nobody believed you."

"Nope. With no gown, there wasn't any physical evidence, just my word. I didn't even have a clear description except that he was wearing a cowboy hat, and that's every guy in Texas."

"And the guest log for that night was missing from the files you gave me. So no proof he was even there."

"You got it. Sheriff ruled it a suicide. And I looked like an idiot."

"Do you remember anything else about Samuels?"

She looked out through the front windshield, shook her head. "Just like every other yahoo you see around here."

"Can you get a little more specific for me?"

"Faded blue jeans, flannel shirt. The hat was pulled down low. I never saw his face very well."

"Age?"

"If I had to guess, maybe in his twenties."

"Anything else?"

She thought for a moment. "I smelled cigarette smoke when I walked up to the trash can."

I paused, contemplated. "You said you were risking your job by giving me the records. So why did you?"

She looked down at her purse, began running her fingers along the outer edges as she spoke. "Faraday didn't want trouble on his watch. He didn't believe me, and he was not happy with me at all for making a fuss."

"So you felt uncomfortable."

"To put it mildly. And it only got worse from there. A few days later, he comes over to me, starts talking about how a psychiatric nurse seeing things that aren't really there is the kind of thing that could get someone fired, and maybe that particular person would be best served not to stir the pot."

"Subtle."

"As a brick."

"So you shut up."

"I was a single mom with a leukemic child and medical bills piling up. You bet your ass I did."

I thought about the photo on her desk.

"Guess it didn't matter anyway." She looked down at her hands, started rubbing them together. "I lost him in eighty-three."

"I'm so sorry..."

"But I would have died for that kid. I would have. And I sure as hell wasn't going to lose my job and my chance to fight like hell for his life. That's what mothers do."

I said nothing.

She looked back up at me, tears in her eyes. "You don't know how many times I prayed for God to take me instead. I was angry as hell that He didn't." She brought both hands up to wipe her cheeks, then shook her head. "I'm sorry, I shouldn't—"

"Don't be." I waited while she found a tissue in her purse, blew her nose. Then I said, "But why now? Why me?"

"It's complicated...most of the people who work at Glenview don't let themselves have feelings for the patients. They can't, and pretty much, neither do I. But Mrs. Kingsley was different."

"Different how?"

"I felt horrible for her. She lost her son, and I had one fighting for his life. I felt a connection. You know?"

I nodded.

"Then what do I go and do? In order to keep mine alive, I kept a secret, one that that did her a horrible injustice." Her eyes began welling with tears again. "I did her wrong. *I* was wrong."

"You did what you had to. What any mother would do."

She closed her eyes. "It's been eating at me for years, this whole thing...the guilt. Then you come along, and you're right, you *are* one of the good guys, you know? Sometimes you can just tell. I knew it when I overheard you talking to Faraday." She shrugged. "I don't know...maybe something changed in me. Maybe I've come to realize that some risks are worth taking, that this was my only chance to make things right."

I gave her a sad smile.

She laughed a little. "Pretty stupid of me to think I could just give you the records and walk away. But I was scared, you know?"

"You did the right thing. I'll make sure everything stays confidential between us. I promise."

"But can you get to the bottom of this? Do you think you can find out what happened? I want you to—I really do."

"I'm sure going to try," I said. "I promise you that."

CHAPTER TWENTY

The skies were closing in as I drove away from Glenview, the rain picking up momentum once more, churning into a storm that was growing angrier by the minute.

Along with a story that was growing more tragic.

I struggled to readjust my perspective. Jean Kingsley, a murder victim. What she and her family endured; what Dennis must have endured.

Dennis. I needed to talk to him. I dialed his number.

"Did Mrs. Kingsley have a nephew?"

A brief pause. "No. She had a niece...why?"

I tried to minimize the concern. "Just researching your family's history. I thought I'd heard someone say she had a nephew, is all. Thanks for clearing it up."

I hung up, dialed Sully's number.

"You're taking too long," I said as soon as he answered.

"Well, hello to you, too, Mr. Manners."

"I know you'll forgive me. Got any answers about Samuels yet?"

He sighed. "Just now. It took some work. And the answer is, nothing."

"Damn."

"The DL number never existed, and the name Michael Samuels doesn't match up with anything close to it, either."

"Phony name and numbers."

"Sure looks that way."

"Okay. Thanks, Sully. I owe you one."

"More than one."

"I'll take care of my tab later."

"Have fun."

"Doubt it."

I hung up, thought for moment. Hiding his identity; I wasn't surprised. Yet another shadow cast upon a case that was already looking awfully shady.

Some things were starting to fall into place, but many others still weren't. Jean Kingsley's being murdered didn't tell me a thing about my mother and Warren's involvement; in fact, it only seemed to confuse things. No clear or logical connection that I could find.

And then there was the other missing link still pulling at my gut: Ronald Lucas. No association, no way to figure out why he killed the boy. Could he have somehow been in cahoots with Samuels? If he was, I had nothing to prove it.

I stopped by the convenience store, grabbed a six-pack of soda, headed back to my motel room; it was starting to feel uncomfortably familiar. Not home, not even welcoming. Just recognizable.

And lonely.

I popped the top off my soda and wrote the word *deformity* twenty-seven times in my notebook.

I'm not sure how much time I spent stretched out on the bed, staring at the ceiling and wondering how long I'd have to stay in Texas. How long until something here started making sense. Then the phone pulled me out of it. I grabbed it midring.

"Mr. Bannister?"

"Who's this?" I replied.

"My name's Abbey," she said, her voice shaky but determined. "I need to speak to you."

"About what?"

She paused, and then, "In person."

"Listen…Abbey. It's late, and I'm tired—"

"You'll want to see me," she interrupted.

"Convince me," I said, my tone quickly changing to match my annoyance. I reached for my notebook and wrote *rummage rummage rummage rummage…*

"I have information you need. About Nathan Kingsley."

I stopped writing. "Okay. You've got my attention. How did you find me?"

"It's a small town, Mr. Bannister. Everyone knows you've been asking questions about the *Kingsley* case. I think I may have some of the answers you've been looking for."

Someone in Corvine who actually wanted to talk to me. "Okay, when and where?"

CHAPTER TWENTY-ONE

I arrived at Jimmy's All Night Diner and spotted her immediately: she had to be the nervous wreck in the booth at the back. Fiftysomething, tiny, brownish hair with streaks of gray running through it. Worry lines all over her face.

She shifted awkwardly and gave a cautious smile as I took my seat.

I waved down a waitress with a coffeepot, who filled my cup and flashed a Big Texas Smile. Abbey was busily folding and unfolding an empty sugar packet.

"So…" I said, wrapping my hands around my cup. "Does Abbey have a last name?"

A single nod. "It's Lawson."

"Pleased to meet you, Ms. Lawson."

"But you'll probably do better with my maiden name. It's Lucas." She watched me with interest as if measuring my reaction, and then, "Ronnie was my brother."

I tightened my feet around the base of the table, fought to keep my face from registering the shock I was feeling.

"He didn't kill that boy."

I gave her an appraising glance, then stared down at my cup, turning it slowly in its saucer. "Ms. Lawson, from what I've read and heard, there was a good amount of evidence against your brother, evidence that left little doubt that he—"

"Was guilty. Yes, I know how it appeared. But I'm here to tell you there's more to this than what you've read and heard, Mr. Bannister. Lots more."

"Okay," I said, motioning for her to continue. "Care to enlighten me?"

She looked down and continued refolding the empty sugar packet. "You're aware that there were a few problems during the trial, aren't you?"

I shook my head.

She gave a cutting grin. "Guess the papers buried that lead."

"What kinds of problems?"

"Well, for one, their star witness? The mailman? Lou Taggert? Let's just say he had some credibility issues."

"Such as?"

"A drinking problem."

"Sounds more like a personal issue than one concerning credibility."

"Not when you consider what happened as a result."

I leaned back in my seat, waited for more.

"Had a few run-ins with the law. Drinking and driving times two, one of them a hit-and-run. Think that might affect his credibility now, Mr. Bannister?"

"It might, yes."

"And if the man had a drinking problem—which it appears he clearly did—who's to say he wasn't also drunk on the job, maybe even the day he supposedly saw my brother wandering through the neighborhood? See where I'm going with this?"

"I do."

"And, in fact, who knows *what* he really saw, anyway…or if?" she said, the wrinkles on her forehead now growing deeper and more pronounced.

"What about the judge? If the mailman was such a lousy witness, why did he allow the testimony?"

She flashed a smile that looked more bitter than happy. "Taggert claimed he hadn't touched a drink in over a year, and since there was no proof he'd been drinking that day, the judge ruled it as admissible. Not that the jury would have held it against him anyway. We're talking about Texas in the seventies."

"Even so," I said, "there was other evidence against your brother."

"Nathan's bloody clothing."

I nodded.

"Well, there's more to that, too."

"Like what?"

"Like, they lost it."

"Excuse me?"

"That's right," she said, nodding. "Lost. Oh, they eventually managed to find it, but there was a gap of a few days in there, certainly long enough for it to get tampered with or contaminated."

"How did that happen?"

"Nobody knows for sure, except that somebody screwed up."

"And the judge still let the evidence into court?"

"Shades of gray, Mr. Bannister, shades of gray. With no proof the evidence was tampered with, he allowed it. Besides, the clothes *were* Nathan's, and they *were* found in Ronnie's apartment."

"So how do you explain that?"

"I don't, really," she said with a sigh. "I've always thought it must have been planted there."

"By whom?"

"I was hoping maybe you could find out."

"Ms. Lawson, I don't have a problem investigating leads, but I usually need something to go on before I do. What you're telling me here is all circumstan—"

"My brother wasn't a murderer."

"It's not my place to say he was or he wasn't. That was the jury's job, and they convicted him."

"Based on lost and possibly tampered-with evidence? Based on bad testimony from a questionable witness?"

"With all due respect, Ms. Lawson, your brother also had two prior sex offenses going into this. Did he not?"

"One," she said, raising her index finger, "and it was for statutory rape. He was nineteen, and she was sixteen. Not the best judgment on his part, I'll grant you that, but it doesn't make him a child-killer."

"And the other charge?"

"Dropped." She was looking into my eyes but still folding and unfolding the sugar packet. "When you're a convicted sex offender, you become an instant suspect in just about anything that happens within a twenty-five-mile radius of where you live, sometimes even farther. But when all was said and done, they had zip for evidence. Couldn't charge him."

I gazed at her for a long moment and thought. Nothing earth-shaking here, but it did raise some questions. I said, "The cops were led to your brother because of an anonymous tip. Ever find out who that was?"

She laughed, but again there was no humor. "Sheriff wouldn't say. No way to know if the person even existed."

"You don't have much faith in law enforcement, do you?"

She leaned forward and looked directly into my eyes; I could have sworn I saw something burning in hers. "My brother went to the electric chair for a crime he didn't commit. How in God's name *could* I trust them?"

"Okay," I said, raising my hands. "I get what you're saying here, and it does appear there could have been some evidentiary issues during the trial—there's no denying that. But to be perfectly honest, what you've told me doesn't necessarily scream out his innocence, either."

She reached into her bag and removed a sheet of paper. Slid it across the table and said, "How about this, Mr. Bannister? Does *this* scream it loudly enough?"

She watched me carefully as I picked it up and read it.

CHAPTER TWENTY-TWO

It was a handwritten statement:

I Emma Louise Stephenson hereby swear the following is true: I was with Ronnie Lucas from the hours of 4 pm to 5 pm on June 29, 1976.

My hand shook slightly as I took it in. I said to Abbey, "Why wasn't this introduced during the trial?"

"Ronnie didn't tell anyone he had an alibi."

"Even though it would've saved his life?"

She was rolling her hands against one another. "It's complicated, but let me see if I can explain. Emma was Ronnie's on-again–off-again girlfriend. Mostly off-again. A real winner, I might add. She was in the process of losing her two-year-old girl in a custody fight. Her ex claimed she was an unfit mother, which she was."

I raised an eyebrow.

"Drug problem," Abbey said, "and the father was worse. Abusive as hell. He liked to beat the crap out of Emma, even smacked the kid around a few times. That's when Emma decided enough was enough, that it was time to get out of the marriage. Of course, she had Ronnie's arms to run into. They'd been carrying on together for quite some time by then."

The waitress came by to refill our coffee cups. We paused, watching and waiting for her to finish and leave. She flashed me another Big Texas Smile as she left the table.

Abbey continued, "So one day, Ronnie calls, wanting to meet, but she tells him she can't, that she has the baby at home and doesn't have a sitter. Of course, he couldn't come to her. His parole officer wouldn't allow him to go near any minors, and obviously, Emma couldn't bring the baby with her, either. But he insisted, told her he was thinking about ending the relationship. Well, that was all Emma had to hear. She put the baby in the crib for a nap and rushed off to meet him at the Alibi bar a few blocks from her house." She saw my response to the name and smiled. "I know, talk about irony, huh?"

"And this is the same time that Nathan went missing..."

"Yeah. The exact time."

I held the paper up. "So why didn't he use this to clear his name?"

She raised her hand. "I'm getting to that. So, they argued for a while, and then they made up...it took a while. Fast-forward to when she gets back home. She finds the baby on the floor, bleeding. She hadn't closed the crib properly, and the baby had fallen out and hit her head. Emma panicked. She rushed to the emergency room and told them the baby had fallen while playing in the driveway."

"Knowing that if she told the truth, she could lose the kid."

"Exactly, yeah. Then Ronnie gets arrested, and here's where it gets complicated: if she provides an alibi, it all comes out in court that she left the kid unattended."

"Tough decision for a mother to make," I said. "Let Ronnie die or lose custody of her daughter."

"Yeah. Of course, he felt partially responsible. I mean, he was the one who insisted she come see him in the first place."

"So what happened next?"

"Emma decided to put the alibi in writing and give it to Ronnie."

"In other words, putting the ball in his court."

"Right."

"But he never used it."

Abbey raised a brow. "Part two—the trickiest part of all. The baby didn't actually belong to Emma's husband." She rested her arms on the table, crossed them, then leaned in toward me. "She belonged to Ronnie."

"Wow."

"Understatement. So there he was, between a rock and a hard place. Use the alibi, they'll take his daughter away from Emma for sure. And then who gets her? The scumbag abusive husband."

"A risk he wasn't willing to take," I said.

"Exactly."

"So it all boiled down to keeping himself safe or keeping his kid safe?"

She nodded, shrugged. "He rolled the dice on a trial without the alibi."

"And lost."

She gazed down at the table and frowned. "Unfortunately, yes."

I thought about what it must have been like for him. The sacrifice. To put his child's life before his own because of love. Then something else crossed my mind. "How come you didn't convince him to use the alibi and then you fight for custody yourself?"

She shrugged. "I never had the chance."

"Why not?"

"I didn't know about the note until after Ronnie died. He left it for me. I guess he wanted me to know he wasn't the monster everybody thought he was." She shook her head, a hint of anger mixed with sadness. "But I already knew that."

I tipped the note up. "And you never gave this to the folks at the *Observer*? They never saw it?"

She straightened her spine as well as her facial expression. "I wouldn't give those people the time of day."

"How come?"

"Because they're scum, that's why." She looked away and sneered. "The way they covered the trial was shameful. They had him convicted before he ever set foot in the courtroom. Banner headlines every day practically calling him a pervert child-killer. They turned it into a damned circus carnival, and when I tried to complain, they wouldn't hear it."

"So after that, Emma ended up keeping the girl?"

She shook her head. "Overdose. She died right after the execution. I wondered if it was guilt about Ronnie, but—"

"Then the little girl went to the ex-husband anyway? After all that?"

Abbey's expression changed to one of determination. "Hell, no. I fought long and hard, but I finally won. She's *my* kid now." And then she smiled.

I smiled, too.

She pulled out her wallet, flipped it open, turned it toward me. With alternating glances between it and me, she said, "Jessica."

"She's beautiful."

"That was at her college graduation. She'll be thirty-five in August. A lawyer, if you can believe it."

I looked from the photo to her and said, "Something good came out of something bad."

A tear filled her eye. She wiped it away, a bigger smile now spreading across her face. "Yeah, something did…after all."

Damage
Damage
Damage

CHAPTER TWENTY-THREE

Trust No One

My mother's needs always came first, with mine getting pushed to the end of the line. Not only that, but she used me to help satisfy those needs, placing me in danger and going places other parents would never tread. I don't know if she understood the damage she caused or the demons she left with me: The demon of *You are Worthless*. The demon of *You're a Sad Excuse for a Human*. The demon of *Nobody Loves You*.

I fight those demons every day.

~

I was eight years old. My mother decided she needed a radio for the kitchen and, as was often the case, dragged me along to Pete's Discount Mart.

She found one she liked, until she saw the price.

"Highway robbery," she mumbled as she shoved the radio back onto the shelf, then shot an angry look toward a nearby salesman. "These people are criminals."

She moved a few paces down the aisle and grabbed another radio.

"Like the price on this one better," she said, holding it up, examining it, "except it's a piece of crap."

Then she looked down at me, and I could practically see the up-to-no-good flashing in her eyes. She put the radio back, pulled me farther down the aisle, then knelt and whispered into my ear, "I'm going to go around the corner to the next row. Once I'm out of sight, you take the price off the crappy radio and put it on the good one. Then put the tag from the good one on the crappy one. Understand?"

"I don't think we're supposed to—"

"It's fine," she said. "Trust me. Nobody will know the difference. These people are making a killing."

"But what if I get caught?"

She laughed and rolled her eyes. "Don't be ridiculous. You won't get caught. Nobody even notices you. It's like you're invisible."

I didn't say anything, just shook my head.

Her expression grew more serious. "Good boys listen to their mothers. If you want me to love you, then you need to trust me."

I looked at the salesman, who was busy flirting with the cashier.

"Go ahead," my mother said, waving me on. "Just do it."

I stepped tentatively down the aisle, my hands clenched, my shoulders tight and stiff.

"I'll be in the next aisle, honey," she said, speaking loudly now so everyone could hear.

My heart began to pound.

I moved over to the cheaper radios. Grabbed one. Glanced at the front of the store; the salesman caught my eye, smiled, then went back to charming the cashier. I turned the box over and found the price tag, began peeling it off.

Then, a short time later, "It's over here on aisle six, ma'am. I'll show you."

I looked up. The salesman was gone, and the cashier was busy reading a magazine.

I kept peeling.

"This toaster is our most popular model, and it's on sale right now."

They were in the next aisle.

The label began tearing in half. My fingertips were sweaty, and I felt like I was about to lose it. Everything was turning into a mess. I wiped my hands on my pants and grabbed another radio. Began peeling again.

Then I felt a firm hand on my shoulder.

I jumped.

The salesman glared down at me. "You mind telling me what you're doing, son?"

Fear and panic silenced me.

"I said, son?"

"I was…I…"

"You want to tell me why you're removing price tags from our merchandise?"

"I…"

My mother stepped around the corner. With hands clamped to her hips, head tilted, and an angry scowl on her face, she said, "Patrick! What have you done now?"

"This your boy, ma'am?"

She walked toward us shaking her head, and with irritation in her voice she said, "Oh, for heaven's sake. What has he gotten himself into this time?"

"I caught him removing price labels from our merchandise," the salesman said, pointing to the shreds still stuck to my pant leg. A group of people began gathering around, watching us.

Watching me.

"You apologize to this nice man!" she shouted. "Do it right this instant!"

And so I did, with tears rolling down my cheeks, barely able to get the words out.

My mother turned to the salesman. "I'm so sorry. I really am. He's a problem child, and I'm just at my wits' end. His father passed away, and me being a single mother and all, you know...I just don't know what to do with him. I'm so embarrassed."

Then she dragged me by my arm, through the crowd and out of the store, shouting the whole way.

I don't remember much about the ride home except for the humiliation I felt.

And this:

"Congratulations," she said, once we were on the road. "You really fucked *that* one up."

Chapter Twenty-four

Yet another storm.

This one came barreling in off the coast, slate-gray skies and rain drifting through the air in sheets.

A perfect match for my mood…and the turbulent feeling in the pit of my stomach.

Figuring out Nathan Kingsley's murder was like peeling away the layers of an onion: the deeper I got, the more it stunk. The less sense it seemed to make, too. No wonder I'd had such a hard time figuring out Ronald Lucas's connection to all this. He didn't really have one.

But if he didn't do it, who did?

The mysterious Sam I Am entered my mind. His role seemed to be pushing its way toward center stage. I wondered if he could have killed both Jean *and* Nathan Kingsley. But why would he want either of them dead? And why then spare Dennis?

And what about my mother and Warren? I still had no idea what they were doing in the middle of all this.

Abbey Lawson helped me fill in a lot of empty spaces where Lucas was concerned. Still, what she told me was just one piece to an already confusing puzzle. If her brother was in fact framed, I had no idea who was behind it, or why.

~

Jackson Wright had represented Lucas during his trial and during the subsequent appeals process. Back at the motel, I powered up the computer and did a search. He was still practicing law in Corvine, with an office on Prospect Street. Good. Hopefully, he could help me take Abbey's information to the next level.

Questions without answers—they were building too quickly. So, too, was my exhaustion, because for the second night in a row, I passed out cold without even turning off the lights.

~

I shot straight up in bed, thinking I'd heard something like a door closing. Not slammed, more like being pulled gently closed. A dream?

I turned the alarm clock toward me: 8:07 a.m. I was still wearing my clothes from the night before. The word *overworked* came to mind and after that, *underpaid.*

I pulled my cell phone from the nightstand and checked messages. Nothing. Then I dialed CJ's number at work.

"Norris," she said, sounding groggy and tired. She wasn't the only one.

"It's Patrick."

"Hey, you. How're things going?"

"They're going. Listen, I need to ask you a question."

"Lay it on me."

"Ever hear the name Michael Samuels?"

She paused for a moment, and then, "No. Should I?"

"Not necessarily. Just wondering."

She spoke her words slowly, and I could hear her smiling. "Whatcha workin', Pat? Wanna tell me?"

"Don't get too excited. So far all I'm doing is running in circles and getting doors slammed in my face."

She didn't respond.

I said, "You still there?"

"Yeah. Uh-huh."

"Why the silence?"

"Oh, nothing. Just trying to figure out why you're giving me a snow job instead of the truth."

"I'm not giving you a *snow job*."

"It's a small town—remember that, Pat. People are talking. Also remember that I'm not stupid."

"Never said you were."

"Hmm. Yeah. Okay. Well, good luck on that. Gotta go." And she hung up.

I stared at my phone for a moment. Smart girl, that CJ, no doubt. Attractive, too, and clearly single; I wondered why, then laughed at myself for asking such a stupid question. I hardly had room to talk.

I started a pot of coffee, went to the door to grab the morning paper.

It was unlocked. I was surprised at first, but I'd passed out so quickly the night before, I figured I'd simply forgotten to lock it.

I poured the coffee, brought it to my bed. Cheap motel, cheap coffee, but at least they gave out free newspapers. Not much going on in Corvine today: the front-page story was "City Council Meets to Discuss New Traffic Light on Fifth and Cedar," complete with a photo of the council, all two of them. They didn't look particularly excited about the issue.

Turned the page for more of the same. Swap meet coming up this Sunday at the Baptist church. Missing German shepherd, answers to "Mike." Wondered who in the world would name their dog that.

I yawned.

From the looks of things, Nathan Kingsley's kidnapping was the most exciting news this town had ever seen—probably enough for them, I guessed. They'd had their fill.

Because both the newspaper and the coffee had failed to stimulate, I decided to get in the shower and get moving. I had an appointment with Jackson Wright in about an hour, figured I'd walk around town for a bit, maybe grab something to eat.

I lathered up in the shower and tried to organize my thoughts. No luck there; far too many of them floating around, and far too confusing. I rinsed off, got out, grabbed a towel.

And froze.

Written on the steamy mirror, a message:

u spy

now u die

Adrenaline pumped up my spine and made me shiver. I sucked in a breath, forgetting for a moment to let it out as I moved closer. This time it sounded like more than a threat. It sounded like a promise.

Things were moving to a bad place.

The door I'd heard closing hadn't been a dream; it was real. Someone had been in my room while I slept.

But the message wasn't written while I was in the shower. It was an old trick I remembered from when I was a kid. Write something on a dry mirror with your fingertip, and the oil residue will cause the words to appear once it mixes with steam.

Clever.

This wasn't just about pushing the envelope anymore; it was about crossing a line. Someone was aggressively pursuing me. I didn't know who, but I knew one thing: the rules of the game were changing at breakneck speed. Although they hadn't harmed me yet, it would be only a matter of time before they did.

Time to be proactive.

I checked out of my motel and into another several miles outside of town. Paid with cash and used an alias. My name was now Ron Braverman, as far as they or my stalker were concerned. Next, to the local gun store—I wasn't taking any chances. Unfortunately, that ended up being a bust. The owner refused to sell to out-of-state customers. I'd have to get by without one for now.

CHAPTER TWENTY-FIVE

A young public defender during the Lucas trial, Jackson Wright was now in his sixties with his private practice, serving as the town lawyer, and handling all matters common. Divorces, probates, bankruptcies—you name it.

His office was a 1930s bungalow converted for commercial use. A grandmotherly woman with flaming red hair and wire-rimmed glasses paused her busy typing long enough to peer over her glasses at me and smile a greeting. After I introduced myself, she directed me to a small waiting area. They had the latest copy of *News World*. I smiled and began thumbing through the pages.

A few minutes later, Wright appeared, a tall, white-haired man with a round, pleasant face.

"Mr. Bannister," he said, reaching out to shake my hand.

"Appreciate you taking the time. Hope I'm not throwing you off schedule."

"Not at all," he said, then led me back to his office. It was a tightly contained mess, bookshelves overflowing and document boxes scattered throughout. Somewhere in the midst, I saw a desk. Found a chair and sat. He reclined in his, a black leather high-back. With fingers locked in his lap, he said, "I figured it was only a matter of time before you got to me."

I smiled. "Who gave you the heads-up?"

He gazed toward the ceiling, eyes narrow, fingers drumming on his desk. "Let's see. Millie at the bar, Dottie at the beauty shop, and Mary at the bank...oh, and CJ Norris over at the *Observer*. But she was more trying to hook us up than gossip. As for the others, well..."

"Strange thing," I said. "Besides CJ, I haven't met any of them."

"Small town," he said with a smile and a wink. "Word travels faster than spit through a straw around here. So, how can I help you?"

I got right down to it. "Do you believe Ronald Lucas was innocent?"

"Absolutely," he said without hesitation.

"Can you tell me why?"

"There was information that never made it into the courtroom. Things that would have made all the difference in the world."

"The evidence that went missing...and the girlfriend's alibi?"

He paused a beat, then nodded. "You've spoken to Abbey, I take it."

"I have."

His mouth slid toward a frown, and he let out a long sigh. "Unfortunately, I didn't find out about Emma's note until it was too late."

"His intentions were noble."

"Noble, yeah, but also pretty foolish. And the real tragedy is that he didn't need to hide that alibi note at all. As far as the kid went, we probably could have remanded custody to Abbey and kept her away from Emma's husband—especially since it turned out she didn't even belong to him. Unfortunately, Ronnie was too unsophisticated about the laws and how they worked to know better. And a bit paranoid. I could hardly blame him after what he'd been through."

"And the other evidence?"

"Well, I'm sure Abbey told you about our mailman."

I nodded.

"But there's even more that she *didn't* tell you. Did you happen to hear about the DA's dramatic performance in court? The one with the window and the much-celebrated Nathan Doll?"

"CJ told me something about that."

"Very impressive, a real showstopper, but more smoke and mirrors than anything else because what they failed to mention during their big production number was that a key piece of evidence went missing. Evidence that would have proved their little dog-and-pony show completely meaningless."

"Really," I said, leaning forward. "Tell me about it."

"A fresh shoe print found in the dirt just below that famed windowsill."

"Whose was it?"

"Not Ronnie's, that's for sure. He wore a nine and a half, and this was an eleven."

"So who'd it belong to?"

"Don't know. Never got the chance to figure it out, since the plaster mold mysteriously got lost on its way to trial. I didn't find out about it until years later. Believe me when I say that if I'd known sooner, I would have been all over it like white on rice."

"How does that happen? Evidence just disappearing like that."

"Well," he said, leaning back in his chair and gazing toward the ceiling, "the story went that someone screwed up, but I think someone *covered* up. That print was part of the evidence that initially went missing, only it never came back with the rest of the stuff. Odd that it was the one thing that could have cleared Ronnie."

"How'd you find out about it?"

"At the Alibi, of all places. I overheard some blabbermouth talking one night. You know the type—five hundred words per minute with gusts up to a thousand. She worked for the sheriff's department and was letting off steam, I suppose, telling everyone about it. At first I thought it was just a bunch of mumbo jumbo—you know, false bravado fueled by liquid courage. But when I looked deeper, it all checked out."

"Any idea who lost it?"

"One of Lindsay's flunkies at the time, guy by the name of Flint Newsome, was in charge of the evidence when it went missing."

"So where did it go during the time it was lost?"

He shrugged, lifted both hands, palms up. "Don't know. Not sure anyone does, really."

"Suspicious."

"As a pink fur coat," he said, eyeing me, nodding slowly. "Indeed."

"And odd, too, that the shoe print was never reported missing. Don't you think?"

"Not really. I mean, they had a...*situation* on their hands." He made quotation marks in the air with his fingers. "So what do they do? Well, the short answer, and the easiest one, is to turn over what they have and keep their mouths shut about what they don't. Then pray to God it all works out."

I thought about Jerry Lindsay and his defensive posture.

He continued, "As far as I'm concerned, the whole thing stunk like someone's rotten trash. They sent an innocent man to the electric chair. That's murder on top of murder in my book."

"What about the shoe?" I said. "Can you tell me anything more about it?"

"It was a boot, actually, and, like I said, size eleven. Tony Lama was the brand, I believe. They knew that because of the logo on the heel. That's what I believe Blabbermouth said."

A cowboy boot. I thought about it, then reminded myself that this was Texas; no shortage of those here. But it seemed a lot of coincidences were beginning to stack up, all of them pointing right to the man who called himself Michael Samuels.

I said, "The guy who lost the evidence, this Flint..."

"Flint Newsome."

"He still around? Can I find him?"

Jackson nodded. "Lives in a trailer up on Highway Seventy-Two. I'm not sure there's even a real address. You could probably stop by the Texaco station off the twenty-four exit, just before Springfield, talk to Judy there. She knows everyone."

"What about tracking him down at work?"

"He got fired from the sheriff's department after the whole mess, then became a permanent employee of the state."

"Doing what?"

"Collecting unemployment, disability, and anything else he could get his hands on. I'll tell ya, that boy's dirtier than tank water." He shook his head. "A real ne'er-do-well, that one."

"Ever talk to him about the evidence?"

"No reason to. By the time I got wind of all this, Ronnie had already been executed. Can't unring that bell. What's done is done, I'm afraid. Besides, the more I find out about this case, the less I like…and then I just get upset all over again." He picked up a paper clip, bent it in half, then tossed it back onto his desk. "Ronnie's dead, and he shouldn't be. That's the bottom line. It's a hard pill to swallow, and believe me, I choke on it every single day."

"One last thing," I said. "Does the name Michael Samuels mean anything to you?"

He shook his head. "Why?"

"Nothing," I replied. "Just wondering."

River red
River red
River red

CHAPTER TWENTY-SIX

You are Damaged Goods

When I was two, I fell on the playground, hit my head, and left a twenty-foot trail of blood along the concrete. By the time I arrived at the hospital, they pronounced me dead on arrival, and it took a team of doctors to bring me back. Twice. This was what my uncle Warren told me—it's how they discovered I had Von Willebrand disease, the one thing we have in common.

There's never been much else.

Being a bleeder was my illness, but, like everything else, my mother managed to make it all about her. Having a son who was vulnerable, who required medical care, was the perfect springboard for taking her plunge into the pool of self-pity. She complained to me, complained to neighbors, complained to anyone who would stand there and listen. Before I knew it, I was the kid with The Disease, the one everyone had to be careful around. After all, I could bleed to death.

That label spelled social death for me. It didn't just set me apart from the crowd—it moved me to the other side of the map.

Gym class was out of the question, as were school field trips and most anything else that was fun. Mr. Jones, the principal, once called my mother to discuss my lack of participation at school, wondering if it was necessary. Of course, she made him regret it.

"Is that so?" she said, her tone rapidly rising to match her indignation. "I'll tell you what, Mr. Jones. Come talk to me after you've had to mop blood off your linoleum floors, after it's soaked into the bottoms of your shoes. Come see me when your hands are so stained from my child's blood that all the soap in the world won't get it out. Come see me after that. And don't you *dare* tell me how much 'more important' his social development is. What's more important is keeping my son alive."

My mother never had to mop up any of my blood, and the only incident I'd ever heard of was the one on the playground. She talked about preserving my life, but really, she kept me from living it. Even worse than that was how she used it to humiliate me.

Spring, my third-grade year. An announcement came over the loudspeaker: summer Little League tryouts were coming up. I wanted to go more than anything but knew if I asked my mother, her answer would be the usual flat-out "No" followed by "You'll bleed."

But I didn't care. I longed to be like the other kids, to be in the spotlight, wear a fresh white uniform on opening day. To have fun and be normal.

So I snuck out of the house and walked over to the playing field. How I figured I'd be able to play the whole season without her knowing was another story. But I was a kid, and I just wanted to play.

I sat in the bleachers, anxiously awaiting my name to be called, the smell of fresh-cut grass filling the air, the sound of bats cracking and parents cheering all around me. I waited for more than an hour, and my excitement grew as each kid stepped up to the plate. Sitting there with everyone felt wonderful. For once, I was just a normal kid enjoying one of life's typically childlike moments. I was *in* the moment, and I wanted it to last forever.

And then, a complete reversal.

I glanced toward outer field and saw my mother moving quickly in my direction, scanning the bleachers with a look on her face that was impossible to misread: she was furious, and I was in big trouble.

Fear and panic struck my gut simultaneously, then twisted through me. I bent my head down quickly, hoping maybe she'd miss me. Then I heard her voice, sharp, loud, and riddled with anger. I looked up to find an expression that matched. With cold, hard eyes, a face as red as blood, she spat her words at me. "What the *hell* do you think you're doing here?"

I was in the spotlight, all right, but for all the wrong reasons. An awkward, painful silence fell over the crowd; every head turned toward me, staring and waiting for my response. I wanted to crawl between the bleacher planks, sink into the ground, then bury myself two thousand feet below the earth's surface.

"*Answer me!*" she screamed so loud that it startled me.

I looked at the wide eyes and dropped jaws surrounding me, felt tension thick as mud. Except, that is, for the kids on the field who were laughing, amused by the show.

She circled around for another attack, screaming even louder now. "*Answer me, I said! Answer me right now, damn it!*"

Her sharp, angry words made me flinch. Throat as dry as field dirt, sweaty palms gripping the bleacher seat, I struggled against my humiliation, my fear, trying to get the words out. With a soft, shaky voice and tears in my eyes, I said, "I just wanted to play."

"Have you lost your mind? Did you *just want* to spill your blood all over this field, too? How about that? Did you want to die?"

Actually, I did. Right then, right there.

The kids were laughing louder now, parents watching and whispering to one another as I slowly got up and followed her down the bleachers. I struggled against my tears; they would only humiliate me further, make a bigger mockery out of me.

She yanked me hard by the arm, then paraded me across the playing field. The place I had so wanted to be—the place I now never wanted to see again.

We drove back home in silence. Back to hell.

I didn't sleep at all that night; I just cried.

CHAPTER TWENTY-SEVEN

The Texaco station off Highway 72 was a slick, modern structure terribly out of place against its desolate and timeworn surroundings. A teenage boy in a cowboy hat leaned against his truck, arms crossed, waiting for the tank to fill. A middle-aged woman came out of the convenience store lugging two small kids and three bags filled with grocery items.

I parked off to the side and entered the station.

A heavyset girl stood behind the counter: jet-black hair with streaks of pink and purple, a silver hoop in one nostril and a tinier one through the eyebrow. Her expression was the picture of indifference. She was busy taking packs of cigarettes from a carton and plugging them into the spots above. She glared at me briefly, then threw the empty carton into the trash. Pulled out another, and went right back to work.

Service with a smile.

Nametag said she was Judy. Just the person I wanted to see, although the feeling didn't appear to be mutual.

"I need directions," I said, skipping the cordial greeting. Something told me Judy wasn't a cordial-greeting kind of gal.

She stopped for a moment, looked me over from head to toe, then went back to working the smokes. "Where to?"

"I'm trying to find someone who lives around here. Guy by the name of Newsome."

At this, Judy became somewhat more animated, but not in a good way; more like how someone might react when she realizes the person next to her has passed gas.

"Flint?" she said, shoving the packs with more vigor now, as if they were the cause of her annoyance. She snickered. "Why would you wanna see him?"

I wanted to tell her it was none of her damned business, but I also needed her help. "Do you know where he lives?"

"He's a big-time loser."

"Can you tell me where he lives?" I repeated.

"Up the road, about seven miles or so. Right side, yellow trailer. Can't miss it. Looks like it got hit by a bus. About three times."

"Thanks, Judy. Sure appreciate the help," I said. As I turned to leave, I couldn't resist adding, "Gotta love that Southern charm."

I heard the word *asshole* mumbled as the door slammed behind me.

A real people person, that Judy.

Got in my car and headed up the road in search of a beat-up trailer, Flint Newsome, and hopefully some missing answers.

A few miles later, I spotted the thing off in the distance. For all her attitude, Judy was right: it definitely looked like a bus had hit it a few times—not only that, but dumped and then abandoned. No road leading to it, just a dirt path. Seemed driveways were optional in this town. An old Lincoln Continental sat parked outside, its condition just as deplorable. The trailer sat on cinder blocks with old wooden apple crates serving as steps. I moved my gaze to the other side and spotted a lanky, rawboned dog tethered to a metal stake. He threatened me with a fierce-sounding growl, low and throaty, which quickly erupted into a full-blown bark-fest. Looked like a cross between rottweiler and just plain mean.

I maneuvered my way around all the clutter. Amid the piles of dried dog poop were rusted beer cans, empty TV-dinner boxes, and various other odd pieces of debris. It appeared Flint liked to use his window as a trash can. As I neared the trailer, an increasingly ripe, rotting stench made my eyes water.

With each step I took, the dog's barking increased in volume and intensity. He lunged toward me, dragging the rusty metal chain along with him. Then he began snarling, upper lip curled, yellow teeth exposed all the way to his gums. I stopped just a few feet beyond his reach and glanced at the trailer, hoping Newsome might look out to see what all the commotion was about.

Wasn't going to happen—not even a hint of movement inside; in fact, no sign of him anywhere.

I weighed the risks. One bite could, in theory, cost me my life. All he had to do was break the skin, and I'd leak like a sieve. But I needed to talk to Newsome.

I thought it over some more, decided to go for it. I couldn't let the dog come between Newsome and me. Now I just needed to figure out a plan to get past him. Alive.

Plan A: I gave Cujo a mean glare. It had zero effect. In fact, it just got him barking again.

Time for Plan B.

I moved toward the rear of the trailer in a wide, sweeping semicircle. The dog ran around his end to meet me there, but his chain twisted under one of the cinder blocks, grinding against it, then pulling him to an abrupt halt. He tried to jerk loose but couldn't. Instead, he began to whimper.

"Nice doggie," I said, then retraced my steps to the front of the trailer. The dog stayed behind—not out of choice, but out of necessity—and I could hear him growling and barking again, pissed off as hell, I was sure.

I climbed Newsome's apple crates and gave the door a few hard and fast raps, all to no avail. I wondered if maybe he was passed out after a long night of hard drinking, so I peered through the sheer olive-green drapes hanging in the trailer-door window.

And that's when I realized something was terribly wrong.

CHAPTER TWENTY-EIGHT

A brown cowboy boot. Sticking out of a doorway. Resting in a puddle of blood.

I placed my fingers around the outer edge of the knob and turned it carefully. Pushed the door open and quickly discovered that the rancid stench wasn't just coming from his trash; it was coming from Newsome himself. I slammed the door, moved quickly toward my car.

At least, that was my plan, but the dog had other ideas. He'd somehow managed to pull the chain out from under the cinder block and was now barreling full bore toward me with a determined look falling somewhere between attack and mutilate. I tried to hightail it past him, but before I could, he knocked me to the ground.

Then sank his teeth into my leg. Hard. And hung on.

I panicked.

I couldn't tell if he'd broken the skin, but if so, I'd have little time to get to a hospital. I'd been warned my whole life to stay away from dogs, from broken glass and sharp objects, from anything that could make me bleed. Other than the playground incident when I was young, I'd managed to make it through without any problems—until now.

My pulse pounded in my head and my breathing accelerated times ten. I had to get the dog off my leg. The longer I allowed him to remain clamped to me, the worse I knew the injury could become and the less successful I'd be in stopping—or at least slowing down—the bleeding. I also knew that any resistance or sudden movement might only exacerbate the potential for further injury.

With his teeth bearing down, the pressure increasing, and my pain reaching an unbearable intensity, I looked around for something, *anything*, to aid me in my attempt to escape. A rusty old carburetor lay just beyond my reach. Sliding toward it would only put more pressure on my leg. A little closer lay an old tree branch. I reached for it and, with all the force I could muster, whacked the dog in the face. He released my leg instantly and recoiled just long enough for me to slip out of his reach. Then he began barking and growling again.

I was still breathing heavily, with sweat dripping down my forehead and off my nose. I inspected my leg: my jeans were still intact with no holes. No indication of blood, either. All good signs. With shaky hands, I pulled up my pant leg.

Then breathed a giant sigh of relief.

Four rounded bruise marks on both sides of my leg, but no breaks through the skin. No wounds. No blood.

I thanked myself for dressing that morning in the thick denim and heavy sweat socks that had most surely saved my life.

Still shaken, I ran to my car, grabbed a rag from the trunk, then wrapped it snug around my leg to ensure that none of the bruises wore thin and started bleeding.

Then I called the sheriff and waited in the car, bruised leg hanging out the passenger-side door, nerves more than a bit on edge. A short time later, the cruiser came charging up the dirt path, lights flashing, siren blaring, and tires kicking up a cloud of dust. It pulled to an abrupt halt beside me.

The sheriff got out of the car and came toward me; he was an older guy, thin, tall, late fifties. I glanced at his nametag: Deputy

Ned Baker. He took one look at my wrapped leg, then my face, and said, "You look like hell, son."

"I'll live," I replied, "but I can't say the same for the guy in the trailer."

He glanced over his shoulder, then back at me. "Flint?"

"I think so. You've got a mess in there, a bloody, stinky one."

He regarded me for a moment, then headed for the trailer, unsnapping his holster and resting his hand on the butt of his gun.

As if on cue, the hell-born hound came running toward him, barking, growling, and baring those nasty teeth. In one swift move, Baker pulled his gun and fired a single shot. The dog flew into reverse, landed on his back, and rolled onto his side. Let out a gasp, then went motionless.

As if Flint's body hadn't been enough.

Baker stared back at me, gun dangling at his side, tough-guy-cop expression on his face. The dog and I hadn't exactly formed a meaningful bond, but the last thing I needed was to see him dead. It wasn't his fault he had a rotten parent. Lord knows I could sympathize there. True, he'd nearly killed me, yet in some strange way I felt badly for him.

Baker continued toward the trailer. I heard the front door suck open and, a few moments later, radio chatter. After about five minutes, more sirens shrieked in the distance, growing louder with each passing moment. Two more cruisers came speeding in; they cut a corner onto the dirt road, kicking up dust that had just started to settle. The cars skidded to a stop beside me, and two deputies got out, glanced my way, then joined Baker inside the trailer.

A few minutes later, they were stringing yellow tape all around the place.

I remained in my car, waiting and watching, as the deputies moved in and out of Newsome's trailer. My leg felt better now; that was the good news. The bad news was my ever-increasing nervousness and the reality of the moment sticking hard in my gut.

I'd managed to walk head-on into a murder scene, and that meant trouble.

About ten minutes later, Baker emerged from the trailer and came walking toward me, snapping bloody rubber gloves off his wrists with an expression that told me he wasn't coming to make social conversation.

"Yep. It's a mess in there, all right," he said, nodding toward the trailer. "Been dead for a while, prolly several days."

"Smells like it," I agreed.

"Let's you and me have a chat," he said and waved me toward his car. He glanced at my leg. "You bleeding there?"

"Just bruised. Dog thought I was lunch."

"Yeah, and then I took care of *him*," Baker replied with a surly grin. Seemed proud of himself.

I felt sick again.

"What's your name, son?"

"Patrick Bannister."

"Got some ID?"

I pulled out my wallet, handed him my license.

"California." He grunted the word. "What brings you all the way out here?"

"Trying to talk to Flint Newsome," I said, "but it looks like somebody else did the talking for him."

"What were you trying to talk to him *about*?"

Internal-dialogue time: I wondered how he could be the only person in Corvine who didn't know about me. My presence here hadn't exactly been a secret; far from it. I stuck my hands in my pockets and said, "I'm a reporter."

"A reporter?" he replied, as if it weren't possible. "Who with?"

"*News World*."

"That national magazine?"

I nodded.

He seemed to think on that for a moment. I noticed his jaw clench, and he gave a slow nod, his eyes now peering directly into mine. It was the same sort of cop look Jerry Lindsay had given me. Must be something they taught them at the academy. Finally, he said, "Not much happening in Corvine…"

"I'm doing a story about Nathan Kingsley," I replied.

"Say what?"

"Nathan Kingsley," I repeated, my annoyance beginning its uphill hike.

He frowned. "Boy who got kidnapped a long time ago?"

I nodded.

"How does Flint Newsome fit in?"

"He worked for the sheriff's department at the time."

Baker laughed. "He *what*? You're joking, right?"

"I'm not."

"Shit. I wouldn't believe that man if he told me it was daylight at noon, let alone trust him to mop the station floors. Where the hell did you ever get the idea he worked for us?"

"From Lucas's attorney."

At this, Baker shrugged, then pulled a pack of cigarettes from his shirt pocket and poked a smoke into the corner of his mouth. It dangled and bobbed while he spoke. "Well, it's news to me."

I matched his shrug.

He found a Zippo in his pants pocket and lit the cigarette. Studying me intently, he took a long, deep drag, then exhaled the smoke through his nose. Reminded me of a dragon. A tall, skinny one.

"Okay. From the start now," he said. "Tell me what happened when you got here."

I told him.

"And you never went inside?" he asked.

"That's correct. I saw the body through the drapes, opened the door to see if he was still alive in case he needed help. As soon as I smelled him, I knew. But I never went in. I've covered enough crime scenes to know better."

"Cover enough crime scenes to know not to touch the door-knob with your bare hands?"

"Just the outer edges, not the front *or* back."

He nodded but didn't seem particularly impressed. "And that's when you called us?"

"Correct. Immediately."

He was studying me again, and it was starting to bug. "Where you staying at while you're here, son?"

The *son* thing was bugging, too. "The Hitching Post."

"How long you gonna be in town?"

"Not sure. Guess as long as it takes to finish my story."

"You check with me first before you leave."

The request didn't seem unusual, but the tone bothered me. Seemed a tad unfriendly. I said, "And the reason for that?"

"In case I got more questions, that's why. Got a pretty nasty murder in there."

"How nasty?"

"Very."

"How nasty?" I repeated.

He seemed to deliberate over the answer. Finally he said, "Someone tied his hands behind his back, stuck a sock in his mouth, put him on his knees, and let him have it right in the back of the head. It was an execution."

We were still exchanging suspicious glances when a Ford Explorer pulled up beside us. CJ Norris got out on the passenger side, a photographer from the driver's side; he went to work right away snapping photos of the trailer. She came over, looked at me, looked at Baker, then looked puzzled.

"What's going on here?" she said, still alternating her gaze between the two of us. I wasn't sure whether her comment was in reference to the tension mounting between Baker and me or to the crime scene behind us.

Baker took another long drag from his cigarette, exhaled dragon-style again, then nodded toward the trailer and said, "Someone killed Newsome."

CJ's face went blank. "Flint? How?"

"Shot in the back of the head," he said.

"Execution-style," I added.

Baker shot me a look.

CJ turned toward me. "And how do *you* fit in with all this?"

Baker said, "Seems our friend here found the body."

She looked at me.

"Long story," I muttered under my breath. "Fill you in later."

She was about to comment on that, but the other deputy came up to us, wiping sweat off his forehead.

"Got something in there, boss. You're gonna want to take a look. There's a safe behind a bunch of clothes in the closet. On its side, open, and empty."

Without a word, Baker moved toward the trailer, his deputy following close behind.

"Looks like we have our motive," CJ said, her eyes following the men as they walked away from us.

"Wonder what was in it."

She gave me a funny look and said, "You going to tell me how you happened to land in the middle of all this?"

I told her.

She looked down at my leg. "I take it that's where the rag came in."

"Yep. Unfortunately, the dog fared much worse."

"Saw that," she said. "Not sure who I feel more sorry for, the dog or Newsome."

"I'll go with the dog."

She smiled, nodded.

A few minutes later, Baker and his deputy came out again. "Not much chance we'll get any prints off the safe, other than Newsome's," Baker said as they breezed past us, "but on the slight chance, make sure we try anyway."

I thought about the boot print that disappeared during the trial and that Newsome was the one who had lost it. Could he have been involved in Nathan Kingsley's murder? The guy was as seedy as they came—it wasn't that much of a stretch.

I motioned for CJ to follow me to my car. When we got there, I said, "What's the story on Newsome?"

She smiled. "Big-time loser."

"Yeah, I get that. Any idea why someone would want him dead?"

She leaned against the hood, crossed her arms. "Not sure. But the empty safe is sure keeping things interesting."

"I'll say."

She looked down at the ground, then back up at me. "Think someone was trying to keep him from talking to you? Then robbed him?"

I shook my head. "Nobody knew I was coming, and Baker said Newsome has been dead for a few days. Sure smelled like it."

She nodded very slowly, staring off into the distance. "Guy like Newsome, there's no telling what he had his hands in. Could've been any number of people who liked him better dead than alive."

I looked at the trailer. "Man, I'd give anything to find out what he had in the safe."

"You and me..." Suddenly she stopped, her attention fixed on something in the distance.

I looked in that direction. "What's wrong?"

She moved forward a few steps, then stopped, eyes narrowed. "Is that dog still breathing?"

I looked, then took off running, with CJ following behind. When we got there, I rested my hand on his back and realized he was trembling ever so slightly.

"We have to get him somewhere. Fast," I said. "Is there a vet nearby?"

CJ had the dog's head in her lap and was stroking it; he let out a soft, helpless moan. "Up the road about six miles. Doctor Shively."

"You stay here with him. I'll bring my car around, and we can load him in the backseat."

In less than a minute, we were speeding off toward the vet's office.

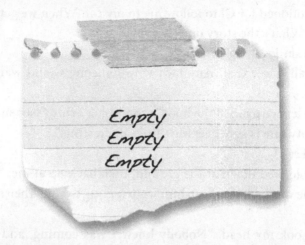

Empty
Empty
Empty

CHAPTER TWENTY-NINE

You have no value

I never much understood holidays. We didn't celebrate them, and to me they seemed like a big party I was never invited to, a time when everyone else got to have fun. The decorations, the music— all of it—seemed so foreign to me, accentuating my feelings of inadequacy and loneliness.

"I hate the holidays," my mother would grumble as we navigated the crowds. "Just a bunch of people getting in my way. Carnal pigs feeding at the trough of material wealth."

But I wanted to feed there, too. I wanted to experience what everyone else did.

It was Christmas Eve. In one of her manic moods, Mother suddenly decided she wanted to paint the bathrooms. As in: it couldn't wait until morning. As in: we needed to go to Wallace's Discount Mart right that moment.

"And don't go wandering off to the toy department, either," she said as we walked through the parking lot. "If you're not with me when I'm ready to go, I'll leave you here."

Inside, colorful blinking lights reflected off silvery tinsel. A fresh piney scent mixed with the smell of hot, buttery popcorn filling the air. Christmas carols played softly in the background while jolly Saint Nick sat front and center, a little girl perched on his lap. Beyond that, even more kids stood along with their parents behind a red velvet rope, waiting for their visit with the white-bearded man in red.

I felt as if I'd landed on Mars.

A sharp jolt snapped me out of it, my mother pulling me by my jacket collar toward the hardware section. I'm pretty sure I was the only kid in the world spending Christmas Eve in the paint department.

"Drop cloth," she ordered, reading the side of a paint can. I walked down the aisle, then turned the corner in search of one, but something else caught my attention about fifty feet away in the gardening section. A life-size Santa sat on a big green tractor, its front end lifting as if taking off in flight. Colorful lights flashed in succession alongside him to give the illusion of forward motion. He had one hand on the wheel, the other waving at me.

I'd never seen anything like it.

As I drew closer, I heard Christmas music, sleigh bells, and Santa's voice saying, "Ho, ho, ho!" The flashing neon sign below him suddenly came into focus. It read: *The only Deere Santa will need this year!*

I was in awe, couldn't stop looking at it.

On the other side of the display, I saw a boy about my age who appeared just as thrilled—and for a moment, it was like looking into a mirror. Then I saw his smiling parents beside him, their hands on his shoulder.

And the mirror cracked.

He had them, and I had my mother. I think it was the first time I actually understood how different my world was from that of other children and how much I was missing out on. I felt an emptiness building inside me, deep and dark. In my child's mind, I wondered what I had done to deserve such a horrible life.

Then it hit me: the drop cloth. I'd forgotten all about it.

I grabbed the first one I found on the shelf, then raced to the next aisle to find my mother.

But she was gone.

I checked several more aisles, frantically searching for her but with no luck. Rushed to the front of the store as well; again, no sign of her anywhere. Then I ran out into the parking lot.

And found my worst fears confirmed. Our parking spot was empty. She was gone, and it was getting dark.

I sat on the curb, buried my face in my hands, and cried.

Christmas Eve: a small boy, abandoned in a parking lot, far from home.

Alone.

CHAPTER THIRTY

The dog was going to live. I gave the receptionist my credit card, told her to do whatever it took to make sure he was well taken care of.

As for CJ and me, we were both tired, and the events of the past few hours were starting to weigh heavily on me emotionally and physically. We were hungry, and I needed a place to rest my leg and settle my nerves. The Italian restaurant on Second and Fenwick seemed to be a safe bet: small, quaint, and nearly empty.

We ordered our food, then sat silently for a while. I was busy processing my afternoon misadventure and watching CJ rearrange her silverware again and again.

Finally, I said, "So what's Baker's problem?"

"You mean besides the obvious?" She moved her fork to the other side of her plate again, didn't bother looking up.

"The guy doesn't like me."

She laughed a little. "I don't think he likes anyone, except maybe himself. Not even sure about that."

"He acted awful suspicious, like he thought I might be involved or something."

"I think he probably just didn't appreciate you walking in on his murder scene. They don't much like that, especially a reporter,

135

and especially one who's not from around here...you get extra piss-off points for that."

I raised my brows, nodded.

She pointed her spoon at me. "But I did warn you about the locals."

"Noted."

The waiter came with our food. Lasagna for me, angel hair pasta with stewed tomatoes and olive oil for CJ. I watched our server leave, then said, "And while we're on the subject of narcissistic cops...what's Jerry Lindsay's story?"

She laughed. "Jerry's okay. You just have to know how to work him."

"Apparently, I don't."

She sipped her wine, wiped her lips with a finger. "Why? What happened?"

"He was an ass. Wouldn't tell me anything."

A needling grin. "Like I told you..."

"Yeah, yeah...I don't know the secret handshake." I gave my lasagna a stab. When I looked back up, she was swirling her wine in the glass, apparently amused by her own thoughts.

"What?"

She leaned back and stared at me for a moment, and then, "Correct me if I'm wrong here, but for someone who's supposed to be doing a story about missing and exploited children, you sure seem awful interested in this one."

"I'm fascinated by it."

"Yeah?"

I took a bite, chewed, nodded.

"And why's that?"

"The death penalty, the lack of a body, the mother killing herself...in a mental hospital, no less. You have to admit it's a sexy story."

She stuck her fork in the pasta and watched as she carefully twirled it. "Yeah, I'm just not buying it."

"Not buying what?"

"The story you're trying to sell me here. About how fascinating you find it all. There are lots of fascinating stories about missing kids everywhere. And like I said before, I'm sure California's got plenty of them. So how 'bout it, Pat, wanna tell me what really gives?"

"What do you mean?"

"All this interest in the *Kingsley* case. What it's all really about?"

"It's not *about* anything. Just looking at some things."

"Things," she said, gazing toward the ceiling as if contemplating the word, then right back at me, "and you won't tell me what those *things* are?"

"Nothing special." I turned my attention to the lasagna, pushed at it with my fork, fully aware she had her eyes trained right on me.

She said, "Keeping secrets, are we, Patrick?"

"No. It's not that."

"Isn't it?"

"Uh-uh." I looked up and made an attempt at sincere eye contact; she wasn't buying that, either.

"Pat…" she said, her tone slowly climbing an octave.

"What?"

"Wanna tell me how come you don't want to play? How come all of a sudden you're taking all your toys out of the sandbox?"

"I never had them *in* the sandbox. And how come you're cornering me?"

"I'm a reporter. It's what I do. And do you always answer a question with a question?"

"Only when I feel like someone's trying to force my hand."

"Force your hand…" She pushed her mouth to one side, looked away, nodding. "Okay. Now I get it. I didn't realize we were on opposing teams. Good to know."

"CJ, it's not like that. I didn't mean it that way—"

"Then what?"

I fell silent.

"You know, Pat, we *are* both on the same side here, just in case you didn't realize it. And if you're worried about me trying to steal your story *or* your thunder, you've got the wrong gal 'cause I just don't roll that way. Not that I expect you to believe that. You barely know me, but—"

"So what's your point, CJ?"

"My point is that we both have the same interests here. That's all. We're after the same thing. It's our job to find the truth. Everything else is secondary, at least from where I stand."

I remained silent.

"Listen, Pat," she said, her voice taking on a tone of diplomacy, "if you've stumbled across something important—and I get the feeling you have—I want to hear about it. But even if you're still looking, I think I can help you there, too."

"What makes you think I need any help?"

"That wasn't what I meant." She closed her eyes, smiled, shook her head. "All I'm saying is, it's pretty obvious you've been hitting some walls, and that's not likely to change. Nobody here wants to talk to strangers about the *Kingsley* case. I told you that. It's just the way it is. Me, on the other hand, I'm from around here. I know the place, know the people, and I know a lot about this story...and people *will* talk to me."

"I'm sure that's true, but—"

"I wasn't finished. I can help you cut through a lot of the crap around here. Why should we spin our wheels separately when we can cover twice the ground twice as fast? Know what I mean?"

I thought about it some more.

"So what do you say, Pat?" She leaned forward, a slight grin. "Team player or free agent? Which do you want to be?"

I wrestled with my thoughts. CJ was right; there was no love for me here. Baker, Lindsay, and the creepy messages at the hotel had all made that painfully obvious. Then I thought about Dennis

Kingsley. The moment I mentioned CJ's name, his whole attitude changed and the wall between us fell. Suddenly, he trusted me and opened up.

But could I trust *her*? I wanted to, but trust and me, well, we weren't the best of friends. There were those old demons…I was used to working by myself. I was used to *being* by myself. It was lonely, but it was familiar. And safe.

"Hello? Still with me there, Pat?"

I brought my focus back to her. "Yeah, I'm here."

"How we doing on that decision? Make any progress yet?"

Take the leap, Patrick. For once in your life, stop being afraid of everyone, and just do it.

I looked into her eyes for a moment longer, studying her eager expression. "Okay. But I need to know something first."

"Name it."

"Are you willing to throw out everything you believed to be true about this case? To entertain new possibilities? Ones you never thought existed?"

She shrugged one shoulder. "Of course."

"Okay," I said and took a breath. "I've found some things that could potentially blow the case wide open."

She leaned forward with her elbows on the table. "Hit me."

"I don't think Lucas kidnapped and murdered Nathan Kingsley."

Her expression fell; her jaw, too. "What the…are you serious?"

"I think he was wrongly convicted and sent to the electric chair needlessly."

CJ fell back in her seat and stared at me for a good five seconds, and then, "That's crazy. Where the hell are you getting this?"

"I assure you I'm not just throwing out theories with nothing to back them up. Since I got to town I've interviewed people extensively, read through scores of records, and gathered quite a bit of information, and my gut tells me they got the wrong guy."

"What kind of information?"

I pulled out a copy of Lucas's alibi note from my pocket and slid it across the table, keeping my eyes on her.

She reached for it, held my gaze for a moment, then read it. The farther down she got, the wider her eyes grew. When she was done, she let it drop onto the table and stared at it. Then she looked back up at me. "Where did you get this?"

"From Abbey Lawson. Lucas's sister." I told her the story, watching her face become stricken as I described Ronald Lucas's choice to protect his daughter instead of himself. Then, after I finished, I said, "And that's not all. I also think Jean Kingsley was murdered."

"She committed suicide."

"I don't think so."

"But she hanged—"

"Staged," I said. "Made to look that way."

"You've got to be kidding…"

"I'm not."

"But why? And by whom?"

"Remember that name I asked you about? Michael Samuels?" She nodded.

"I came across something interesting—and disturbing—while going through the visitation logs at Glenview. There was a guy lurking around the place while Jean was a patient. Signed in under that name, claiming to be her nephew. Jean didn't have a nephew, and the DL number Samuels left in the guest log comes up as a fake."

"And you think he killed her?"

"The hospital records put him there, and so does an employee statement."

"Who? And what did they say?"

"Can't say who. I promised confidentiality." Then I told her about the stained gown, how it got dumped, and about the missing guest log from the night Jean died.

"But you have no idea who Samuels is…or even why he did it?"

"That's the part I can't figure out."

"What about Nathan? Do you think this Samuels guy also killed him?"

I let in some air, blew it out quickly. "There's a chance."

"Wow," she said, now staring vacantly across the restaurant. "Just wow."

"I know."

She looked back at me. "But why would he have wanted them both dead?"

"Good question. I don't know."

"And how did Lucas get drawn into all this?"

"I think he was a pawn."

"But whose?"

"Can't figure that one out, either. But if I had to guess... someone with an awful lot of power. Someone with the ability to manipulate the system."

I had an idea who that might be.

CHAPTER THIRTY-ONE

The rest of dinner was very quiet.

CJ appeared deep in thought, probably trying to make sense of what I'd just told her and, by the look on her face, without much luck. For me, the reality of my mother's and Warren's involvement was setting in.

I was driving CJ to the *Observer* to pick up her car. For a long while, neither of us spoke. Finally she shifted in the seat so her whole body faced me and said, "I don't know what I'm going to do if it turns out Lucas was innocent. I don't know if I can deal with that."

I kept my eyes on the road and nodded, not knowing what to say. There wasn't an easy answer.

"Even if we clear his name," she continued, "it doesn't seem like that would be enough. It would be way too little, way too late. He's dead."

"If we find the person who really killed Nathan, it'll make a difference."

She answered with silence, staring out her window, slowly shaking her head.

It was quite a change from the salty reporter I'd come to know, the one who just earlier had been trying to corner me. CJ

Norris may have had a tough exterior, but I was discovering that the inside was very different. For the first time, she seemed vulnerable and uncertain. I thought about the contrast, the complexity, wondering why I found it so appealing. Was I attracted to her? Of course, but I had a rule I'd never broken and didn't intend to now: I don't date other reporters. Ever. I have a hard enough time holding on to women with normal lives; being with one of my own would only complicate matters to the nth degree. And with CJ, our strong personalities together would be like adding gasoline to a fire.

CJ screamed.

I turned to her and saw a large SUV outside the window just before it rammed us hard, sending us careening onto the shoulder. I overcorrected, tried to aim the car back toward the asphalt, but the SUV rammed us again, this time from behind. The impact threw the car forward and jerked us like a pair of floppy rag dolls.

u spy now u die

The words flashed through my mind like a grenade explosion.

The SUV punched into us from behind, this time harder. I could feel the sweat dripping down my forehead and my pulse banging through my body. There seemed to be no escape as our car—and our lives—went out of control.

I checked the rearview mirror and caught a glimpse of them coming up on us again, fast. They moved alongside us, just enough to nudge the side of the car with their front bumper. I fought for control of the wheel as they started to force us off the road again. Beyond it was a drop. We were riding the shoulder now, loose gravel flying up against the car's undercarriage, the SUV now right alongside us, preventing us from getting back onto the road. I wondered how much longer until we went over the edge.

And then, with a final burst of power, the SUV sent us right off.

Our car went down diagonally across the steep embankment. All I could do was hang on to the wheel and try to keep us at an angle, rather than heading nose-first straight down the slope.

We finally hit the bottom, crashing into a dense group of scrub brush that brought us to a stop. My hands were clenched so tightly on the steering wheel that they had cramped closed.

Complete silence.

I wasn't sure if I'd been hurt, felt no pain, but knew the power of shock, how it can have a numbing effect. I'd just narrowly escaped a bleeding crisis with the dog; now I was facing yet another.

Bleeding. Was I?

Just the thought was enough to renew my panic. As soon as my hands relaxed, I felt around my body, furiously patting my clothes like a man who'd lost a wallet full of hundreds.

mending mending mending...

The words repeated in my head as I kept checking for blood.

And then, relief: pants, shirt, head, neck, and arms all dry. I leaned back, closed my eyes, and took a deep breath; it felt like the first one since this whole thing had started.

But that relief had a very short shelf life. Panic returned when I glanced over at CJ: head back, mouth wide open, unconscious. Blood spilled down the side of her head.

"CJ!" I yelled, then leaned over and grabbed her shoulder. "Can you hear me? CJ?"

No response.

I fumbled in my pocket for my cell phone to call for help.

And noticed the single drop of blood on the seat between my legs.

Dark it
Dark it
Dark it

Chapter Thirty-Two

You will never be safe

Random images often invade my dreams. Some I can identify; others are elusive. Dark, formless, and gritty, they slip through the folds of my inner consciousness; most leave as quickly as they come, but the ones that stay with me seem so real...I can feel them, smell them, sense their emotional charge. It's as if they speak to me in a language that doesn't use words.

I've had these dreams since I was a kid. Don't know why. Don't understand them.

The dream about the woods is the most frequent, the most vivid, the most disturbing. I'm flying through a forest facedown. Rain is falling hard, loud claps of thunder slapping at the air, water filtering though the trees and soaking my body. As I continue, I realize there is blood—lots of it—dripping onto the forest floor, covering the dead, wet leaves. The farther along I move, the more the blood seems to pour, until finally, the ground beneath me is a rich, velvety red.

Am I bleeding to death?

In the distance, I hear a voice, like someone singing. It echoes through the trees. Haunts me. Sounds like a little girl or—I'm not sure who it is. I can barely make out the words:

> *Never fades*
> *Never lies*
> *Never dies*

Then I am standing in the middle of a clearing with a little boy blocking my way. He smiles and motions for me to follow him, turns to head deeper into the woods. His back is horribly disfigured: gnarled flesh with two gaping wounds from shoulder to waist. I ask him what happened, and he tells me he was once an angel, but someone ripped the wings from his body.

And then the dream jumps again, and we are standing together on a bridge, overlooking a stream. He stares at the water, his expression sad and troubled. I look, too, and as I do, some-thing powerful shoves me forward. I burst through the railing. Everything is happening in slow motion as I sail through air, pieces of wood flying all around me. I see the bridge above me. The little boy is no longer there; instead, watching me, laughing, is my mother.

I begin my downward spiral.

CHAPTER THIRTY-THREE

I threw my hands up to my face, ran my palms over it, and felt something wet. I checked my face in the rearview mirror. There was a gash above my eye, no more than a half inch long, but there's no such thing as a small cut in my world. For the first time since childhood, I was broken open, my blood betraying me. I felt it trickling down the side of my head and neck now, faster, faster. How long before I bled to death? Minutes? Seconds?

I heard a wild scream and, for a split second, thought it came from me.

No, no…it's the sound of sirens in the distance, coming closer, getting louder. Help on the way.

Soon firemen and paramedics were sliding down into the ditch. They pulled the doors open. One group began loading CJ onto a stretcher. Another reached for me. I had my hand pressed tightly against the wound; I could feel my palm full of blood, and my shirt was wet. "I'm a Type Three VWD!" I said to the nearest paramedic.

He yelled up the hill with urgency, "Get me some desmopressin! We've got a bleeder here!"

~

By the time they got us to the ER, they'd managed to slow the bleeding but couldn't make it stop completely. Desmopressin has its limitations for certain people; apparently, I'm one of them. Next line of defense: factor concentrate, a stronger agent that would hopefully shut down the flow.

After several minutes, it did. They closed the wound, then took me to radiology to check for internal bleeding. Thankfully, everything came up negative. I was out of the woods. Such a tiny hole, yet so dangerous.

A tiny hole that could kill me.

Luckily, I hadn't lost enough blood to cause any serious problems, but it was a reminder of just how fragile I was, how vulnerable.

After checking my vitals to be sure I was stable, they parked me in the waiting room. I sat there wringing my hands, worrying about CJ, and trying to process the past few hours. Someone had just tried to kill us.

But who, damn it?

I wasn't sure—all I did know was this wouldn't be the last of it. Whoever was coming after us would continue until the job was done, until we were out of the picture.

I buried my head in my hands for a moment, then I heard my name. Looked up and saw the doctor gazing down at me, his expression one of concern. Just over his shoulder, I spotted the last person I wanted to see right now—Baker—heading toward us at a rapid clip, his expression revealing not a trace of concern, only that suspicious glare I was growing accustomed to.

"Mr. Bannister?" the doctor repeated.

I took my attention away from Baker and gave it to the doctor.

"Your friend's going to be okay," he said. "A pretty severe concussion and a nasty laceration on the side of her head, but all in all, she came out of it pretty well."

"Thank God," I said, standing up. 'Any idea when she'll be released?"

"I want to keep her overnight for observation, but she won't have it."

I grinned a little, not a bit surprised. I thought it might take more than a whack on her head to curb CJ's stubborn streak.

"We'll have her out of here in a while," he assured, then left me there with Baker, who was studying me with crossed arms and conspicuous contempt.

"Well, well, well," Baker said. "Murder scenes. Hit-and-runs. You sure do get around, partner."

"Partner?" I replied. "Gosh, and we haven't even been on our first date."

"You're funny," he said, "but no time to joke, son. Looks like you got yourself in the middle of another mess."

"I assure you it wasn't intentional."

"So you say…," he replied, nodding. "Curious, though, isn't it?"

"What is?"

"Barely here a week, and already you've had more excitement than most folks around here get in a lifetime. Kind of funny."

"Hilarious," I said. I was tired and my head hurt.

"Care to tell me what happened, son?"

I rubbed the back of my neck. "With all due respect, Sheriff, isn't it your job to figure that out?"

"Wasn't asking you to solve the crime," he said, almost snarling at me. "I think you know what I meant."

"I do, but in all honesty, it's been a rough evening, and you've given me plenty of reason to get defensive."

"And you've given *me* plenty of reason to be suspicious."

I dug my hands in my pockets and gave him the benefit of full eye contact. "Are you accusing me of something, Sheriff?"

"I didn't say that—"

"Then what *are* you saying? If you think I've committed some sort of crime, I'd like to know what it is."

"Just that things have gone sort of…awry since you came here, and it's my job to figure out why."

"So let me make sure I understand you correctly: You seriously think I'm somehow the cause of all this?"

A vague nod, keeping eye contact. "Could be. In some manner."

"Can you define 'in some manner' for me?"

"If I knew that, I'd have this all figured out now, wouldn't I?"

I moved in closer so we were face-to-face, gave him a burning glare. "You're playing games with me, Sheriff, and I don't like it."

Keeping his eyes locked on mine, over-pronouncing each word now, "I'm doing my job, son, and whether or not you like it really isn't my concern. And since it *is* my job, I'm just gonna go ahead and keep on doing it. If that's okay with you."

"It's not the *doing your job* part I have a problem with. It's the part where you harass innocent citizens."

His lips spread into a smile, but it was cutting and unpleasant. "I did a little checking on you. Quite a colorful past."

I said nothing.

"A nasty drug overdose." He pursed his lips and shook his head with mock dismay. "Shame, shame, shame."

I did my best to conceal my surprise, but what I really wanted to do was smack the stupid-assed grin off his face.

Just then, the ER door swung open and an orderly pushed CJ out in a wheelchair.

"Hey," I said. "How are you doing?"

She rubbed the side of her head and frowned. "You know, I think I've been better. Hey, Sheriff."

"Ms. Norris."

CJ looked from Baker's face to mine, and I could tell she sensed the tension. "God, I hate hospitals," she said to me. "Can we get out of here?"

"Absolutely," I replied, then nodded to the orderly; he began to push the wheelchair toward the exit.

Baker stood like a stone statue, eyes trained on me. "Son, you're not going anywhere until I get a statement."

I heaved a sigh, then looked at CJ and said, "I'll just be a minute."

~

It was more like fifteen. When we finally got into the car, CJ said, "What the hell was that about? It looked like you were about to clock the sheriff."

She had no idea.

"Long story. Tell you about it later. For now, let's get you home and into bed."

CHAPTER THIRTY-FOUR

I had no intention of leaving CJ alone. She had a head injury, and it was abundantly clear that neither of us was safe. There's strength in numbers, and in my way of thinking, we were better off together than apart. After stopping at the motel and gathering up my belongings, we headed to her place. I put her to bed and settled myself on her couch.

I was lying upright and writing *shelter shelter shelter*. At number twenty-two, I glanced up and found CJ standing in the doorway, staring at me, the moonlight catching part of her face.

I turned the notebook over a little too quickly.

"What are you doing?"

I forced my voice to sound casual. "Just writing some things down, trying to make sense of everything. Why aren't you in bed? You should be sleeping."

"Can't," she said, still staring at the pad in my lap.

"What's wrong?"

"Somebody tried to kill us tonight—that's what's wrong." She came over, sat by my feet, moved a lock of hair away from her face. The bruise on her forehead looked nasty. She said, "I have a feeling you know what this is all about. Wanna tell me?"

I paused a moment, thinking before speaking, and then, "Someone wants me dead."

"I figured that after our little game of demolition derby."

"No, before tonight even. Someone's been trying to rattle my cage ever since I got into town."

"Rattle it? How?"

I reached down into my bag and pulled out the note. "Somebody stuck this under the door of my motel room."

She read it, pursed her mouth, and then, "Who do you think did it? And what exactly were they hoping to accomplish?"

"To mess with my head, I'm guessing. I've been doing a lot of digging lately. Someone wants me to stop."

"And they thought this would do it?"

"That's just part of it." I took a deep breath, let it out slowly. "Someone came into my room while I was sleeping the other day. And left me another message."

She held out her hand. "Let me see it."

"I can't. They wrote it on the bathroom mirror."

"The mirror," she repeated, as if doing so would help her understand better. "What did it say?"

I ran my fingers through my hair. "*You spy, now you die.*"

She stood up, started pacing, then stopped and turned toward me. "Why didn't you tell me about all this?"

"Because I didn't want to scare you. But after tonight, I knew I had no choice."

"You should have told me."

"Okay."

She placed her hands on her hips. "No. You *really* should have."

"*Okay*," I said.

She stared at me for a moment, came back to the couch, sat down, then stared at the floor instead. She whispered, "Jesus Christ."

"I know."

"What the hell do we do *now*?"

"We stick together. At least that way we can watch each other's backs."

"Okay. Then what?"

"I don't know. But I think we'd have an easier time figuring out our next move if we got some sleep."

"Yeah...that's just not gonna happen. I mean, seriously, Pat. After hearing all this, you honestly think I can sleep?"

"I'm exhausted, and you have a concussion, for crying out loud. Neither of us is in any shape to make logical decisions right now. Get back in bed. We'll figure things out in the morning."

She didn't get up, didn't say anything.

"Hello?" I said.

"I'm thinking."

"Stop thinking and get some sleep. At least try."

She was about to say something but stopped herself, then got up and headed back toward her room.

I leaned back and closed my eyes, trying to imagine how to get us out of this mess.

But I didn't get far because CJ screamed from the other room. I jumped off the couch and ran to her, found her standing in the bathroom doorway, visibly shaken, eyes opened wide.

Hanging from the shower curtain rod by a strand of rope around its neck was a small doll, no bigger than my fist. A little boy doll. Dripping with what appeared to be blood and a note tacked to its chest that read *Kill me.*

I put my hand on CJ's back. She startled and let out a gasp.

"Pack up your things," I said. "We're getting out of here."

CHAPTER THIRTY-FIVE

Nowhere to hide. No place safe, not even CJ's house.

The hanging doll pretty much clinched it. Someone had been there before we'd ever arrived. That meant they knew we were coming, and *that* meant whoever was running this campaign of terror was tracking our every move—not only one step behind us, but one step ahead of us, too.

My rental car was still drivable, more or less. It had suffered substantial damage to the side and rear during our dance with death and now had an annoying rattle. But we were alive. My insurance would take care of the rest.

I stared out at the open road as the headlights carved a path into darkness without so much as a clue as to where we were going or what to do next. CJ rode open-eyed next to me; any chance of sleep now fell into the slim-to-none category.

"Any ideas?" I said.

"Yeah. I've got lots of them. Which one would you like?"

"How about where to stay for the night?"

"Sorry, that went out the window around the same time the strangled Kewpie doll showed up in my bathroom."

"How about a motel?"

She allowed herself a mild laugh, but nothing about it showed any amusement. "Not in Corvine, that's for sure. There's only three; it wouldn't take them long to figure out which one we were at."

"Okay. How about somewhere off the beaten path?"

She yawned. "There's a little hole-in-the-wall town called Jerome about twenty miles up ahead. There's a motel, I think. Can't guarantee it'll be livable. Or even clean."

About fifteen minutes later, we rolled into town—or something like one. It had a gas station, a drive-through liquor store, a drive-through post office, and drive-through cleaners. Seemed folks here didn't like getting out of their cars much. The main road brought us to a bridge so old and rickety that I feared we might not live to see the other side.

"I told you," CJ said in a singsong voice.

"I didn't think it would be quite this bad."

If it hadn't been for the sign, I might have mistaken the motel for an abandoned warehouse. The place looked dark. And empty.

"Think they're even still in business?" I asked. We walked toward something white hanging down from a rafter, which eventually revealed itself as an OFFICE sign.

"There are two other cars in the lot," she offered. "They have to belong to someone."

"Yeah, the two people who work here probably." I pulled on the door: locked. Peered inside. Saw nothing but darkness.

"Push the button," she said, nodding toward it.

I did. Heard a buzzing sound inside. Looked at CJ.

She shrugged. "It works. That's a good sign."

"Or not."

A light flickered on, and a shadowy figure appeared toward the back.

CJ said, "Hooray." But the expression on her face—and tone of her voice—implied the opposite.

More lights came on, and the shadowy figure became a man. He cupped his hand against the window and peered out at us, his eyes tired and squinty. He was a heavyset guy in his fifties with messy hair, an unshaven face, and a neck that looked like a pile of pre-oven pizza dough. All nicely packaged in a wifebeater undershirt with stains down the front.

"Nice," CJ muttered under her breath.

"Zip it," I muttered back.

He opened the door, said nothing.

"Have anything available?" I asked.

He burped under his breath, motioned toward the parking lot, and said, "Does it look like we got a waiting list?"

Then he walked back into the office. We took this as an invitation to follow.

"All that and charm, too," CJ whispered. "Catch me—I think I'm falling in love."

I elbowed her, then to Pizza Neck, "We need a couple of rooms."

"Well, it's your lucky night. I just happen to have about twenty. Take your pick."

∾

My room smelled nasty, like a cross between stale socks, stale air-conditioning, and stale cigarette smoke. A few seconds after hitting the light switch, I heard a knock on the connecting door.

"Hate it here," CJ said, standing in the doorway, expression stoic, arms pulled tightly to her sides. She came in without waiting for an invitation. "Did you see the bathrooms." It wasn't a question; it was a declaration.

"That bad?"

"The dirt has dirt on it, and what's not completely filthy is corroded. I'm calling this a serious case of the nasties. Who stays in a hole like this?"

"Apparently we do."

"There you go throwing that logic at me. Don't do that."

"It's just for the night, until we can figure out what to do next. And it's not *that* bad."

"You're right. It's far worse. But hey, at least we get a free newspaper." She lifted it off the bed as if it were a dead fish, then carefully laid the pages across the bedspread. "Which doubles as a bed condom, don't you know...very handy." She sat.

I sat next to her. The paper crunched under my ass. She looked at me and, for the first time in a long time, started to laugh.

I gave her a look. "What?"

Still laughing. "This."

"You think it's funny?"

"No, I think it's horribly pathetic, but if I don't laugh, I'll cry. And I don't want you to see me curled up on the floor in a fetal position, twirling my hair. Not pretty." She was laughing harder now.

Then I began to laugh, too.

Chapter Thirty-Six

I woke up to the sound of knocking. It took me a few seconds to realize it was coming from the partition between my room and CJ's. I rolled out of bed, stepped into a pair of sweatpants, and pulled them up on my way to the door.

CJ stood on the other side, wide awake, fully dressed, and holding the morning paper.

"It's four a.m.," I said.

"I actually never went to sleep."

"I *actually* don't find that hard to believe."

"Sorry. It's this place."

"That ought to help your concussion heal well. Just what the doctor ordered." I returned to my bed, sat on the edge, rubbed my eyes. She followed me in.

"I was thinking," she said.

"About how sleep is something you should try to get every day?"

"Very funny. No." She was busy spreading sheets of newspaper across the bed.

"That sleep is something *I* should try to get every day?"

She sat on the newspaper and began ticking points off on her fingers. "Samuels kills Jean. And we think he may have killed Nathan, too. And framed Lucas. What's the connection?"

I thought for a moment and then, "You've been here for a long time, talked to lots of people about this case. Is there anything we've missed? Someone you've spoken to at any point that was somehow connected to Jean, maybe?"

She chewed her lip for a long moment, then answered, "There's one woman, but I honestly didn't see a connection then, and I don't see it now."

"Who?"

"Her name is Ruth Johns. She called me several years ago and claimed her son-in-law was somehow involved in the *Kingsley* case. I never could make it fit."

"Why did she think he was involved?"

"Well, she didn't like the guy much, then her daughter fell off a boat on Chambray Lake and drowned. It was ruled an accident, but Ruth thought he killed her. Only she had nothing to prove it."

"So what made her think he did it?"

"They'd been having marital problems for years, and the daughter—Kristen Johns was her name—was scared of him. Guy was into all kinds of shady stuff."

"And the connection to Kingsley?"

"I'm getting to that. The couple lived with Ruth for a short time. After the daughter died, Ruth started digging through all these notes he'd left behind—you know, hoping to come up with something to implicate him in Kristen's death."

"You read them?"

"I skimmed them. Most of it was just scribble, unintelligible, really. Couldn't make heads or tails. But Jean Kingsley's name did pop up a few times. There were also other vague references to a boy. Ruth insisted to me it was about Nathan. I didn't see it."

"But Jean's name *was* mentioned, right? You didn't find that unusual?"

"Unusual, yes," she shrugged, "but this was all a long time after everything happened. Jean was dead. Lucas had been tried and convicted. In terms of the case, it seemed incidental at best."

"Think it may be worth talking to her again?"

She threw her hands up, shook her head. "I don't know. I think it's a long shot."

"She still in town?"

"Yeah, over in Wentworth Hills. South side of Corvine. That's big-bucks territory around there."

"Think she still has the papers?"

"I could call her and find out."

"We've got nothing else at this point," I said. "Might as well have a look, right?"

She nodded.

"And the son-in-law? What was his name?"

"It was Bill. Bill Williams."

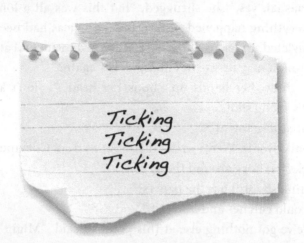

Ticking
Ticking
Ticking

CHAPTER THIRTY-SEVEN

Question your Beliefs

Mother's little helper came in the form of a small white pill. Only Mother wasn't the one taking them.

The pattern was always the same. I came home from school, did my homework. Then we had dinner, and that was the last thing I remembered. The next morning I'd wake up with few or no memories of ever going to bed. At first, it happened only occasionally, but through the years with more regularity.

"That's how it is when you're young," she would tell me in a tone that belittled my concerns. "It's perfectly normal."

I believed her.

But the symptoms I began having weren't normal at all. I'd wake up feeling dehydrated, with stomach problems and headaches. In the beginning, they weren't too bad, but over time they got much worse. The stomachaches sometimes turned to nausea, and I'd sweat a lot.

She continued to explain it all away, saying my food allergies were the cause or that I wasn't drinking enough water. But she never seemed to know what I was allergic to, nor did she make any effort to find out. Instead, she'd ply me with Gatorade, bottles and bottles of it. Our refrigerator was always full of them, and I got so tired of drinking the stuff that just the sight of the label was enough to make me ill all over again.

Through the years, the symptoms came and went, as did the strange sleeping patterns. I had periods when everything was fine, until it wasn't again.

By the time I turned twelve, the sleep issues were more pronounced, as were the symptoms of my so-called allergies. Then I started having problems with slurred speech—so much that one of my teachers called my mother to express concern.

"Yes," my mother said affirmatively, "I know about it, and of course I'm very concerned, too. I took him to see the doctor, but he can't seem to find anything wrong. He thinks it may be somehow associated with the Von Willebrand. But thanks so much for letting me know. I'll keep an eye on it, and please do call me if you notice it's getting more severe."

Then she put the phone down with a snort, and that was the end of that.

But not for me.

More and more, I couldn't account for large blocks of time, felt confused a lot, disoriented. If I pressed her about it, she turned nasty and combative, as if I had no right to ask. But the funny thing was that usually after we fought about it, the symptoms would dissipate. For a little while.

These on-again, off-again bouts became a normal part of life for me, but through it all, my mother's casual attitude and overall lack of concern continued to unnerve me. I think on some level I always knew she was behind it all—I just didn't know how. I'd developed a belief system over time that she was the cause of most everything bad in my life, so really, why would this be any different?

It's amazing how the mind—especially that of a child—can be so easily manipulated. For years, my mother could bend my reality in whatever way she chose, as outlandish or ridiculous as it might be. Blackouts were normal. Frequent headaches and stomach problems were normal. A warped sense of time was just a part of life. Living with an emotionally unstable and abusive mother was something not only to be tolerated, but to be accepted. She could act as cruel as she wanted, tinker with my sense of reality. and, perhaps worst of all, invalidate my emotional reactions—all of it was status quo. Family business as usual.

But that was about to change.

CHAPTER THIRTY-EIGHT

Bill Williams.

Jean Kingsley's murderous alter ego. Faraday had said he wasn't real, that she'd made him up.

I swallowed hard, tried to speak past the lump in my throat.

"What's going on?" CJ asked. "You look like you just saw a ghost."

"Close."

"Tell me."

I did. Explained about Bill Williams: how Jean had taken on his identity during her final days at Glenview, how they'd told me he was nothing more than a product of her imagination. That it was a lie—either that, or they never knew.

After I finished, CJ said, "This just keeps getting weirder."

"And creepier. The guy scared the crap out of me when I thought she was making him up."

"What kinds of stories did Faraday tell anyway? What exactly did Jean say?"

"Awful things. Horrible things. He wouldn't tell me all of them, said he didn't want to talk about it...or think about it.

According to Jean, Bill Williams was a sadistic sociopath, a killer, who started accumulating bodies at a very young age."

"How young?"

I hesitated for a moment. "Nine."

She shivered and rubbed her arm.

"And I'll spare you the details. You don't want to hear them."

"You think they're true?"

"Who knows?" I said. "Jean's mind was all over the place most of the time. It's hit or miss where she's concerned. But the part about Bill being real sure was."

"Okay. Next question. You think he and Samuels are one and the same?"

I sighed, contemplated. "Jean claimed Bill was the one who kidnapped and killed Nathan. I didn't put much stock in that then because Faraday insisted he didn't exist."

"But now that we know he's real…"

"Certainly makes me wonder. I mean, we were already moving toward the idea that the same person killed both Nathan and Jean."

"So if Samuels killed her," she said, "And Bill killed Nathan…"

"Then maybe Williams used the Samuels name as a cover to gain access to Jean at the hospital."

"And don't forget motive," CJ added. "Jean was telling people that he was Nathan's killer."

"So maybe he got nervous and wanted to shut her up before someone figured out she wasn't just ranting?"

"It would make sense."

I began formulating a theory in my head. Jean believed Bill killed her son, and in her deteriorating mental state, the only way she knew to communicate it was to assume his identity. Then one night she woke up and there he was, standing over her. I tried to imagine what that must have felt like, the horror—nobody to call out to, nobody to protect her. Victimized all over again by her child's murderer.

CJ echoed my thoughts without even knowing it. "What kind of monster is this?"

"Call Ruth," I said. "Call her right now."

～

On the road once more.

And heading right back toward Corvine, back into the danger zone. I reminded myself that someone wanted us dead. Whoever that was could easily pick up our scent again, putting us back on their radar.

Then I thought about Bill Williams. Was he still alive after all these years? I hoped for our sake that he wasn't. Being killed would be one thing—but if Jean's stories were true, being killed by him would be completely another. We were tempting danger, for sure, but the clock was ticking in double time, Nathan Kingsley's disappearance and murder becoming an even bigger and more bizarre mystery with each passing minute.

I needed to call Sully. Dialed his number but got no answer, so I left Bill Williams's name on the message. Told him it was urgent he get back to me ASAP with anything he could find.

～

Wentworth Hills had no hills that I could see, but it did scream money from every rooftop. Ruth's home was no exception: a sprawling colonial affair with giant pillars and windows everywhere and situated on several impeccably landscaped acres.

We pulled up to the wrought-iron gate, pushed the buzzer but got no response.

"Look," CJ said, pointing out through the front windshield.

I followed her gaze to a camera situated high up a tree and saw that it was slowly turning in our direction. It stopped on us. Past the gate, I saw more.

Concrete walls encircling the perimeter, a gate fit for a politician or dignitary, and cameras everywhere. Heavy-duty security, I thought, for a little old rich lady.

The gate opened. We drove in and followed a longish driveway leading to the house. A man stood out front, waiting for us. White pants, green polo shirt, mid-to-late forties, with salt-and-pepper hair. On the stocky side. As we climbed from the car, he stared at CJ's bandaged forehead for a moment, then at the gash on my head. He gave me a look that seemed to ask for an explanation.

I said, "Car accident."

He nodded but still appeared a little concerned, then extended his hand for me to shake. "Sebastian Johns, Ruth's son."

He led us inside and past a living room filled with old and expensive-looking mahogany furniture, then to an office down the hall. A smallish woman with a warm smile was waiting for us.

"Mrs. Johns," CJ said, "I'd like you to meet Patrick Bannister. He's a reporter for *News World*. We're working together on a story."

Ruth's face lit up; so did the ring on her finger as she extended her hand to shake mine—it was the biggest damned diamond I think I'd ever seen. That same hand was also trembling, barely detectable, but enough to give me the sense she was on edge.

They say everything is big in Texas; Ruth might not have been, but most of what she owned certainly was. A grand piano–size desk sat in the center of the room, piled high with cardboard filing boxes, all overflowing with papers. Enormous oil paintings set in ornate carved frames hung on each wall—no Walmart specials here—all originals, all hand-signed by the artists.

"Beautiful place you have here," I said.

She acknowledged the comment with a nod and smile, then moved behind her desk, nearly obscured by the boxes. All I could see was a tuft of gray hair above the stacks of paper.

"Are all of these your notes?" CJ asked.

Ruth materialized at the other end of her desk. "The rest is in the attic."

"There's more?"

Ruth rested a hand on one of the boxes, then glanced at it. "What I gave you years ago were the things that I felt pertained to the *Kingsley* case. I'd been gathering information on Bill long before that...and long after."

CJ nodded.

"He killed my daughter." She placed a firm hand on her hip. "There's not a doubt in my mind. I was never able to prove it, but I know."

I said, "Mrs. Johns, do you have any idea where he is now?"

She raised both hands, palms facing out. "God only knows. Hopefully as far from here as possible. I'm scared to death of him, even after all these years."

CJ and I exchanged glances, then I said, "When's the last time you saw him?"

"He disappeared right after Kristen died."

"And they were never able to prove he killed her?" CJ said.

"I wish. The sheriff couldn't show it was anything other than an accident, so case closed. Just like that."

CJ eyed me for a moment, then returned her attention to Ruth. "It's been a while since I looked at the notes. There were references to Jean, if I recall."

"And her boy, too," she added.

"Nathan?" I asked.

"Well, not by name. But I could tell it was him because he'd refer to Jean, then mention *the boy* shortly after. There was no mistaking who that was."

CJ said, "Mrs. Johns—"

"Call me Ruth, dear."

"Very well, Ruth. Did you know the Kingsleys at all?"

"Knew *of* them, just through all the media attention, but if you mean personally, then no, I'd never met any of them."

"Did Bill?" I asked.

Ruth shook her head back and forth quickly. "Not that I'm aware, which is why I was so surprised when I came across them in the notes."

"We'd like to see them again, if you don't mind," CJ said.

"Sure," Ruth replied, "not a problem. But just so you know, there's nothing about the Kingsleys you didn't see the first time. The rest are my own notes on my daughter's death."

CJ gave the boxes a quick glance. "We'd like to look through all of them, if you don't mind. Even the ones in the attic."

Ruth seemed to be contemplating the idea but not at all falling in with it. Speaking very slowly now, she said, "I'm not sure why you'd need the information about my daughter, and I'm a little hesitant to let it go. It took years of hard work. I'd really rather not."

"We just don't know what might pertain to the *Kingsley* case," I said, "and we want to be sure we don't miss anything."

She looked at me, looked at CJ, but still looked troubled. Said nothing.

"I promise we'll take good care of them," CJ said. "You have my word."

A cautious nod. "All right. I suppose. But it'll take you a while to go through them all. They're not very organized, and there's a lot there."

"By the way," I said, changing the subject before she changed her mind, "what did Bill look like?"

She rolled her eyes. "Quite unremarkable as far as I was concerned. Never understood what Kristy saw in him. It was rather a sticking point between us. She always did go for the rough-and-tumble types. A beautiful girl, my Kristen, could've had any man she wanted. Why she chose him, I'll never know."

"Rough-and-tumble?" CJ asked.

She smiled. "That's a nice way of saying *redneck*, dear."

CJ grinned.

"About six feet tall," Ruth continued. "Brown hair. Blue eyes."

"Did he wear a cowboy hat?"

"All the time. Don't think I ever saw him without one. It was all part of his image, you know, tough guy, Mr. Macho. Made me ill."

"Did he smoke?" CJ asked.

Ruth gazed at her with curiosity. "Like a chimney. Why?"

"Nothing special," CJ said. "We're just looking at a few loose ends that never got tied up in the case."

I added, "Trying to figure out if Bill has any connection."

"I see," she said, nodding slowly, watching me a little more carefully now. "Well, then, I hope the notes help you find what you're looking for. I'll call Sebastian to help move boxes, if you'd like."

"Won't be necessary, Mrs. Johns...I mean, Ruth," CJ said. "I think we can manage."

We each grabbed a box, began moving them out.

"Just one thing," Ruth said just as we reached the door.

We turned around.

She alternated her gaze between CJ and me, appeared to be stuck on a thought, and then, "I don't know how much you really know about Bill...but the man's evil. To the core. I knew it from the day I met him. If you find out he's alive, stay away from him." She frowned. "If I just could have convinced Kristen of that, maybe she—"

"But it never stopped you," I said. "I mean, knowing how dangerous he was and all, it didn't stop you from going after him for your daughter's death. Weren't you afraid he'd come after you?"

She raised a hand. "Oh, I was plenty afraid. Still am."

"But you seem just as determined as ever, dead *or* alive."

She looked directly into my eyes, and hers began to glisten. "Do you have any children, Mr. Bannister?"

I shook my head.

"Then you may not understand this...or maybe you will. Losing a child is the most painful thing a mother can endure. It rips at your soul, like a part of your heart's been torn right out. I truly sympathized with that Kingsley woman, I really did, and I suppose in some way I identified with her, too. I know what she went through. It never seems to get better, either. In fact, it just gets worse every day. I guess what I'm trying to say is, sometimes even fear is no match for a mother's love."

I thought about that, and then, "So you're not really worried he'll find out…"

"Oh, I'm plenty worried."

"But not enough to stop."

"I'll never stop. I'll go to my grave trying to see justice is served where my daughter's concerned. I owe her that much. It's just that I seem to go back and forth between pursuing the man and being scared to death of him."

The reason, I now realized, for all the security precautions.

I noticed her hands trembling even more so than before. Then I looked up, met her eyes, and saw fear in them, plain and raw.

"If you want to know the truth," she continued with a shaky voice, "I can't tell you the number of nights I've sat up worrying that someday he'll come back and *I'll* be the one floating in a lake…or maybe something even worse."

CHAPTER THIRTY-NINE

We loaded the car full of boxes, putting most of them in the trunk, the rest stacked so tall in the backseat that they blocked the rear window as we drove off.

"You see the look on her face?" CJ said once we were on the road.

"You mean toward the end? When she was talking about Bill?"

"Yeah." Staring out her window now, shaking her head slowly. "She's terrified."

"And with good reason. He's one bad dude."

She nodded, deliberated. "But she didn't get us any closer to connecting Samuels and Williams."

"Cowboy hats and cigarettes…could be lots of men in these parts," I agreed, "but it still does match."

"Think he's even still alive?"

I glanced at her, then back at the road. "Guys like that don't often go away very easily."

"And he sounds like an expert at flying under the radar."

"Which reminds me." I grabbed my mobile phone, dialed Sully's number, and got his voicemail immediately. Clicked it off and shook my head.

"Your contact?"

"Yeah," I said. The irritation must have been evident.

She sat up straighter and started counting on her fingers. "So Williams kidnaps and kills the son, then he starts visiting the mother in the mental hospital. Then she assumes *his* identity before he kills her?" She paused a beat, shot me a blank look. "Reality really *is* stranger than fiction."

"And don't forget Lucas," I added. "We still don't know how *he* got sucked into this."

She nodded. "Yeah, there's that."

When I glanced over, I saw she was staring into the rearview mirror.

I said, "What is it?"

Still looking, squinting, "That car was behind us when we left Ruth's, and it's still there."

I couldn't see a thing—all the boxes obscured my view. I adjusted the side-view mirror, saw a late-model SUV with black tinted windows. Looked ominous as hell. CJ shifted nervously in her seat. "Pull off at the next exit. See if he goes with us."

I glanced ahead. There was one coming up. CJ saw it, too, and with urgency in her voice said, "Take it."

I did. Drove up to the stoplight at the end of the ramp, looked in the side-view mirror. But the SUV hadn't followed. I gazed over the railing and saw it go flying down the freeway. Then I looked over at her.

She shot me a suspicious glare and said, "You think I'm paranoid."

"After what we've been through these past few days? All that we've seen? Do I think you're overreacting? Nope. Not a bit."

She revealed a shadow of a smile.

I tightened my grip on the wheel, felt the sweat in my palms as I merged back onto the freeway. The urge to list was overwhelming me. I struggled against it, fought it back.

Not now. Not in front of CJ.

But the pressure was almost unbearable, and I knew where it came from. It was becoming a way of life for us: always looking over our shoulders, always afraid someone was on our trail.

Hunting us. Like animals.

~

CJ insisted on finding another motel in a different town. She'd had her fill of Jerome—come to think of it, so had I. Next stop: Virginia, Texas, about fifteen miles up the road.

After realizing we hadn't eaten all day, we picked up Chinese takeout, then checked into our new digs, the Desert Inn. At least it was clean. Seemed to pass CJ's inspection.

Then we got down to business, sifting through the multitude of paperwork.

"She said this stuff wasn't organized." CJ shoved a pile of papers away. "She wasn't kidding."

"What a mess." I reached for another stack, started shuffling through it. "Most of it I can't even read. Looks like a bunch of chicken scratch."

"A whole lot of nothing. Even the so-called references to *the boy* that Ruth mentioned—most of them aren't even on the same page as the ones about Jean. Hardly as incriminating as she seemed to think. Could've been talking about anyone." She held up a sheet, stared at it, then tossed it aside, shaking her head. "God, it's sad."

"What is?"

"Losing her daughter," she said. "Knowing who killed her and not being able to bring him to justice."

I said, "It happens every day."

"I know. Still, no matter how many times…"

I looked up at her. "Got something?"

"I'm not sure," she said, examining a sheet of paper. Then she handed it to me.

I took it. Read it. And felt a burn in the pit of my stomach.

"Patrick?" CJ asked.

Her voice was nothing more than a distant echo. I tried to zero in on her but only saw white.

"Pat? What's going on?"

After finally gaining focus, I said, "There's something I need to tell you."

CHAPTER FORTY

The names in the note weren't spelled out, but they didn't need to be. I knew exactly who it was to, who it was from.

> B–
> Meet at 5:30pm
> Usual place.
> –W

I recognized Warren's handwriting, and as cryptic as the note was, it seemed clear to me. A letter from Warren to Bill. *Usual place*: it wasn't their first meeting, either.

It was the one thing I hadn't shared with CJ—about my mother and Warren, that I knew they were somehow involved in Nathan Kingsley's kidnapping and murder. A big thing, and I needed to tell her. So I did. I also showed her the note and the necklace.

"So let me make sure I understand you correctly," she finally said once I was done. "This Warren guy—the senator—is your uncle?"

"Right."

"And all this time, you suspected he was behind this…along with your mother?"

I gave a single nod. "Also correct."

"And the reason you're just now mentioning it?"

"Because of this note."

She looked at me for a long time, biting her lower lip, and then, "Yeah, I get that. Now tell me why you held out on me. This information is kind of important, Pat, kind of relevant. And you didn't share it until you absolutely had to."

"It's not like that…"

She crossed her arms and tilted her head. "Really?"

"No."

"Then tell me, what *is* it like? Because I need to tell you, Patrick, this one-way-relationship thing—it's not working for me."

"What's that supposed to mean?"

"*This.*" She held up the note and necklace, one in each hand, giving them a single shake. I saw veins sticking out of her forehead. "*This* is what I mean. You sat there and lied to me, Patrick. You told me it was just a damn news story! It wasn't—this is all about you."

"What was I supposed to say? 'Yes, I think my mother and uncle are involved, but I don't have a thing to prove it'?"

Her smile looked angry. "You know, it's funny. I wasn't aware that we had an agreement to only discuss what we can prove. I must've been absent the day you sent the memo out, because I clearly don't remember."

"C'mon, CJ. Give me a break here," I said, hands spread out, shaking my head. "You know what I mean…"

"No, I really don't. So please enlighten me. Tell me why you haven't been honest. Tell me why I've been spinning my wheels, working my ass off on a story with someone who doesn't reciprocate, who won't share the most important facts of this case."

I stood up. "I did share. I just told you."

"Sooner."

"Huh?"

"You should have told me sooner. Much sooner. And the only reason you did it now was because the note forced your hand." She walked to the vanity area, placed both hands flat on the counter, locked her elbows, and stared at her angry reflection in the mirror.

The silence that stretched between us only added to the pressure I was feeling. I threw my hands up. "Okay. I apologize. I was wrong. I should have told you. You're right."

She spun around to look at me. "I'm about this close to making you a memory. As in, *history*. As in, *see ya*. Do you get what I'm saying here?"

"Don't do that."

"Give me a reason why I shouldn't."

I didn't have one.

"God!" she said. "You've got walls around you that are stronger than steel."

I looked away, shook my head. "I don't know what you're talking about."

"Oh, yes you do. You know exactly what I mean. It's not even anything that you say. It's more what you don't...like some unspoken language. I can't even describe it...like you carry a wound so deep it'll never heal. What the hell happened to you?"

It was brutal, it was honest, and it was truthful. It made me feel exposed and vulnerable and raw. The pressure inside me was almost too much to bear. I said in a choked voice, "Look, I'm sorry. I mean it. It won't happen again. I promise. It's just...I'm not used to working with other people. I'm used to going at it alone, and I get scared sometimes. But I'm trying, I really am, and believe it or not, I've shared more with you about this story than I've done with anyone else. Ever."

"All I'm asking is that you—"

My phone rang.

I looked down at the caller ID. "It's Sully. I've got to take this call."

Grudgingly, she nodded her approval.

I cleared my throat, tried to act unaffected. "Hey, Sully."

CJ got up and moved slowly across the room. She took a seat on a chair. Sully's voice pulled my attention away from her.

"Think I got a location on your boy Bill Williams," he said.

"Talk to me." I put the phone on speaker so CJ could hear.

"Now, this isn't confirmed, so you're going to have to do some legwork here. Write this down."

I grabbed the pen and paper from the nightstand. "Go ahead."

"Telethon, Texas."

"Say what?"

"Exactly. Near the Mexican border. Population four hundred fifty-five at last count about six years ago, but I can't imagine they've had a baby boom since then. We're talking the middle of nowhere."

"What makes you think he's there?"

"Couple things. He has a cousin there by the name of Nancy Skinner. And believe me, Skinner's a real winner. She's a tweaker, and her rap sheet reads like a never-ending story. According to the police report, your boy Bill was at her place when she got popped for a probation violation."

"When was this?"

"June of last year. That's why you'll need to do some legwork. He may be long gone by now."

I said to CJ, "How far is Telethon from here?"

"About seventy miles," she replied. "A little over an hour's drive."

"Thanks, Sull," I said. "Anything else?"

"Actually, yeah."

"Shoot."

His voice got deeper. "This Bill guy is one nasty son of a bitch."

"Yeah, we've heard…"

"No, I mean bad. *Real* bad. If you do find he's there, do not approach him. Call the cops. Or call me."

I started writing down the word *shelter* repeatedly. "He have priors or something?"

"Negative. He's too smart for that. But he'd just as soon kill you as look at you, and you'd never know what hit you. Neither would anyone else. He's that bad."

I glanced at CJ. Her eyes were wide and blinking fast. Back to Sully: "How do you know all this?"

"I got people."

"I need details, Sull."

He paused and then, "The bureau's been following the guy for years but can't get him on anything. He's a suspect in several murders."

"How many?"

"A lot."

"What about—"

"Nothing with the *Kingsley* case. I checked. But I'm telling you, he's dangerous as hell, one bad-assed bastard."

"Sully. The details, *please.*"

"Okay, okay...one of the stories goes like this: A couple of agents came looking for him at his mother's house one evening, and she made the mistake of telling them he was at the local bar. When they walked into the place, he darted inside the john, escaped through the window."

"And this makes him dangerous?"

"Hell, no. It was what he did after that."

"Which was?"

"Put it this way—it was the last mistake his mother ever made. They found her the next day floating in a lake. When they pulled her up, her larynx had been cut out. His way of telling her to shut up, I guess. Permanently."

"Jeez."

"At first they thought he'd taken it with him. But the ME found it during the autopsy."

"Where was it?'

Sully paused. "Shoved up her ass."

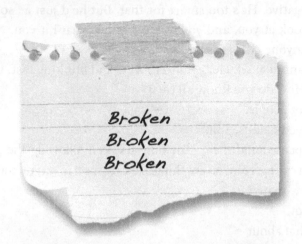

Broken
Broken
Broken

CHAPTER FORTY-ONE

You will Never be Okay

Up and down. Up and down. My life had turned into a sickness seesaw, one episode following on the heels of another. I was tired, depressed, and fed up. Fed up with my mother, fed up with my life.

Fed up with everything.

During the spring semester of my senior year, another round of symptoms hit, this time so severe that I ended up missing school for several days. But being at home wasn't exactly restorative, so I went back to class as soon as I could—although I was hardly up for it.

It was my first day back. On my way out of the building, I stopped in the bathroom, gazed in the mirror, and barely recognized myself:

dark circles under dull and lifeless eyes, pale skin surrounding them. I looked like the walking dead.

Out of the building and through the courtyard.

"Patrick?"

Without turning around, I recognized Tracy Gallagher's voice. If there had been a rock to crawl under, I would have been there in a heartbeat. Of all the times for her to see me. I pretended not to hear her, kept my eyes ahead, kept walking.

"*Patrick.*"

I turned around and saw the shock register on her face, but I was equally bewildered. It had been years since she'd spoken so much as a word to me—not since the social order had shifted.

"Patrick?" she said once more, head jutted forward now, as if trying to see if it was really me. "What happened? You look horrible."

"Thanks." I looked at the ground.

"No, I..." A bashful smile, pushing her hair behind one ear. "I'm sorry, I didn't mean it that way. Really. It's just...are you okay?"

"Fine," I said, and then after my lie, "Why?"

She moved closer, still staring at me. "You don't look like it."

I started feeling dizzy and nauseous, stumbled to catch my balance. Tracy lunged forward and caught me just in time.

"Patrick," she said, "*what's going on?*"

I turned my head away, tears filling my eyes.

She placed a soft, gentle hand on my shoulder; still, I couldn't look at her.

"Patrick?"

"I'm fine." But my voice broke despite my attempts to sound strong.

She leaned in. "Tell me what's wrong."

Eyes back toward the ground now, I shook my head, saw a lone tear splash onto my shoe.

She placed her hand under my chin and gently pulled my head up so we were face-to-face, then looked into my eyes—hers were so gentle, so worried—and in a soft, low voice said, "What is she doing to you?"

It was the first time in so long that someone had showed concern, actually cared, let alone touched me with a loving hand.

And it was her.

I lost it.

She wrapped her arms around me and pulled me in close, her shoulder muffling my sobs, neither of us saying anything for a long time. It felt warm, like coming home, and in that instant, there was no social order, no division, no time that had passed between us. Just her and me. I wanted to tell her everything. I felt like I could.

The sound of screeching tires startled us both.

A car came driving up, kids screaming and laughing, horn honking. I looked inside and saw a cluster of letterman's jackets and bright, attractive faces.

"C'mon, Trace, we don't have all day!" one of the Jackets yelled to her.

She glanced at me, then at him. "In a minute, Rob. I'm in the middle of something."

"You can pick up with Pasty Face later," he said. "Not like he's got anywhere to go except home to his loony-tunes mother."

Laughter all around from the Jackets, the dagger hitting me square in the chest.

"Shut the hell up, Rob!" she said, then turned back to me.

"Jeez!" he said. "Sorry, babe! Didn't mean to interrupt your *charity* work."

Dagger.

More laughter.

I looked at the Jackets, looked at her. Saw white and felt another wave of nausea sweep through me. Then panic. Something inside told me to run as fast and far as I could.

And that's just what I did.

I made it as far as the shrubs about twenty yards away before I threw up. Heard a roar of hysterical laughter from the Jackets.

"Check it out! Pasty Face is bush-barfing!" one of them said.

More laughter.

"What's the matter, Pasty? Get a look at yourself in the mirror?"

Laughter again.

Then they all starting singing, *"Tracy and Pasty sitting in a tree!"*

The laughter grew louder; it struck me like wicked thunder. I bowed my head and squeezed my eyes shut, forcing tears to roll down my cheek. Wanting it all to go away.

Then I heard tires squealing, looked up, and they were all gone.

Tracy, too.

CHAPTER FORTY-TWO

CJ was right next to me in the passenger seat but so lost in thought that she might as well have been a hundred miles away. The conversation with Sully and his frightening news about Bill had managed to upstage our disagreement, her annoyance now replaced by fear.

I wasn't exactly feeling so great myself. Reality hit hard: who we were dealing with, what we were up against, and that Bill could still be alive.

I took my eyes off the road every few minutes to check on CJ. Finally, I said, "What are you thinking about?"

She kept her gaze straight ahead, but I doubted she was seeing much. "Three guesses."

"Bill?"

"Smart boy."

"Smart-ass."

That made her smile. Just a little.

"Care to share your insights?" I asked.

"Just that Jean may not have been so crazy after all, at least where Bill was concerned."

"She seemed to know a lot about him," I offered.

"Yeah. I wonder how."

We stopped at a hole-in-the-wall barbecue/beer joint on the outskirts of Virginia, Texas, called Shea's Hog Heaven. Nothing heavenly about it, but the hog part certainly fit. Not exactly what I'd call Texas dining at its best—not even at its worst. Maybe somewhere just beneath that.

I watched CJ mindlessly stab at her food, never once bothering to take a bite. Finally, she looked up at me with deadpan eyes and said, "This shit looks like shoe leather. I can only imagine what it tastes like."

I stifled a laugh. She was still grumpy, but her dry humor seemed to be making a comeback. It was a good sign.

She tossed her fork onto the plate, rolled her eyes, then said, "Not that I'd eat it even if it *was* suitable for human consumption."

I gazed around the room. The company wasn't much better than the food. In one corner sat a robust dude who seemed to be wearing his meal more than eating it. In another corner, two guys covered in tattoos were shooting pool. From the looks on their faces, you'd've thought they were solving world hunger. Serious business, that pool.

"A psycho," CJ finally said. "Guess it shouldn't come as much of a surprise."

It was my turn to move my food around the plate. "I'm really starting to wonder if we should pursue this guy."

"We can't just quit now. It's not an option. Not at this point."

"The man cut his own mother's larynx out and shoved it up her ass. Do you really need a better reason than that?"

"Not an option," she repeated, then picked up her fork, went back to stabbing her food. "We're already invested in this."

"Invested?"

More stabbing now, with an irritated look on her face. "You know what I mean."

We both fell silent for a moment, then she said, "He may not even be there. And he wouldn't know who we are anyway, right? So what's the big deal?"

"The big deal," I said, "is that the town only has four hundred fifty-five people in it. How exactly do we keep a low profile in a place like that?"

Our waitress came by, a skinny little twentysomething gal showing the latest in tattoo wear: a snake that wound its way around her upper arm, then slithered into her boob region. I knew this because I could see it peering out from between her cleavage. It looked like it was smiling.

CJ caught me looking, glanced at the boob snake, then rolled her eyes and muttered under her breath, "Lovely."

The waitress narrowed her eyes, then slapped the bill down on our table and walked off without a word.

CJ mumbled, "No, we're fine. Thanks for asking, though." She snatched the bill up. "Jeez. Thirty bucks for lousy service and a shot at ptomaine poisoning? Hardly seems worth it."

"You're getting cranky."

"I've *been* cranky."

I circled back to the issue at hand. "Are you getting the part about it being a small town? As in, you can't even buy a loaf of bread without everyone knowing about it?"

"Yeah. I get that. And I still think we can pull this off. Patrick, listen to me. This is what we do. This is who we are. It's not the first dangerous situation either of us has ever faced, and it won't be the last, right?"

I offered no response.

"And we have each other. We can do this."

I studied her face and wondered who this woman really was and, more importantly, how I'd gotten mixed up with her. Tough and angry one minute, fragile and vulnerable the next, she seemed to change like a shadow crossing under the sun. She could drive me out of my comfort zone so easily, like no one had ever done before, yet I had no idea how.

Finally, I said, "Well, you're determined, that's for sure."

She smiled a little more.

"And I'm pretty sure I'll regret doing this…if I survive."

"You'll survive."

"Not feeling so confident."

Then, in that matter-of-fact intonation I was learning to recognize—and sort of hate—she said, "Stick with me. I'll bring it out of you…one way or the other."

CHAPTER FORTY-THREE

I watched an overpass sign fly above us: *Something*, Texas. I hadn't caught the name—they were all starting to look alike, the signs *and* the towns.

CJ napped on the way to Telethon, probably her first good sleep in days. Of all the times, I thought. We were, after all, headed for big trouble.

But it gave me time to think things over. We needed a plan to keep us alive and safe from Bill, the psycho who, by all accounts, had a heart the size of a peanut. Unfortunately, I couldn't come up with much. I blamed it on exhaustion, both body and mind.

Instead, I took in the scenery, which wasn't much to marvel at, but at least it sort of kept me awake. Harsh desert on both sides of the interstate, filled with lots of dead stuff and a few run-down outbuildings, most of which looked as though they'd outlived their purpose. Finally, I saw an indication that the next cluster of breathing humans was coming up, a sign that read *Calamity: 10 Miles Ahead*.

Man, they said it.

CJ woke up—or rather, bolted up—as if a bad dream had frightened her. She got her bearings, looked out her window, and said, "Where in God's name are we?"

"Calamity ahead, both literally and figuratively."

She looked at another sign as we passed by; it said Calamity had a population of 560. She rubbed her eyes. "Don't you just love the way they tell you how many people *don't* want to live in these godforsaken places? Almost like it's a warning."

"Apparently a few do."

"What?"

"Want to live there."

"Yeah. The ones who couldn't get out," she said with a yawn, her eyes following a semi as it passed by. "And they're mad as hell about it."

"Are you originally from Texas?"

"Born and raised."

"Corvine?"

She laughed. "Hell, no. Dallas. I moved to Corvine to pay my dues. Six years later, here I am, still paying them."

"How come you never moved on?"

"Oh…I don't know. Guess I settled, in a way."

"For what?"

"For…" She stopped. "I'm not really sure actually. What about you?"

"What *about* me?"

"What did you settle for?"

I gave her a quick glance, then turned my attention back to the road. "Not sure I ever did."

"You're avoiding."

"Huh?"

"You just did it again."

"What are you talking about?"

"The guarded thing. What's up with that anyway?"

"I'm not *guarded*. Is it okay to just not have an answer?"

"Sure." She gazed out through the windshield with a combination nod and shrug. "If you don't really have one. I just think there's more to Patrick than what Patrick lets us see."

Our conversation stalled, the rhythmic humming of tires the only sound.

CHAPTER FORTY-FOUR

"Mind if we stop at the next rest exit?" I said a short time later, nervously shifting my weight. "Nature's calling."

She nodded, shrugged, and kept her gaze ahead.

A few miles up the road I took the off-ramp, then pulled into a service station. Told CJ to lock the doors behind me and stay put until I returned. After getting a key from the clerk, I headed back toward the restroom.

I was washing my hands when something caught my attention on the floor under the sink. A child's fat red marker. I stared at it for a moment.

I had to pick it up.

I had to remove the cap, had to press the tip against the mirror, and, very slowly, had to write the letter *d*.

And then I had to finish the word.

danger

I stared at it for a moment and felt a rush of relief. Did it again. Felt the rush again. Did it one more time. And now I wanted to stop, but I couldn't. I'd started scratching the itch, but the itch was only getting worse.

So I kept scratching, kept writing…

danger danger danger danger danger danger danger danger danger...

It just went on and on, covering all four walls, the stall door, even the trash can.

I turned to look around as I was leaving. Danger was everywhere.

Walked outside and quickly away, feeling relieved of my stress and yet thoroughly disgusted and sick, like some hungover junkie.

When I returned to the car, CJ said, "Finally! My turn."

I froze and stared at her. "Huh?"

"I've gotta go, too," she said, irritation in her voice.

I felt a flash of panic, heat rushing through my body, feet heavy as lead. The word *exposed* blinked inside my head.

"Pat? What's wrong?"

"I'm just worried about you going alone," I heard myself say.

"I'll be fine," she replied and got out of the car.

I got out, too, and followed her.

She turned to look at me. "What are you doing?"

"Nothing," I said, struggling against my thoughts and my nerves. "I just...I have bad vibes about this place. That's all."

She gave me a lingering stare. "All of a sudden?"

"I think we should get out of here. Quick. Let's find a restroom up the road."

She placed her hands on her hips, tilted her head. "I can't wait until *up the road*. I have to go *now*. I'll be okay. *Sheez.* You can watch me go in if you want."

She turned around and started walking toward the station, and I continued following. She went inside to get the key.

I waited there, ran my fingers through my hair, and realized I was sweating. CJ came out holding the key and gave me a quick, troubled glance, then moved on to the restroom.

I watched her go inside, knowing I was about to be caught. My dirty little secret brought out in the light. My world turned upside down. All these years I'd managed to keep it a secret. Now I was about to be...

Exposed.

A few seconds later, the door swung open and CJ came out, her face colorless, her eyes wide, staring right at me.

Exposed.

I lowered my gaze to the pavement in shame, closed my eyes tightly as she moved toward me. Slowly.

Exposed.

"*Pat*? What the hell's going on?"

I said nothing. There wasn't much to say.

Exposed.

"How could you?" she said, voice trembling.

Head bowed, slowly shaking it. "I'm sorry...I..."

"How could you let me go in there? And how in the hell could they have known?"

I looked up. "What?"

"How could they have known we'd stop here?"

I swallowed hard.

CJ crossed her arms, looked away, and shook her head. "Behind us, now even ahead of us...it's like they know our next move before we do. What the hell? Did they follow us here?" She looked around. "We'll never get away from them, will we...ever? They'll never let us go."

I kept silent.

"Let's get the hell out of here. Fast." She began moving toward the car, then stopped and turned to me. "For God's sake, Pat. Why didn't you say something? Why didn't you tell me?"

"I didn't want you to go in there," I said quietly. "I tried to stop you."

～

Once inside the car, I locked all the doors, pulled out of the lot, got back onto the road. CJ was visibly shaken; so was I, but for different reasons.

I should have felt guilty for what I'd done in that restroom, for what I'd allowed CJ to think, for upsetting her. And part of me did. But the other part, the part that I couldn't control, was bathing in the release of tension. That part of me thought it was much better for CJ to fear whoever was chasing us than to fear me.

And that part of me won.

CHAPTER FORTY-FIVE

For the rest of the way, I managed to separate from my act, telling myself I was under extraordinary stress, that it wasn't me in that bathroom.

That it was the disorder's fault.

Telethon, Texas, finally announced itself with an antiquated clapboard sign. Beyond that, it was no different than anything else we'd seen for the past seventy miles: more desert, more nothingness.

We drove past a service station with no customers, not even an employee in sight, then an old hardware store, and then—to my complete lack of surprise—a drive-through liquor store.

"Welcome to Telethon," I said, enthusiasm absent from my voice.

"Welcome to hell," she replied in a tone that matched.

Nowhere to hide. Not even a dumpy diner for strategizing. My stomach hit another nervous jag. Seeing the town made me realize even more what a big mistake this was.

"Just keep driving," CJ said, jolting me from my thoughts and apparently reading them. "There's got to be more to this place."

"Yeah, the other side of hell."

A few miles later, we hit the other side of Telethon and the Paradise Motel—an oxymoron if I'd ever seen one. Nothing remotely beautiful or tropical about it, just your basic motor inn: a single-story, nondescript, U-shaped affair with twenty or so homogenous rooms facing out.

"Pull in there," CJ ordered, pointing to a vacant gravel lot.

"Turning in," I said. "Bates Motel, here we come."

"Not funny," CJ replied.

"Not trying to be."

I pulled up in front of the office, turned off the ignition, then gazed at CJ—or maybe it was more of a glare. "Now what?"

"Let's go in and meet Norman," she said with her usual wry smile. "I don't think his mom's gonna be around, though. I hear she's hanging back at the house."

"Not funny."

"Not trying to be."

"Touché."

We walked in past a rack of literature, presumably about Telethon, although I couldn't imagine what there was to promote about the place. CJ grabbed a handful of brochures and shoved them into her purse.

About ten feet away sat a man behind the counter, fiftyish and heavyish. He lifted his head as if we'd awakened him from a hundred-year nap.

"Looking to stay the night," I said.

"Single or double." It sounded like an automatic phrase.

CJ offered me a quick glance, then said, "We actually need two rooms."

He dragged himself to the rack, grabbed two keys, then dragged himself back. The task looked painful.

I said, "Can we get adjoining rooms?"

"They are," he replied.

"Is there anyone else staying here?" CJ asked.

"Nope."

"Why's that?"

"Off season."

"When's in season?"

"Summertime."

"What happens then?"

"Nothing, really." He shrugged. "Just…you know…summer."

"I see," CJ replied, but the look on her face said she didn't.

~

Before even settling into my room, I sat on the edge of the bed and started writing *forgiveness* repeatedly. It hadn't escaped me that my urge to list was becoming unmanageable, that I was out of control. I wondered where I'd be, who I'd be with, if the urge hit so strongly that I couldn't stop it.

I made it to *forgiveness* thirty-five when I heard a knock on the connecting door. I shoved the pad into a drawer, then opened the door to find CJ waving a handful of pamphlets at me. The look on her face screamed, *Get me the hell out of here.*

"It's official," she said. "This place sucks."

She came in and inspected the bedspread for cleanliness before sitting down beside me. "According to these pamphlets, the town's attractions are the jail, the water tower, and the train station…oh, and the cemetery. It's a bad sign, Pat."

"I didn't need a pamphlet to tell me that. Did you happen to figure out where there is to eat around here while you were doing your research?"

"In fact, I did." She opened one up and read it. "We have Covey's Diner, famous for their cow's tongue."

"Seriously?"

"And if that don't strike yer fancy, well, a half mile on up the road is the Hash House, where they serve…" She held out her hand as if waiting for my answer.

"Hash."

A smile, one of those wry ones again. "Which one you got a hankerin' for? Besides the tongue place, that is."

"I'm gonna say hash."

She pointed at me. "I'm gonna say good guess. We can save the tongue place for our special night."

CHAPTER FORTY-SIX

The Hash House was everything we'd hoped it wouldn't be: another filthy dive at the end of a dusty road. Country music twanged through ceiling speakers with sizzling grease doing background vocals. I started to wonder whether Texas had any decent places to eat or if we were just missing them at every turn.

The sign said to seat ourselves, so we found a booth in back. Across the aisle from us sat a kid sporting a T-shirt that looked as if he'd spilled a can of oil down the front. He had a greasy ball cap to match and a serious case of teenage acne. He stared at us with his mouth half-open and a faraway look in his eyes—one that seemed to state the obvious: *nobody's home.*

And then there was the young couple a few rows down who looked as though they hadn't spoken a word to each other in years. She'd clearly used a fork to style her hair. He had a tattoo on the side of his neck that said *Mercy.*

My feeling exactly.

Finally, CJ said, "Okay, the mouth-breather over there is totally creeping me out."

"What, you don't think he's cute?"

"If you mean cute in a Charles-Manson-had-a-baby sort of way, then yeah, okay, I can see it."

A sheriff's deputy walked in, young, probably in his mid-twenties. Brown hair, blue eyes, nice-looking guy. He sat in the booth behind us with a smile of hello.

"Well, there's a welcome sight," CJ said, giving him a little wave and smile in return.

"What's that? Someone who doesn't look like they were derived from a chicken embryo?"

"Yeah, and he even knows how to smile."

"Y'all from out of town?" he asked.

CJ nodded. "Just passing through."

"Whereabouts you from?"

"Dallas," she replied.

"Not much going on around here, is there?" I added.

"Nope," he said through a laugh. "The town's so small, our New Year's baby was born in March."

CJ and I laughed, too.

A waitress breezed past our table—another ninety-eight-pound twentysomething—and dropped two menus in front of us.

As she opened one, CJ said, "Is it me, or is there only one waitress in Texas?" Then she gazed around the room appraisingly. "It does have a certain charm, this place. I especially fancy the dead moose head on the wall over there."

"I'm glad you like him," I replied, nodding toward it. "He's tonight's special."

"Very good, Pat," she said, eyes wide with pleasant surprise. "It's official. You're now a card-carrying member of the Smart-Ass Club. Welcome."

"I proudly accept."

CJ smiled, then her face grew more serious. "So what's next?"

"Salad for me. I'm staying away from the mystery meat. The moose over there's making me nervous."

She gazed over the top of her menu, shot me a look. "You know what I mean. Our plan of attack."

Before I could answer that, the waitress came to our table. She cracked her gum and took our order, never once bothering to make eye contact. Then she left.

"So...," CJ said, "Bill."

"I've got the cousin's address. Let's start there."

"And on the slight chance he's there..." She reached for her purse, opened it, tilting it forward so I could see inside. The butt of a gun stared back at me.

Suddenly acutely conscious of the deputy sitting behind me, I said out of the side of my mouth, "You brought a *gun*?"

A smile lit up her face.

"Jesus...do you know how to use it?"

She gave me a *what do you think?* look, and then, "This *is* Texas."

"You're just full of surprises, aren't you?"

"You have no idea," she replied with a wink. "Pull up a seat. The show's just about to start."

Exactly what I was afraid of.

CHAPTER FORTY-SEVEN

The sun had barely peeked over the horizon the next morning as we drove through the center of town, everything looking orange and radioactive. Adding to the eeriness was a warm, prickly wind blowing from the east like oven fire. The feeling reminded me of the Southern California Santa Anas. Warm, early mornings always make me edgy. It doesn't feel natural. The farther we drove, the more the winds seemed to pick up, blowing dust and loose debris into our path, making my nerves even more ragged.

"I didn't think it was possible," CJ said, "but this place looks even worse in the daylight."

"Weirder, too," I added.

"Seriously," she said, watching a tree branch as it tumbled alongside us. "It's like the bastard child of *Jerusalem's Lot*. Like one of those movies where two innocent travelers wander into some godforsaken desert town and everyone's half-crazy...and half-related."

I made a sharp and sudden turn into a service station. Two guys sat on a bench; one of them had to be pushing eighty, the other, a skinny guy, probably in his twenties. Both wore vacuous, stoic expressions.

"Roll down your window."

She did.

I pulled up to them, leaned across her, and said, "Excuse me, fellows. Either of you know a gentleman by the name of Bill Williams?"

Nothing. No sign of movement except for the wind blowing through their ears. The wooden expressions remained that way.

"Our father's an old friend from high school," I continued. "We heard he's living around here. Promised Dad we'd stop and say hi if we ended up passing through."

Finally, a sign of life: the young guy looked at the old guy. The old guy shook his head, then the young guy looked back at us and shook his head, too. I waited a second or two, just in case one of them had a flash of recollection. Wasn't going to happen; in fact, I had a feeling they'd already forgotten the question.

CJ took a crack at it. "What about Nancy Skinner?"

A lightbulb seemed to go off in the young guy's head. He leaned forward, slowly raised his hand, and pointed up the road.

"Okay. Thanks," I said with a smile and a wave, then pulled away.

"I swear," CJ said, "it's like Valley of the Dolts in this place, starring Loose-Brain and Lunk-Head over there."

A few miles up the road we came to Nancy Skinner's street, although it was hardly a street—more like a dirt trail about ten feet wide with ruts so deep it forced the car into a tumbling motion. Scrub oak overgrew both sides, their branches whipping against our windows. No sign of a house.

"This doesn't look right," CJ finally said.

"It's what Sully gave me."

"Where's she living these days, in a lean-to?"

"It has to be somewhere," I said, leaning forward slightly and looking from side to side through the windshield.

"Hold on," CJ said. "I think I see something."

I strained to look ahead. Off in the distance was a house or something that looked like it might be one. As we drew closer, I could see the front door wide open, swinging back and forth to the commands of a howling, angry wind.

"Okay," she said, staring at it, "definitely not cool."

We pulled up a very rocky, very bumpy path leading to the house. As we got out of the car, CJ said, "I'm not loving the atmosphere around here." She put a hand into her purse.

"Not sure I am, either."

"And it's not abandoned." She had the gun out now and was using it to point at the front door. "I can see furniture."

"Would you put that thing down?"

"What? We may need it."

"It's not the needing part I have a problem with. It's the waving-it-around part."

She rolled her eyes, lowered it to her side.

We made our way toward the front of the house. I thought about Bill and wondered if CJ's gun would be enough to defend against a man like that.

The wind whistled loudly, and I felt something tug at my leg. I lurched back, startled, then kicked away a dead branch that had blown against me.

Then we heard a loud bang.

Both of us jumped, then looked toward the house just in time to see the wind grab the front door and blow it shut again. Even though we saw it coming this time, we both still jumped as it slammed. CJ looked at me, palm flat against her chest. I breathed deep. If houses had minds and mouths, this one would have warned us to get the hell away.

But instead, we moved forward, CJ holding the gun out in front of her, finger poised on the trigger, ready to fire at the first sign of danger. When we got to the porch, she turned and stared at me.

I motioned ahead to her. "You've got the gun…"

"So I get to have all the fun? Is that it?"

"That's how it goes when you're the one packing heat."

She aimed the gun at the door, spared me a glance, then said, "So be it. Locked and loaded."

"Okay, Ms. Oakley."

She climbed a few steps, then, without looking back, said, "You know, most men would feel emasculated letting a woman take the lead."

"Not me. I'm an equal-opportunity masochist."

I caught an acerbic smile, then she placed a palm against the door and held it there.

"What are you doing?"

"Feeling for vibrations."

"What kind?"

"A TV, stereo, even people talking inside will cause them."

"Feel anything?"

She held her hand there a bit longer, shook her head, then said, "Ready?"

"Yep. Let's do it."

Rolling a sleeve over her hand, she turned the knob ever so gently and pulled the door open.

She moved forward into the entryway, gun extended, gaze sweeping the room. I followed. She was right: furniture and pictures on the walls. Somebody still lived here.

We moved first to the kitchen. Freshly dirtied dishes in the sink. Then we moved out into the hallway, toward two more closed doors.

CJ eased open the one on our left. "Holy shit."

She stepped aside to reveal a woman lying in bed. Well, sort of: she was on her stomach, lower body under the sheet, upper body hanging over the edge. Her arms dangled loosely, and her head barely touched the floor.

We moved in closer, and CJ pointed to a syringe next to one hand.

"Looks like Nan fell off the wagon hard this time."

"Doubt she ever got on," I said, then placed two fingers on the woman's neck.

"Dead?"

I nodded.

We moved into the other bedroom, and it didn't take long to figure out whose it was: a mattress on the floor, a pair of jeans, two pairs of cowboy boots, and an empty pack of Marlboro Reds beside an ashtray overflowing with butts.

Between the mattress and the wall was a duffel bag.

I clambered across the mattress and began digging through the bag.

"*Hurry*," CJ said.

Inside and beneath the layers of clothing I found a receipt for a box of .40-caliber rounds from Dolittle's Gun Exchange. Next, a cell phone bill with a string of calls to Black Lake, Georgia. I recognized at least one of the numbers: Warren's cell phone.

I swallowed hard, then said to CJ, "It's him."

She motioned for me to keep looking through the bag.

I shoved the bill and receipt into my back pocket, continued rummaging.

Then I felt the hair on the back of my neck stand straight up. I looked at her. My face went bloodless.

"*What?*"

I shook my head. "We're not the hunters anymore."

"What are you talking about?"

"We're the hunted."

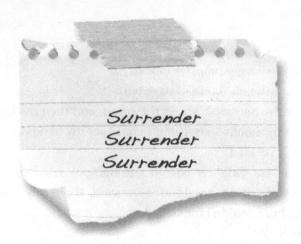

Surrender
Surrender
Surrender

CHAPTER FORTY-EIGHT

You'd be better off dead

The Jackets' laughter echoed in my head all the way home. I was fighting dizziness, fighting nausea, and fighting mad—or sad. I wasn't sure which. All I really knew was that if there was a breaking point, I'd reached it.

I flew through the front door and into the kitchen. No sign of Mother anywhere. Ran upstairs to my bedroom, slammed the door. Grabbed my notebook.

And started writing *persecute* over and over.

Not right. Ripped the page out.

Desecrate.

Still not right. Ripped it out.

Violate.

Ripped.

And then, finally...

monster monster monster monster...

Filled the whole damned page with it.

Threw the notebook across the room, and then the lamp, the desk chair, my books—anything I could get my hands on.

And I screamed.

The Jackets' laughter roared through my head once more, louder now. I put my hands over my ears, shook my head back and forth, but I couldn't make it stop.

Make it stop!

Everything was spinning around me, then came the cold sweats, the nausea.

Ran to the bathroom, threw up. Cried with my head in the toilet, tears dripping off my nose and into the water.

What is she doing to you?

Tracy's words ran through my mind, and something clicked. A low, guttural moan started inside me, then came out as a full-blown, agonizing scream.

I stumbled from the bathroom, headed downstairs and into the kitchen. Started opening cabinets, pulling things down. It was here, somewhere, and I had to find it. HAVE TO FIND IT. Took out a box of rice and dumped it onto the floor. Spaghetti, tossed. Can of coffee, dumped. All of it into the sink.

Nothing.

To the pantry. Dumped the flour, dumped the cookies, dumped whatever I could find. The place was a mess, the sink, the floor, everything, filled with food and empty boxes. Didn't care. DON'T CARE. Moved on to the next set of cabinets. Pulled down a box of cereal, a bag of oatmeal, all the contents spilled into the sink.

And there it was: something wrapped in a paper towel inside a plastic bag. Two plastic vials, one with capsules, another with finely ground white powder. Both read:

Camilla Bannister
Diazepam 2 mg capsule
Valium
Take one to two pills daily as needed for back spasms.

I continued searching some more. Found a total of six vials, all strategically hidden throughout the kitchen.

I held up one of the bottles and stared at it—just stared—tears streaming down my cheeks. Then, in a soft, broken whisper, I said, "You're supposed to love me."

More tears came; I wiped them away with my sleeve, then, through my sobs, almost pleading now, "Why can't you just love me?"

Because, Patrick, quite simply, you can be rather unlovable.

I slid to the floor and sat, hugging my knees, rocking myself. Then I buried my head and began to cry, a sadness, dark and profound, rising up through me. Sadness that now owned me, more powerful than any I'd ever felt and from the innermost part of me. Sadness over a life filled with the deepest of hungers, one I knew would never be fed. If my own mother couldn't love me, no one ever would. I lifted my head and through my sobs said, "Unloved isn't living."

I pulled myself slowly to my feet, turned toward the counter, and picked up one of the vials. I removed the cap. I poured all the capsules into my hand. I washed them down with Gatorade.

And went into peaceful sleep.

CHAPTER FORTY-NINE

Bill Williams had photographs.

Lots of them.

All of me, all taken during my time in Corvine: going to and from the motel; knocking on Jerry Lindsay's door; waiting outside Dennis Kingsley's house; walking in and out of Glenview; sitting in Penfield's car at the rest stop; leaving Jackson Wright's office; talking to Baker outside Newsome's trailer; and even one of CJ and me eating dinner together.

It was like watching part of my life whiz by in reverse.

But by far, the most shocking one of all: me, fast asleep in my motel room, with the tiny Nathan Doll propped against my shoulder—the same doll we found later, hanging from CJ's shower rod, soaked with what appeared to be blood.

What kind of twisted game is this guy playing?

All along, it had been Bill who was a few steps ahead of me, a few steps behind me, and every minute of it—without fail—hot on my trail. Watching my every move, snapping away.

Even while I slept.

A spiky chill ran up my spine. He knew who I was long before I ever had a clue he existed.

But how?

"Would you please tell me what the hell's going on?"

CJ's voice pulled me from my thoughts. I handed her the photos, watched her expression turn to shock as she shuffled through them. She looked up at me, cheeks blanched, mouth hanging open. *"What the..."*

I thought I saw something shift outside the window and shouted, *"CJ! Step away from the window! Now!"*

She gave a choked scream and dropped to her knees.

"Holy shit, Patrick! He could be out there. Or even in the house! We've got to get out of here!" She pulled the clip from her gun, checked the rounds, slammed it back in. Her hands were shaking.

"CJ. Listen to me."

She looked up and gave me her attention.

In the calmest voice I could muster: "If he were in the house, we'd know it by now. He would have gotten to us before we ever started going through his things. I think we're okay."

She nodded quickly.

I stuffed the duffel bag under my arm, then said, "Follow me."

We moved from window to window, searching for any sign he might be outside. Nothing. Then I led her down the cellar stairs. "Here's the plan: if he's here—"

"Of course he's here. He's everywhere!" She began fumbling with the gun. "Don't you get it? He's out there somewhere, waiting for us. He has to be!"

"If he's here," I repeated, "then he's probably sitting at a vantage point and waiting for us to leave the same way we came in. Our car is parked ground level to this cellar window. If he's out front, he can't see the space between the window and the passenger-side door."

"Right." She took a deep breath. "Okay. Let's do it."

And then we heard footsteps upstairs. Someone with heavy heels.

I pointed at the window. "Hurry."

CJ stuck the gun into the waistband of her jeans, climbed into the sink, eased the window open, and shimmied through. As I followed, I could hear footsteps coming down the basement stairs, getting closer by the second.

CHAPTER FIFTY

We flew down the highway as fast as the car would take us. The rattle was getting worse, and I wondered if some loose part was about to fly off. I kept my foot to the pedal, alternating my gaze between the windshield and the rearview mirror, searching for Bill.

But I didn't even know what to look for; I'd never seen the man. He'd sure as hell seen plenty of me, though, and had the photos to prove it.

I looked over at CJ and barely recognized her. Bags under her eyes, worry lines on her forehead—it was like seeing a different person. The gash on her head looked like it was starting to swell.

"That cut on your head is getting worse," I said. "We need to have it looked at."

"Yeah. Maybe Bill can recommend a good doctor. Or, better yet, maybe he can have a look himself."

"I mean it. Seriously."

CJ took a deep breath, and I watched her get control of herself, start thinking again. She turned to me and said, "Why is he chasing us?"

"Because we know too much."

"It can't be that," she said. "He started snapping those pictures the minute you got to Corvine, before you even knew he existed."

"That doesn't mean he didn't know about me."

"How could he?"

"Warren must have given him a head start. He had to."

"But Warren didn't know you came here, right? Let alone that you're on to him."

"I didn't think so, but somehow he had to…" Then it hit me. "*Son of a…*"

"What?"

"That damned box."

"You're losing me, Pat. What box?"

"The box of belongings I took from my mother's house after her funeral. The one with the necklace in it."

"How did he know what was inside?"

"I dropped it. Everything fell out, and he tried to help me pick it up."

"And you think he saw the necklace then?"

"I know he did. It was right there, right in front of him. *Damn it!* I should have known. The way he started grabbing at the stuff, the way he was staring at me."

"But do you actually think he'd put a hit on you because of it? His own nephew?"

I looked at her. "We're talking about protecting his career, his wealth, his public image, the only things that have ever mattered to him. He'll preserve those things at any cost. Look what he did to an innocent three-year-old boy. A child!"

She looked down at her hands, clenched them together, then brought her attention back to me. "And if there's a hit on you, then there's one on me, too."

"I think that's a given."

"What are we going to do?"

"It was a mistake to come here. We put ourselves right under his nose. We've got to get as far away from him as we can, *fast* as we can."

"That's if we can," she said. "The guy's like a ghost. He seems to know where you're going even before you do. How does he do it?"

"My God," I said.

I pulled onto the shoulder and hit the brakes.

"What are you doing?"

"*Damn it.*" I said. "Why didn't I think of this?"

"Think of what? What the hell are you talking about, Pat?"

I got out of the car. CJ did the same and followed me, watching my every move as I knelt, ran my hand under the bumper, then pulled out a small metal device. Held it up. "Here's how."

CJ stared at the tracking device with a sickened look.

"He's going to have to work harder if he wants to find us now," I said, and hurled it as far as I could into the brush behind me.

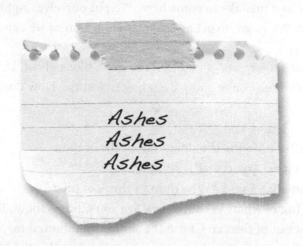

Ashes
Ashes
Ashes

CHAPTER FIFTY-ONE

The Biggest Lie

My mother found me in time and called for help. I never could figure out why. It would have been much easier to let me die and then claim she'd found me that way. It would have solved all her problems.

She told the authorities I'd been troubled for years and was gradually turning more self-destructive. Then she threw in the struggling-single-mother bit for extra measure. It worked.

The story went something like this. I'd gotten hold of her prescription pills after she'd stepped out for a moment. When she came back, she found the place trashed and me passed out on the floor. All true, of course, except she left out the most important detail: what she'd really been using the pills for all those years. I didn't bother arguing with her story. I had no fight left in me. She had won.

I spent weeks in the psychiatric ward at Black Lake Memorial, undergoing extensive counseling for my supposed nervous breakdown, where they warned me about the dangers of abusing drugs.

"Valium is highly addictive," the doctor told me.

It might have been the only time I ever laughed during the whole experience. I didn't tell him that thanks to my mother, I'd been addicted to Valium for years—living like some junkie, only I'd never known it, alternately overly sedated or in the throes of withdrawal.

For a long time I beat myself up, asking how I couldn't have known. But I ended up making peace with it. My mother had kept me locked within a strictly controlled environment where she could bend reality in any manner she wished. The brainwashing had started while I was very young, and as long as nobody on the outside challenged it, and as long as she kept me isolated, I remained in the dark, never stood a chance of finding the light.

When I returned home from the hospital, I was a changed person. I'd been to the bottom, and in that process, finally got to see what was left.

Nothing.

I was tired of keeping secrets, tired of being the victim, tired of my mother and all her lies. She knew it, too, and kept her distance. We barely spoke a word to each other throughout the summer.

Soon September came, and thanks to Warren, I was out of there. I went off to college, finally freeing myself from hell, the one she'd owned and operated. As the years wore on, I had less and less to do with her, and as that happened, she continued losing the hold she'd once had on me.

But not all of it.

I could travel to the far ends of the earth, off the planet even, and it wouldn't have mattered. Her ghosts still lingered, always would; they'd become a part of me. That's the most tragic thing about child abuse and its effects—they never leave, just take on another form. The abuser goes on living as if nothing has ever happened, while the victim pays the price.

And that's the biggest lie.

CHAPTER FIFTY-TWO

It seemed as if the Texas Plains were becoming the backdrop for our lives and perhaps the saddest of metaphors: a never-ending road. Muted shades of brown flanked both sides of a dusty blacktop, one that seemed to go nowhere.

Just like us.

The events of the past few days were catching up to me, and I could feel my mind and body quickly approaching overload. Now our lives were in more danger than ever, all because of a note and a necklace.

We drove on.

"We can't go back to Telethon," CJ said. "That's the first place he'll look for us. It feels like there's nowhere else left to run."

I sighed. The Road to Nowhere was getting longer all the time.

About ten minutes later, I noticed CJ looking at me funny.

"What?" I said.

She sniffed. Sniffed again. "I think we've got a problem."

I took a deep breath through my nose and smelled something burning. "Oh, no," I said. "No, damn it, *no!*"

I drove onto the shoulder and pulled to a stop—and as soon as I did, smoke began to drift from under the hood.

"Just when you think it can't get any worse…" CJ said.

"It does."

We both got out of the car. I popped the hood and jumped back as a stinking cloud of smoke boiled out.

"I don't believe this," CJ said, leaning against the car, crossing her arms and shaking her head. Then she kicked a little dirt.

I knelt and looked under the car. A puddle was already forming on the ground. I stuck my finger in it, took a whiff, looked at CJ. "It's the radiator. We need to get to a service station."

"There's nothing for miles around here," she said. "Where will we go?"

"Maybe we can flag someone down for help," I said.

"But what about Bill?"

"Just make sure the safety is off on your gun."

CJ took the gun out of her purse.

And we waited.

About ten minutes later we saw a car coming, off in the distance.

"It's a patrol car," CJ said, looking ahead and looking relieved, her hand over her forehead to block the sun.

The wind had picked up again, and the air was thick with dust. I squinted as the green-and-white sheriff's vehicle rolled toward us.

CJ stowed the gun in her purse, then began flagging him down. She glanced over at me. "It's the deputy from the diner!"

The car slowed down, came to a halt. The deputy leaned over toward the passenger window.

Before he could say anything, CJ said, "We've broken down. Can you get us some help?"

"The nearest service station is up in Boulevard," he said. "It's a good fifty miles from here."

I roofed my hands over my face to shield it from the blowing dust and dirt, tried to speak over the whistling wind. "Can you call them for a tow?"

"No point," the deputy shouted back, also pitching his voice over the forceful winds. "Jim Shemple's closed on Wednesdays. It's his fishing day."

CJ threw her hands up and said, "You've got to be joking."

The deputy shook his head.

"What can we do?" I asked.

Another strong wind came rushing through, blowing sticks and dirt in our faces and nearly forcing CJ off the road.

"I could drive you there," he shouted. "We might get hold of his nephew, Jessie…he lives just a few blocks from the station. He tows for Jim. But it'd be best if you come with, just in case we can't find him."

I gave him a nod. "That would be great. We'd sure appreciate it."

"Hop in then," he said.

We piled into the front because the back was filled with all his gear. CJ sat next to the deputy, and I got in after.

"Thanks so much for the help," CJ said once we were on the road. "I don't know what we would have done if you hadn't come along."

The young man kept his eyes on the road, nodded, smiled politely.

"Something was leaking from a hose," CJ continued. "It might be an easy fix if we can find the mechanic."

Then I glanced over at his waistband and something immediately caught my attention.

Both of his holsters were empty.

I heard what sounded like the slide of an automatic handgun clicking into place, then cold steel on the back of my neck.

"Gawd a'mighty, this conversation's as dull as dishwater," Bill Williams said. "How 'bout we liven things up some?"

CJ gasped.

The car kept rolling.

The gun's barrel slid from the nape of my neck to the soft spot on the back of my head. I felt the burn in my stomach.

"So nice to finally meet you folks," Bill said with a thick Southern drawl, now moving the barrel over to CJ's head and teasing her curls with it. I could see him in the rearview mirror, all big grin and cold, cold eyes. "Although I kinda feel like I already know y'all. And I guess in a way, I sorta do."

He returned the gun to me, pressing the barrel deep into the back of my neck; I clenched my teeth, then swallowed hard.

"Hey, sport," he said to me. "Mind handing me the little lady's purse? And don't try nothin' foolish or I'll throw a quick bullet to your brain. It could get messy."

I lifted the purse over the seat to him.

"I thank you kindly," he said, then shook it around so he could view the contents. "Well, looky here. Missy's got herself a gun. I love me a woman who ain't afraid to shove some steel around."

The deputy kept his attention on the road; his grim expression told me he was fighting back his own anxiety.

Bill tilted his hat back with his other hand. "You know, funny thing happens when you pull a radiator hose out ever so slightly. Eventually, thing's gonna give out, car's gonna overheat." He grinned, exposing teeth the color of too many cigarettes. "Got that done while I seen the car parked out front. C'mon, y'all didn't think I was *that* dumb, did ya? That I'd just let you scurry on down the road? Merrily on your way?"

We answered with silence.

He gave the gun a shove against the back of my head. "I believe I just asked a question."

I shook my head.

"Then all I had to do was scoop up this handsome young man—Telethon's finest—and have him give me a lift to y'all. He didn't mind much. Well, not sorta." He poked the deputy's shoulder with the tip of his gun, flashed the wide, yellow grin again. "Thanks for helping me with my flat tire, son. So much for being a Good Samaritan." He laughed at his own joke.

The deputy showed no reaction.

Bill brought the barrel over to CJ and began stroking her hair again. She flinched, and he responded by jabbing it deep into her neck. She closed her eyes and took in a deep breath. I felt my pulse pounding into my throat, then something warm and tinny on my tongue. I wondered if it was the taste of fear...or maybe fast-approaching death. I grabbed CJ's hand and squeezed it, could feel her shaking.

"Turn here," Bill ordered the deputy.

He did, onto a dirt road. The car began to rattle as dust flew up into the air behind us.

"Where are you taking us?" CJ asked, her voice shaky.

"Never you mind on that, missy," he said, "but not to worry. You'll find out soon enough. Turn again, handsome."

The deputy took a sharp left onto another dirt road. A few hundred feet later he headed down an embankment and contin-ued on. The farther we drove, the thicker the brush, the rockier the road, and the deeper into trouble I knew we were getting.

About five minutes later, Bill directed the deputy up a gravel drive and past a large sign that read *B&D Meat Processing Inc.* I could see the plant ahead; the place looked run-down, like it hadn't been open for years.

"That's right, boys and girls!" Bill said, his voice filled with a peculiar sort of enthusiasm. "We're taking a little field trip to the Meat Puppets' Ball. Gonna have us some good times. I can hardly wait."

The car pulled to a stop.

"All righty, folks," Bill said. "Fall out. Now's when the *real* fun begins."

～

He made us line up against a concrete wall, began pacing back and forth, then, as if hit with a sudden thought, said, "*Jeez-us*. Where the hell are my manners? Thanks for the help, Deputy. You can go now." Then, calmly, he put the barrel against the young man's head and blew his brains out.

The blast echoed in my head, echoed everywhere. The deputy dropped to the ground, facedown, blood and brain matter staining the wall where he'd stood. CJ began sobbing. I closed my eyes as tight as I could, wanting it all to go away, wanting this to be some bad dream. It wasn't. It was real. It was hell, and I knew we were next.

"Okay, friends," he said, shoving the deputy's body out of his way with one foot, his voice with an overly enthusiastic kick to it, "here's how it's all gonna go down. Y'all get in line, Gossip Girl in front, Wonder Boy behind. Gossip Girl raises her hands just above her shoulders, palms up, and Wonder Boy places his—palms down—on top of hers. Then we move forward. *Do not* let your hands become separated from one another at any time or you both get dead in a hurry, just like our friend here. Understood?"

Neither of us said a word. CJ was still trembling and crying. I don't know what I was doing.

He shoved the gun barrel into my ear. "I *said*, understood?"

We both nodded.

He continued, "Now let's see how good y'all are at following directions. *Move it!*"

With hands joined together, we moved forward until we came to a pair of rusted steel doors. Bill held one open and motioned us through with his gun. Then he marched us down a long hallway with tiled floors and tiled walls. Our echoing footsteps were all I could hear, apart from the pounding of my own heart.

We came to another pair of doors. Once through, we moved into what looked to be the main processing plant.

I don't know how long the place had been shut down, but a rancid odor still lingered. Row after row of conveyer belts ran along the ceiling, with stainless-steel meat hooks dangling from them.

I took my attention to the far corner and saw two chairs positioned side by side. A roll of duct tape rested on one of them, and directly behind them was a third chair with a pair of semiautomatic pistols on it.

Clearly, he'd been expecting us, and clearly, he had plans.

I got that metal taste again, tried to ignore it, instead choosing to focus on how to get us out of this mess. How to survive.

"Wonder Boy, take a seat," Bill said. "Missy, you tape his wrists together."

CJ and I exchanged timorous glances, then moved forward. I sat while she taped my wrists. She tried not to do a good job. Bill made her sit while he taped her wrists, waist, and ankles. Then he checked the tape on my hands. He gave CJ an unpleasant grin and taped me up as thoroughly as he'd done her.

I stole a glimpse at CJ. Her expression appeared stoic, but she was trembling something fierce. She caught my gaze, and in a split second, reality seemed to hit us both, telling us our lives were about to come to an end.

But not if I could help it. I looked around for something to use as a weapon. Looked up high along the walls for some heavy or sharp object, one I could possibly force down on him. There were old tools all over the place. The only question was how to get to them.

"Here we go, kids!" Bill said, interrupting my thoughts. He was standing before us now, grinning, eyes wide and animated: the face of a madman. A killer.

He said, "We're going to have ourselves a good old-fashioned double execution. That sound like fun?" He didn't wait for an answer. "But we're adding a new twist. I've done a lot of these, you see, and they get...a little boring. Have to liven things up some, keep myself entertained, you know." He raised his hand as if taking an oath. "No worries, folks. This ain't my first rodeo. I'm a pro at this. Won't screw it up. I'll do ya right. Promise. Scout's honor. Now, here's what I got planned."

He began pacing in front of us, then he stopped and pointed toward the empty chair behind us with his gun. "I'm gonna take a seat right there behind y'all with my girls, Kitty and Miranda—better known as Smith and Wesson. Then I'm gonna sit a spell and think. And then I'll blow one of your brains out first, and then I'll let the other live just a little longer. Of course, that's more for me than it is for you. See, it's those few extra seconds of life that'll put the fear of God in ya, and I just *love* to watch that. Sometimes the person'll wet themselves…or shit their britches. Sometimes both even. I've seen it happen. I have."

"You don't have to do this," CJ said.

"Well, darlin', yeah, actually, I do. Oh, there was a point in time where that mighta been true. But that point's done gone. You can blame yourselves for that. If y'all just could've left well enough alone, none of us would have to be here. But ya couldn't do that, could ya? Ace Reporter and his little sidekick had to start digging, had to try and figure it all out." He turned to me. "'Course, you didn't quite figure *everything* out, now, did you, Nathan?"

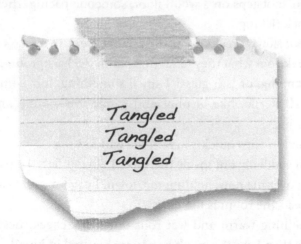

Tangled
Tangled
Tangled

CHAPTER FIFTY-THREE

People will hurt you

A world I visit only at night. While I sleep.

A run-down shack surrounded by trees. An old white pickup parked alongside it. An angry storm brewing overhead.

This is how the dream always begins.

Thunderheads pick up speed, rolling through turbulent skies, casting a shadow of darkness over everything. The rain begins to fall, lightly at first, then with gathering intensity. A flash of lightning explodes, followed by a violent clap of thunder. The wind howls.

Even though I'm looking at the scene from outside the shack, I have a strong sense that inside there is chaos. Something bad is happening. Something evil.

I hear footsteps on a wood floor, someone pacing, rhythmic, like a clock ticking.

A door slowly creaks open, then slams. Next, two men's voices. I can't make out what they're saying, but in the background I hear metal clanging; or is it glass? I smell something, too, something medicinal, sterile, like alcohol and gauze. Makes me anxious, frightens me.

A shadow slips quickly across the window.

Then suddenly I'm inside the shed. Laid out flat, the two men standing over me now, holding me down. I can't move. I can't see their faces—the room is too dark.

Something warm and wet rolls down my cheek, tickles my skin, and then I see the men's hands are covered in blood.

I scream as loud as I can. The other man quickly shoves his hand over my mouth to muffle my cries. I can breathe only through my nose now, but it's difficult. I feel as though I'm being smothered. The room starts spinning. I'm suffocating.

"Do it, Raphael. Do it now, damn it. Right now!"

A needle.

And everything goes black.

CHAPTER FIFTY-FOUR

"It's like a stupid fucking dog chasing after his own tail, I tell ya!" He let out a hysterical laugh, which erupted into an uncontrollable coughing fit. "All this time you been tryin' to figure out what happened to *poor little Nathan*, and all this time, you didn't have a dang clue!"

"You're lying," I said.

"Am I?"

"Either that or just plain crazy."

"That, my friend, may be right, but the truth is the truth. You ain't nothin' but a bastard child, a whore-son. Warren ain't your uncle—he's your papa. And your momma, Jean, well…" He shook his head in mock disappointment. "She was spreading it all over town. Wave some cock in front of the tramp, and she'd fold over faster than a cheap lawn chair." He allowed himself a short, contained chuckle. "And Warren never *could* keep that eleventh finger in his pants. No sir. Those two'd been carrying on for years."

I saw white, felt light-headed, could hear my heart go racing.

"Then things got a little complicated—well, actually, *a lot* complicated—the day you fell and hit your head on the playground. That changed everything. Momma Jean had to rush you to the hospital when they couldn't stop the bleeding on account'a that disease you got. But the plot thickens. Yessir. It's passed on by one parent. Well, Momma Jean didn't have it. Neither did Daddy Dennis. But Warren did, and everyone knew it. And so little Nathan became a walking time bomb. *Tick, tick, tick.*"

The room began to spin. I closed my eyes tight, tried to get my bearings.

Bill continued. "So they had a bit of what they call a *situation* on their hands. Had to do something about it. I mean, they couldn't risk word getting out that he'd had an affair, let alone a love child. No-sirree-Bob. After all, he had a political career to think of, and *she* didn't want Dennis finding out. Nope. Damage-control time. So Jean and Warren made a deal with the devil." He tipped his hat, smiled big. "That's me."

Breathing shallow, heart pounding in my head, I felt my whole body go warm, tried to speak from a throat as dry as wool but couldn't force out so much as a word.

"So Warren hires me to kidnap you, take you to that wack-job sister of his. You didn't really believe she could be your momma, did you?" Big laugh. "The woman couldn't raise a turnip. But Warren didn't care so long as he could stay close, watch his boy grow up, and keep his political career from falling apart."

Images flashed through my mind. The white pickup truck, the shack, the boy in the woods. Suddenly, I blurted out, "The thunderstorm."

"Huh?" Bill looked at me with raised brows.

"There was a thunderstorm that day."

Nodding, smiling. "Yep. Sure was."

It was all coming back to me now, the dreams, the images. I wasn't flying through the woods; I was being carried under his arm. "You tripped…or you dropped me…or…something. I hit my head on a rock. There was blood everywhere, all over the leaves."

He pointed at me. "Bingo! And what a pain in the ass *that* was."

"You took me to the shack."

He clapped his hands together, spoke with excitement. "Right again, hoss!"

"*Do it, Raphael. Do it now, damn it. Right now!*" I said, tears now streaming down my cheeks. "The needle! The damned needle!"

He shrugged. "Had to settle your ass down so we could stop the bleeding."

"You fucking *animal!*"

"Now, now, Nathan," he said. "No need to pull your britches up in a wad. All in a day's work, partner, all in a day's work."

I caught CJ's gaze and saw a pair of sad, sympathetic eyes looking back, searching mine. Then I looked at Bill and gritted my teeth so tightly that my temples began to burn. I spat my next words at him, "You did this to me! You sick—"

"Well, not exactly," he said, looking down, shaking his head. "Not really. Technically, your momma did it. She and Warren did. Me, I was just the go-between, did all their dirty work."

CJ said, "But Jean was the one who paid the price for it. Not Warren."

"True. Can't argue there," he said, nodding. Then back to me, "And you were just their sacrificial lamb, Nathan—that's *all* you was, all you'd ever be. Warren slept fine at night, like a little baby, but she couldn't, and in the end it drove her nuts, right into the loony bin."

"Where you ended up killing her," CJ said.

"Had to," Bill said, throwing his hands up. "Had to shut the whore up. Warren needed her gone. And fast."

All of a sudden Bill glanced down at his watch, then up between CJ and me, his expression one of pretend surprise. "*Criminy*, would you just look at the time? Where does it all go, I ask you? I think story hour is over, kids."

He looked at CJ. She glared back at him.

"'Course, I wouldn't mind a little pre-execution bonus right about now. Nope. Not one bit." He walked up behind her and pushed his crotch up against the back of her head, began thrusting against it, giggling like a thirteen-year-old boy. CJ closed her eyes and pursed her lips as he forced her head to bob back and forth. "So, how 'bout it, darlin'?"

"Leave her alone," I said.

"Put a lid on it, Nathan. You ain't got nothin' to say here." He looked down at CJ. "So whad'ya say, sugar? How 'bout givin' up some of that sugar? Ever been with a real cowboy?"

"No, but I'd settle for a real man."

Bill smacked her on the head with the butt of his gun, and blood began oozing down the side of her face. He came around, grabbed her by the collar, pulled her close to his face, then through gritted teeth said, "You're makin' me hard, darlin'. Nothing I like more than a good grudge fuck."

I shouted out, "*NO!*"

"Shut it, *Bastard Boy.*" He pointed the gun at me. "Or I kill you first and *then* fuck her."

Panic and anger twisted through me and came out as fiery words. "*Leave her the hell alone, you stupid, inbred prick! What's the matter? Did your whore of a mother knock the crap out of you when you were a kid? Treat you like her little bitch? Is that why you have to beat on women just to stay hard?*"

Bill swung his head toward me with a cocked eyebrow and a maniacal grin that told me I had his full attention. He walked over and began ripping away the duct tape, leaving just my hands bound in front of me. Grabbing me by the collar, he jerked me straight up into a standing position, then hoisted me onto a meat hook so I was hanging by my wrists. He spun me around toward him, held me in place with his right hand, wound up with his left, and delivered a powerful left hook to my gut.

Everything blurred. I gasped for air but couldn't draw much in—the pain in my abdomen prevented it. I knew I could be bleeding internally, the lifeblood inside flooding my body, drowning my organs until they could no longer function.

My vision returned just in time to see Bill coming at me with something long, something metal.

Something sharp.

"It's been a long time since I seen you bleed, Nathan," Bill said, full malice in his voice. He began pushing the rod against my body, the tip barely tearing through my clothes, forcing me to swing back and forth. He used that same momentum to drive the end into my leg; it felt wet and warm with intense pain. Then he plunged the point into my shoulder, more pain and more blood now trailing down my arm.

CJ screamed.

I caught a glimpse of her, wondering how much longer before I bled out and died.

Bill stepped back and prepared to take another jab, but as he did, the end of the rod snagged on a panel behind him. I heard a sharp click, followed by a long, squeaky whine, and the machine came to life. A hook swooped in from behind, caught the back of his jacket, and lifted him into the air. Now we were both moving along the track within an arm's length of each other. He grabbed hold of my shirt, and I kicked him away with all the strength I could muster, forcing him to release his hold and swing away. He came back and slammed into me with such force that the hook began tearing through the tape around my wrists. Before I knew it, I'd dropped onto the floor.

I scrambled to my feet, gasping in pain. I was soaked in blood, could see it now, oozing out fast from my shoulder, my leg, too. I couldn't see what might be happening inside me but knew one thing: I wasn't going to last long.

I spotted Bill moving along the track, heading for a junction where the conveyer split in two directions. To the right, the track was broken—if he continued on that course, he'd eventually derail, then come off and fall to safety. I didn't know where the track to the left led, but I made up my mind that's where he was going.

I needed to get to the rail switch and change Bill's course before he reached the junction. I stumbled to the control panel, pushed the button.

And nothing happened.

I pushed it again. Nothing, again. Damned thing was broken, and Bill was coming up quickly to the end of the track. I could push him onto the other track manually, but that meant having to run alongside him. I looked up at the hooks rolling past with their spear-like tips angrily tossing back and forth, clawing at the air. Telling me to stay away.

I couldn't. I'd spent my whole life terrified of my own blood and in the process became terrified of living. Not anymore. My anger had arrived; it was strong, it was powerful, and it would drive me through this. I'd use it to make sure that bastard never took another breath.

I found a screwdriver sitting on top of a machine and stuffed it in my back pocket, handle first. I caught up to Bill, ran ahead of him, and reached for the manual wire. He kicked out and wrapped his legs around my neck, squeezing hard. Now he was dragging me along the ground by my neck, choking me. I reached up, tried loosening the grip, but he was holding on tightly, his boots locked together. I pulled the screwdriver from my pocket and buried the end in his thigh. He shouted and his leg twitched, releasing his hold, dropping me to the floor.

Bill continued on, grunting in pain, now barely a foot from the juncture. I rushed up beside him, pulled the manual wire, and forced him onto the other track just in time. He swung in the other direction and began moving away from me. Suddenly, the hook released, dropping him into a chute. When I got there and looked down, I saw him lying faceup, eyes wide open, with a metal stake pushing up through his chest.

And covered in blood.

But I had no time to revel in his death because I was bleeding too, the red running wild from my body. My vision blurred and I began to shiver. I knew these were all effects of severe blood loss. It wouldn't be long now.

I staggered back toward CJ, leaving a trail of blood along the way. I think she said something, but I didn't hear it; I was too focused on ripping the duct tape from her arms, legs, and waist.

And that was the last thing I remembered.

CHAPTER FIFTY-FIVE

My eyes shot wide open.

The packing plant was gone, replaced now by white light—in fact, everything was white. And clean. It took me a moment to realize I was lying in a hospital bed.

I looked up and saw CJ standing beside me, head tilted, watching me with studied concern.

I smiled.

She did, too, and then in a soft voice said, "How you doing there, kiddo?"

"Pretty lousy," I said, "but thanks for asking."

She smiled wider, brushed a hand across my forehead, pushing the hair away from my eyes. "You know, that was some pretty crazy stuff you pulled back there. You almost died."

I frowned, closed my eyes, nodded.

Another voice said, "You know, being a hero is not such a great idea."

I opened my eyes. "Sully...holy...how did you...?"

CJ grinned. "I found your phone on the floor while they were loading you into the ambulance. It rang, so I answered it."

"Guess who?" Sully said with a wave and a smile. "So I had to come see for myself if you were all in one piece." Then he said, more seriously, "And I'm glad you are."

"He flew out here right away," CJ added.

Sully pointed to me. "I warned you not to take that bastard on yourself—so what the hell do you go and do?"

I looked at CJ and gave her a scolding grin.

She said, "Guilty, but you're partly to blame."

"Me?"

CJ put a hand on her hip. "It seems once again you've been holding back on some very crucial information. Doing that guarded thing. The bleeding? Good *Lord*, Pat. You want to explain why you never told me about it? And you'd better make it good."

"I didn't want you to worry?"

Her voice had a little anger in it. "I never would have let you do half those things if I'd known."

"Which is the other reason why I didn't tell you."

"They had to revive you twice," she said. "The second time you almost didn't make it."

I struggled through my memory. It was all coming back to me now, the rolling chicken fight with Bill, seeing him dead. I looked up at CJ. "It was worth it putting that bastard to the metal. I'd do it again."

She fought back a smile, and her eyes began to glisten. Then, barely above a whisper, she said, "He was going to kill me first."

I turned my gaze toward the window and nodded, squinting against the harsh sunlight. *Alive.*

Then I felt CJ's hand gently cup my chin. She turned my face toward her and looked into my eyes. Hers were full of tears.

She said, "Thank you, Patrick."

CHAPTER FIFTY-SIX

It was time to head home.

Suddenly, the thought of going back to my empty apartment didn't seem so bad anymore. I wondered why. Maybe Corvine, in some way, had managed to correct that distortion for me.

Maybe life had.

But there was still one final matter weighing heavily on my mind, and I couldn't leave until I took care of it.

I rode Highway 72 to exit 24, parked in the lot, and went inside. The woman's expression brightened as soon as I walked through the door.

"Is he still here?" I asked, worried she might say no.

She nodded. "He sure is."

"How's he doing?"

"Wonderful. Want to see him?"

I felt my smile widen. "Yeah."

She got up, then hurried toward the back.

A few moments later she was standing in the doorway, leash in hand and one big, happy-looking dog on the end of it.

I couldn't believe my eyes. He was a completely different animal. About ten healthy pounds heavier now, he had a full-bodied coat that was slick and gorgeous and an expression that told me he'd finally tasted happiness.

Like a phoenix rising from the ashes.

I was smiling so big that my ears began to hurt and then, to my surprise, felt tears fill my eyes.

He brought his gaze to mine and jutted his head forward a notch, mouth hanging open, almost as if making sure he was really seeing things right. Then his expression changed into a flash of enthusiastic recognition.

A sudden burst of energy broke him free, propelling him right toward me, slipping and sliding his way along the slick linoleum floors. He leaped up, threw his paws over my shoulders, and with furious excitement began licking my face, my ears, my neck... anything he could cover. Then he pulled back for a moment and held my gaze, watching me smile through tear-filled eyes. He gave one of those sideways tilts—the canine equivalent of a shrug—and then went back to work, licking the tears from my cheeks.

"I think he likes you," the receptionist said with a wink.

"Yeah," I said, trying to speak around his canine kisses, "who ever would have thought?"

She smiled. "Sometimes a little love is all it takes."

No truer words...

She told me the poor thing had been abused and neglected for years. The talk around town was that Flint had kept him chained to that post ever since he was a puppy. Day in, day out, nobody paying attention to his needs, physical or emotional.

All alone in this world.

"Where's he go from here?" I asked, still kneeling and running my hands through his fur.

The receptionist shrugged and frowned.

And that was the beginning: a whole new life.

For us both.

CHAPTER FIFTY-SEVEN

The mighty lion tumbled.

Warren Samuel Strademeyer, the beloved senator, was exposed for the entire world to see. A kidnapper. A murderer.

The trial lasted nearly a month, and I sat through every minute of it, listening to all the lurid details. It would have felt like some horrific movie, only it was all about me.

Warren and Jean's peculiar connection to the notorious Bill Williams was finally revealed. As it turned out, they both knew him. He also grew up in Rose Park, Georgia. While Warren and Bill were never friends growing up, he knew exactly who to call when he needed someone to carry out my kidnapping. Warren had the money, and Bill had the mind for it; they were a perfect match. I never figured out whether those horrible stories Jean had told about him were actually true, and to be honest, I didn't want to.

Flint Newsome was another one of Warren's casualties, albeit a very shady one. During my kidnapping investigation, Warren had paid him to lose the evidence—well, the boot print anyway—but he couldn't just take that; it would have seemed too obvious. So he paid Flint to take it all, hide it for a few days, then return it, minus one very important piece, of course.

Apparently, Newsome owed somebody money for a bad gambling debt and figured he could dig into Warren's deep pockets to get it. Around the same time we started investigating in Corvine, he called Warren, trying to blackmail him, saying he still had the boot print, which he'd kept in his safe all these years. He chose the wrong man. Bill was already in town, and Warren gave the go-ahead to get rid of him. Bill took the print and then Flint's life.

Camilla never had a son named Benjamin. It was Patrick, and he hadn't died when I was two. He died while she was a pregnant, unwed sixteen-year-old. Warren convinced her to abort the child, then later sold her on the idea that I could be a replacement for him.

But I couldn't, even after she gave me his name.

It took the jury only about four hours to come back with their verdicts. Kidnapping, murder for hire, obstruction of justice, and evidence tampering—guilty on all counts. No mercy from the judge, either, who gave him three consecutive life terms. The distinguished gentleman from Georgia became inmate number 23433-068 at the Federal Correctional Institution in Talladega, Alabama.

I watched as they loaded him into the van headed for prison. A horde of reporters and photographers jockeyed around me for a good position, all trying to capture the moment. Just before getting in, Warren looked up at the commotion, and our eyes met briefly. Somewhere in the unspoken conversation between us, we knew that this was really the end. Then he climbed inside and the door slammed shut.

I never saw him again.

Warren died of a massive heart attack after serving less than twelve months of his sentence. Of course, the press covered it heavily. I watched file video taken while he was in prison and barely recognized the man, saw a mere shadow of the powerful politician I'd once known. Though he'd only been there for the better part of a year, it might as well have been twenty. Bound, shackled, and shuffling along, he was at least fifteen pounds lighter, appearing disheveled, diminutive, and weak. The once-burnished silver hair had turned ashen, as had the flawless, tanned complexion. Gone, too, were the custom-tailored suits, once his hallmark, now traded for a drab prison uniform. A pathetic image if I'd ever seen one: the picture of a man who'd lost it all. A man waiting to die.

I chose to continue living as Patrick Bannister. Nathan Kingsley seemed like a fable to me, a story I'd never read. Nathan may have been the name I was born with, but Patrick was who I had become. I stuck with what I knew.

And it seemed that Patrick Bannister was destined to become an overnight celebrity...for all the wrong reasons. *Good Morning America, Dateline NBC, 48 Hours Mystery*: I appeared on all of them, but even that wasn't enough to quench the public's insatiable thirst for the unsavory. It was hard to go anywhere without flashbulbs shooting off in my face, the tabloids constantly hounding me, the attention reaching a fever pitch. For a while I spent a good part of my time hiding out. Eventually, fresh new scandals hit and the press moved on from me. I was finally able to begin my new life, assimilating it with the old—the one I'd never come to know. The real one. Nathan Kingsley never really died, and Patrick Bannister never really lived. It took me some time to come to terms with the irony that my entire life had been nothing more than a lie. Warren and his clan of misfits had robbed me of something essential, something that most people take for granted: an identity, a sense of self—and the worst part of all, just to save his lousy career. Of course, in the end it did just the opposite.

The fact that my kidnapper was also my father would be a burden I'd have to bear. I would live with that. Seeing justice served made it a little easier. Finding out that Camilla wasn't my mother, for some reason, didn't seem quite as hard—maybe because she never felt like much of one to me anyway.

I still speak to CJ often. She's now one of my closest friends, always will be. After my story broke, I gave her the exclusive rights. My wounds were still too tender, and I wasn't comfortable writing about them. But I wanted the story told fairly, and that's just what she did. The book came out a year later and shot to the top of the *New York Times* Best Sellers list, and then the awards began piling up. She moved back to Dallas, became the star reporter for the *Tribune News*, and married a coworker shortly after. She'd finally paid her dues, finally got everything she deserved, and I couldn't have been happier for her.

We met at LAX after the book went to number one; she was making her way to Hollywood for a consultation with one of the major film studios. Her book was on its way to the silver screen. So was my life.

I barely recognized her when she got off the plane.

"My God," I said, still locked in her hug, "you look amazing."

She pulled back, took me in, then shook her head with a great big smile and a tear in her eye. "You don't know how much I've missed you, Pat. You just don't know."

Then we stood there for a long time, just grinning at each other like two stupid teenagers. We couldn't help it—we'd been through so much together.

We had dinner and spent every minute of it laughing and catching up.

She put down her menu and gazed at me. "You look wonderful, Pat, you really do. I still can't figure it out—as good-looking as you are, as nice as you are, how come nobody's snagged you yet?"

"Guess I'm not snag-able."

"Nonsense," she said, waving it off with a hand.

Just then the waitress came over.

"Iced tea for me," I said, "and a Tom Collins for—"

"Actually," CJ said, placing her hand over mine, "just a soda water for me."

"Soda water?" I asked after the waitress left.

"Well, as much I love me some Tommy…I can't. But I'm sure I'll be needing one about every hour after Baby's born." Then she grinned.

I fell back in my chair, widened my eyes. "You're kidding me…"

"Nope." Bigger grin. "Can you believe it?"

"What…*when*?"

"In about seven months. We just found out."

"Oh, man, CJ…I'm so happy for you. That's wonderful."

"Well, it wasn't planned, I assure you. Guess we had a little too much fun on the honeymoon. But what the hell, right? I mean, we're doing okay financially, and we're happy. It'll all work out."

It sounded like she was asking for my assurance, so I gave it to her. "I know it will."

"But what about you?"

"What about me?"

She leaned back, crossed her arms, and deadpanned me.

"What?"

"Avoiding?" she reminded.

I looked away and grinned. This was starting to sound familiar. It was us all over again, three years ago. Just for old times' sake, I did it again: "Am I?"

She sighed. "Just answer the question, smart guy, will you? How are you doing? And I mean, *really* doing. Don't bother giving me the usual stuff you throw at other people, either. Got my BS meter turned up to high."

"I'm okay," I said. "You know. Not gonna say it's been easy."

"You'd be lying if you did…"

"But I'm making progress, I really am."

She nodded, seemed to drift away, then came back with a serious look on her face.

"What's wrong?"

She studied me for a moment before speaking, and then, "I need to show you something."

"Okay…"

She opened her purse, pulled out an envelope, and handed it over while holding my eye contact. I had a hard time reading her expression. Anxious concern...or maybe something else. Inside the envelope I found a sheet of paper—very old, yellowed by age.

As soon as I saw the first line, I knew who'd written it. I looked up at CJ. "Where did you...?"

She lifted her hand off the table and placed it on top of mine. With a sad smile, she shook her head. "Just read it."

I did. It was a letter written the day after I was kidnapped.

July 30, 1976

My dearest Nathan,

I'm writing this note, hoping it will someday find its way to you. I honestly don't know if it ever will, but at this point, hope is all I have. There's so very little else left in my life. When I lost you, I lost everything.

My dear sweet boy, if you only end up knowing one thing about me, please let it be that I love you with all my heart. You became my world the minute you entered it, and you will be my world until the day I die. I never knew I had so much love to give until you came along.

And that's why it's so important to me that you know the truth. I didn't give you up. I would never, ever do that. You were taken from me, literally ripped from my arms. I told them they'd have to kill me first, and I meant it. I fought like hell. But I was no match for them.

I tried so hard but couldn't save you. My precious boy, I failed you in the worst possible way, and it's something I live with every single day. They might as well have ripped the heart right from my chest, and in a way, I guess they did.

They say nothing is more powerful than a mother's love. So I'm hoping that somehow, in some way, you can feel my love no matter how many miles stand between us. Remember that it's always here for you, my love, whenever you need it, and it will never fail you.

You probably won't remember this, but when you were a baby I used to sing to you whenever you cried. No matter how upset you were, it always seemed to bring a smile to your face. You had the most beautiful smile. I bet you still do. Oh, what I wouldn't give to see that smile once more. How I miss it. Please think of this song whenever you're troubled and whenever love is missing from your life. May you hear it and let it fill any voids where love is lacking. Because with it comes all the love you'll ever need. From me.

Through the smiles
Through the frowns
Through life's ups and downs
Through distance, no resistance
A mother's love never fades
Never lies
Never dies

I love you, Mom

And she did. The love I'd so desperately been searching for, so desperately needed, had been there all along. I just didn't know it.

I closed my eyes and felt a tear roll down my cheek, then CJ's warm hand on mine. She kept it there for a long time but said nothing. I opened my eyes and ran my fingers gently across the words, unable to look up at her. Not yet. It was just too hard.

"She loved you, Patrick," CJ finally said.

I nodded, still staring at the note, wiping away fresh new tears.

"More than anything, she did."

I looked up at her, and through a broken voice, I said, "Where did you get this?"

A gentle smile filled with warmth. "Aurora found it going through old records."

Aurora. My guardian angel.

Something within me healed that day; a question found its answer, an empty space became filled. My world came full circle, and it felt as if my pain had finally found a place to rest—a safe one. I could go on now.

I *would* go on.

I still make my lists, although not as often as I did—at least, I don't write *danger* on bathroom walls anymore. I'm in therapy. We're making progress. I've learned that a relapse is just a relapse, and it isn't the end of the world. More than anything, though, I've found peace and have a better understanding of my obsessive-compulsive disorder. It took me a long time just to be able to say those words, to admit that they even applied to me. I'm no longer ashamed of it. I've learned that I share my pain with more than three million other people and find great comfort in that.

I know it'll take time to heal the wounds Camilla and Warren left. I also know that I'll eventually need to forgive them. I'm not there yet, but I'm working on it. My Road to Peace is a long one, but I'll get there. Besides, it can't be any worse than the road that brought me to this point.

The dreams still come, though not nearly as often as they once did and not nearly as disturbingly. The little boy is no longer there. He's gone. I now know that it was Nathan standing on that bridge. Like wings ripped from an angel, so, too, was his identity, his innocence. I'd like to think that I've set him free, set myself free, that in some way he still lives through me.

The dog and I got off to a rough start but found our happy ending together. I named him Bullet. A single gunshot brought us together, and that single gunshot forever changed our lives for the better. The receptionist gave me the actual round they removed from his shoulder; I carry it in my pocket, a reminder that no matter how bad the circumstances, you can always rise from the ashes. Not that I really needed it: he and I are living, breathing proof.

He's my best friend, and I love him dearly. Sometimes while we're napping on the couch, his head tucked comfortably under my arm, he'll suddenly awaken in the midst of what appears to be a bad dream. When he looks up at me, his fearful, restless gaze gives way to one of those priceless canine expressions that no words could ever communicate. He licks my face, tucks his head back under my arm, then goes quietly off to sleep again, thankful we're together.

Me too, buddy, me too.

ACKNOWLEDGMENTS

When I sat down to work on my first book, *While the Savage Sleeps*, the biggest question on my mind was whether I could write a novel. It turned out I could, and thanks to you, my amazing readers, it exceeded all expectations. So this time around, the question seemed to have changed; now I found myself wondering if I could write a *better* novel.

It's my nature to want to improve, stretch, and grow with each new experience, but for some reason this seemed different. I didn't just owe it to myself—I owed it to you, my readers. After all, you were the ones who made the first book a success, lent your unwavering support and enthusiasm, and anxiously awaited the release of this one. Simply put, without you, I wouldn't have a career as an author. I don't take that relationship lightly, nor do I ever lose sight of how important you are to me. To offer you anything less than my absolute best is something I could never consider.

And so it began: an irresistible concept, a fascinating main character, and a blank screen. Add some sweat and tears, some twists and turns, and the final product was a complex psychological thriller called *The Lion, the Lamb, the Hunted*. Did I write a better book? I'd like to think so, and if emotional investment is any indication, then I'm pretty confident I did.

It's funny where a novel can take an author, in both the figurative and the literal sense. Admittedly, I'm a seeker; I love finding out things, and in the course of writing this book I found out a lot. I also found myself, once again, entering into worlds I never would have otherwise explored. Of course, that meant having to bug *a lot* of people for information, but, as has always been the case, I was fortunate enough to meet people who were gracious and beyond helpful at every turn; to those individuals, I send my warmest and most sincere thanks. One side note, by the way: any inaccuracies in this book are my own, and I take full responsibility. In addition to the experts, I also offer thanks to the many others who gave their love, support, and good wishes as I struggled to write this novel. The words on these pages would not have been the same without the people who gave of themselves.

To Kelley Eskridge at Sterling Editing, a big thanks, not only for being a ridiculously talented editor, but also for being a genuinely sincere and kind person. She catered to my every neurosis throughout this process, sometimes humoring me, sometimes encouraging me, and quite often sharing her depth of knowledge about writing, something for which we both share a profound passion. She made sure every word in this novel counted and helped make this book everything I wanted it to be. I have enormous respect for the people who do this often-thankless work because I also know how difficult it can be. To do it with constant enthusiasm and good cheer can't be easy, yet that's just what she did.

To Patty G. Henderson at Boulevard Photografica for her amazing cover design and assistance with the interior design for the paperback version of this novel. She never fails to amaze me with what she comes up with—not only that, but she does it all with enthusiasm, excitement, and talent that blows me away every time.

On the technical side, thanks to Dana Lerner, LCSW, who was instrumental in helping me develop the many complex facets of Patrick's character and personal struggles. With her knowledge, I was able to breathe life into him. Also of great help on this front was Dr. Byron Egeland from the Institute of Child Development at the University of Minnesota, who helped me gain a deeper understanding of child abuse and its devastating effects. He generously offered his knowledge so that I could portray Patrick's tragic past and current battles in a realistic, meaningful way.

My sincere appreciation to Jeff Bell at the International OCD Foundation and Dr. Jonathan Abramowitz, professor and associate chair of psychology at the University of North Carolina at Chapel Hill. Their insight on obsessive-compulsive disorder was, without question, vital to this novel. I wanted to present the issue in a compassionate, moving, and informative manner, and they helped me do it. I came away not only with new knowledge about OCD, but also with new respect for the people who suffer from this debilitating and challenging disorder. I hope I did them justice by portraying it through Patrick Bannister.

Thanks to Lori Boggs of Oregon State Hospital for sharing her professional experiences and giving me the details I needed to write the Glenview chapters. I wanted to give the reader a visceral sense of what this environment is like, and she helped me achieve that goal.

On the legal front, Barbara Smith, attorney at law, shared her knowledge about the death penalty and all things legal and helped me map out Ronald Lucas's story of injustice. We bounced a lot of ideas back and forth, and she let me know which would fly and which wouldn't. With her guidance, I was finally able to come up with a story that worked.

To Marty Weiner of Atlantic Veal and Matthew Leone—thanks for helping me understand the inner workings of a meat-packing plant. Staging the book's climax there was a challenge—mapping out an action-packed, meat hook–suspended, rolling chicken fight, even more so. But with their help I was able to pull it off—or at least I hope so.

A very special thanks to my good friend Linda Boulanger at TreasureLine Books & Publishing for her unfailing professional and personal support. Even though she was busy running a publishing business along with a demanding and heavily populated household, she never once wavered as a friend and professional comrade. There aren't enough pages here to list all the times she stepped up to the plate for me (including her beautiful work formatting both the e-book and the paperback interior), but it never went unnoticed or unappreciated. You just don't find friends like her very often, and I'm beyond thankful and pleased to call her one of mine.

To my team of beta-/proofreaders (in no specific order): Diane Harrison, Barbara Richards, Jenny Hilborne, Linda Boulanger, Jaimey Grant, Peg Brantley, Kyle Myer, Deanna Rickrode, Chris Janzen, Gayla Catrett, and Jodie Renner: you don't know how much I value your input and the time you spent reading my earlier drafts so I could make this book shine. Having those eleven extra pairs of eyes was a crucial part of this process.

To my good friend Barbara Richards, who has always been there for me throughout the years. It's great having someone to lean on when life gets a little wobbly, and she never hesitated to step in and offer a dose of stability whenever needed; it wasn't always easy, but it was always genuine, always greatly appreciated. To Kyle Myer for his thoughtful insight, advice, and guidance, which he offered with generosity and sincerity. To Kay, Paul, and Deanna Rickrode for looking after me and treating me as one of their own.

Much love to my mother, who I know is smiling down on me from up above, and to my dad, who's got my back here on Earth.

And finally, to my readers: I am in awe of you. In this day when the publishing industry changes by the minute and when the reading choices multiply almost as quickly, I'm amazed and thrilled beyond measure that you choose to read my work. All I've ever wanted was to tell my stories, and you've given me a place to do it. There are no words to express what that means to me. How I got so lucky, I have no idea, but I'm thankful for it and humbled by it more than you can know. It's for those reasons and many more that I dedicate this book to you.

I

Dead bolts.

Steel bars.

Metal slamming against metal.

This is my unyielding world, where I mend ruptured minds and fuse cognitive wires. A world that—if emotions were physical—would be a tangled mess of hooks and thorns.

But it's not just the sights and sounds: it's the smell, a musty hybrid of human waste and perspiration. Even the steel has a fug all its own, a mineral tang seasoned by rust and time.

The stench of insanity.

How long have I been here? Six years? Eight?

Sometimes it's hard to remember, and sometimes I forget who's serving time.

"Welcome to the jungle, gentlemen," my boss says, brittle shades of cynicism coloring his words. Jeremy Firestone's sentiment is not unwarranted, but it's hardly necessary. Calling Loveland Psychiatric Hospital a jungle is at best an optimist's euphemism, much like calling hell a tropical destination. And right now we are moving deeper into its cavernous underbelly, a subsurface passageway that dead-ends at a high-security plaster box called Alpha Twelve. Home to the worst of the worst.

The killers.

The rapists.

The dark souls with an incurable addiction to evil.

Dr. Adam Wiley and I exchange vigilant glances. Neither of us knows the purpose of this trip. I steal a glimpse at Jeremy, his steps determined, his gaze aimed ahead, his expression set. On a normal day, our boss is the consummate image of emotional economy, but on this day, reading his face is like studying the side of a concrete slab.

We hit Security Checkpoint One, a gateway that leads to the long corridor, which will take us into Alpha Twelve. The guard spares us a prudent nod, punches a button, and the buzzer goes off. A yellow light flashes once, flashes twice, then turns to green. The gate slides open, and we enter; its bars slam behind us, letting out a thunderous *crack* that cuts the air and ping-pongs ahead through formless shadows.

Something hard and icy pushes through me.

This place is so cold.

But I wonder if my perception is driven more by emotion than climate, whether this hole in the ground is cheating my senses and blowing a chill through my mind.

I try to chase the thought away with a deep breath, but my only payoff is a double shot of noxious-nasty that fills my lungs. I force the air out and with my gaze set ahead, keep walking.

It would be fair to say that Loveland is by no means a modern or up-to-date facility. Calling our setup archaic would be a compliment. Three years ago, Arizona officials agreed. They stepped in and slapped us with numerous building code citations. Once we were on their radar, allegations of human rights violations went flying. Feeling the heat, our board acted quickly, and plans were soon under way for a new building and a complete program overhaul. But it will be years before everything is up and running. In the meantime, we make do with what we've got, watch our Ps and Qs, and keep guardedly mindful that we're under a microscope.

"So, Chris, how's that beautiful boy of yours doing?" Adam asks. An obvious attempt to cut through the tension, but I appreciate it.

"Growing too damned fast," I say.

"And the more-than-beautiful wife?"

"More beautiful than ev—"

"Gentlemen." Jeremy interrupts our small talk, his voice booming louder as we round the next corner. "There's a new patient at Loveland."

Neither Adam nor I respond. Our boss didn't bring us all this way just for that.

"And I can't stress enough how important this case is," he continues. "It's one of the biggest we've ever had. Needless to say, we have to get this right."

Adam raises a brow. "And the mystery patient would be . . ."

Jeremy's gaze drops to the floor, and for the first time, I see worry break through his stoic demeanor—worry that pulls us closer toward Alpha Twelve.

"Donny Ray Smith. He's been transferred from the Miller Institute in Northern Arizona."

"The reason?"

"A court-ordered eval. His lawyers are going for the insanity defense."

"How come Miller sent him to us?"

"*Miller* didn't—the judge did. The institute had an internal shake-up just as their review of Smith was near completion. A neuropsychologist working the case is about to get her license yanked. When the DA found out, he put in a request for reevaluation."

"He got nervous," I say.

"Very nervous. This story's been all over the news up there. Another reason why we must proceed flawlessly. With everything that's been happening around here—"

"We don't need more negative publicity."

"Exactly," Jeremy agrees. "Incidentally, because of all the delays, the judge has us on a tight turnaround."

"How tight?" I ask.

"Your evaluations are due in a week. Until then, I'll be clearing your caseloads."

"Did the folks at Miller reach any decisions before trouble broke out?" Adam asks.

"The psychologist's findings were inconclusive, but the neurologist begged to differ. He concluded that Smith is memory malingering."

My gaze sharpens on the doors leading into Alpha Twelve. "What's his crime?"

"How many would you like?"

"I'd like as many as you've got."

"Murder." Jeremy nods once. "So many young girls, you can count them on two hands. Unfortunately, so far they've only been able to nail him on the last, a six-year-old."

The same age as Devon.

Jeremy eighty-sixes my thought. "That crime will be your primary focus. As the case widens, more charges will likely come down the pike. For now, since Smith's involvement in them is as yet unproven, the information on those cases is for background purposes only. The judge wanted to make this very clear. That said, because the last victim was under the age of fifteen—and multiple murder charges may eventually come into play—this could end up being a death penalty case. So it would be wise to keep in mind the impact of your diagnoses."

"Ten kids? And they couldn't get him until now? How does that even happen?"

He stops to look at me. "It happens when you can't find the bodies."

"Including the last."

"Including the last, yes."

Adam shoves his hands in his pockets and observes Jeremy. "So how come he's being held down in Alpha?"

"It's taken three years to get him into custody, and the DA's not about to take any chances. He requested that Smith be placed within a maximum-security setup. Naturally, we agreed to accommodate."

"Suicide watch?"

"You bet."

We reach Alpha Twelve. Jeremy swipes his card through a scanner slot. The door responds with a sharp, motorized *click*; when it opens, sounds roar out. The kind that can penetrate marrow, the kind that few people—if they're lucky—ever have to hear. Ululating, wordless lamentations. Shrill cries of base terror. Cackling, eerie laughter from men who would not only rather murder you than look at you but also do it in the most heinous and barbaric ways their depraved minds can imagine.

We step out onto the floor. A row of doors faces us on both sides, each punctuated by a steel-gridded window. I see fingers and faces, all eyes aimed directly at us. I see expressions that run the gamut from glazed to goofy, maniacal to menacing, and the rest Just Plain Mad.

"Hurry up!" An urgent whisper sounds from behind me. I turn my head and find Stanley Winters staring at me with pleading distress.

"What the hell are you waiting for?" he asks. "Time is running out!"

I look at him calmly.

"This place is broken!" His voice ramps with frenetic urgency, his body jouncing up and down. "We have to get out of here!"

Stanley tied his wife and three kids to their beds, then set them on fire and watched while they burned to death. He isn't going anywhere. Ever.

"Hey, pretty, pretty . . ."

I swing the other way and lock onto a pair of hungry eyes, a predatory smile dangling just beneath them. On closer examination, I realize the eyes are growing wide as saucers and keenly focused on my forearm, the predatory smile evolving into a shit-eating grin.

"Gorgeous and lovely," the mouth says, nearly salivating. "Gorgeous and lovely."

Adam is now watching, too.

"Gerald Markman," I inform him under my breath.

Adam, a neurologist, works on the medical side of things. He studies imaging tests, lab work, and other diagnostic data, so most of his encounters occur in examining rooms. He rarely makes it down here, but as a psychologist, I often visit Alpha Twelve to observe my patients in their surroundings.

"You know about Gerald, no doubt," Jeremy jumps in, apparently overhearing us.

Adam nods. "Just never had the pleasure of meeting him face-to-face."

"The *pleasure* would be his."

No lie. I've treated Gerald, and he's arguably the most dangerous patient to ever set foot inside Loveland. One of only three serial killers in history to have successfully used the insanity plea, he murdered seventeen people that authorities know of. The news media nicknamed him The Husker—a moniker he earned because killing his victims wasn't enough. Gerald also degloved them, separating their skin from flesh with near-surgical precision. According to detectives, walking into his house was like pulling back the curtain on a grisly horror show. The place was chock-full of biological mementos that included a "mammary vest" fashioned from a woman's torso, a belt adorned with nipples, and Mason jars with preserved human vulvas. When they asked what he'd done with the remains of one particular victim, Gerald Markman smiled broadly and pointed to his shoes.

Everyone at Loveland knows that if you catch Gerald staring, it can mean only one thing: he wants to skin you and wear you.

He's still looking at my arm.

"Back it up, Gerald," Jeremy warns.

Gerald returns a lazy, apathetic I-just-wanted-to-play shrug. I bet he did.

I shift my attention away, but where it lands offers no deliverance. There's a guy standing toward the back of his room. I know this because, through the window, I can see his head. Not the one on his shoulders—the other one.

"Put it away. Right now," Jeremy scolds.

The patient walks to his window, and I realize it's Nicholas Hartley, revealing his rawboned face and a trembling mouth not indicative of fear.

All up and down the hall, more screams, more laughter, more indeterminate noise.

"An interesting group of patients here," Jeremy comments with a single, downward nod.

"I'm mostly concerned about the one at the end of this trip," I say.

Jeremy holds silent.

"Come on," Adam says, "help us out here. What exactly are we walking into?"

"I'd prefer to let you decide."

A response equivalent to nothing.

We proceed to the end of Alpha Twelve's barrel-vaulted hallway, where an antiquated fixture hangs by a dusty chain, throwing dingy light against the last door on the left. Evan McKinley, one of Loveland's uniformed police officers, stands guard out front. Members of the security staff are normally charged with keeping watch over our more challenging patients, but seeing Evan here underscores the importance of this case: the hospital isn't leaving anything to risk.

A nerve-shattering scream goes off inside the room.

McKinley and I lock gazes, and from his, I get the message: *You've got a live one in there.*

Adam looks at the door. "But we haven't even had a chance to see the patient's files yet."

"You'll get full access to them," Jeremy says. "For now, I've provided most of what you'll need."

"And the rest?"

A guttural yowl, then the sound of rapid-fire chain rattling. Then a bed skidding and squealing along the floor, followed by more screams.

"It's all waiting for you in there," Jeremy says.

He turns and walks away.

2

Evan McKinley peers through the window and into the room, then flashes what might be a mild smirk . . . or maybe I'm just imagining it. He takes a key ring from his uniform belt, unlocks the door, and motions for us to enter.

The moment we step inside, my focus locks onto Donny Ray Smith, but I'm still not quite sure what I'm seeing. I was expecting a monster; instead, this guy looks like he was sent here by Central Casting rather than by another psychiatric hospital. It would appear he wandered onto the wrong set, though, because our new patient in no way fits the role of a serial killer. Striking is the word of the day, and he owns it. With his well-defined physique, jet-black hair, and sculpted jawline, Donny Ray Smith could have leaped from the page of an Abercrombie ad.

A child killer? He's nothing more than a kid himself.

Barely into his twenties, is my guess.

Lying in bed, Donny Ray blinks a few times, then looks down at himself to examine the Posey Net that covers his entire body. Arms, neck, and legs pulled through the openings. Ankles and wrists secured with loop straps. He's sweating, trembling with fear.

Refusing to look at us.

Adam says nothing, but I instantly sense he isn't buying into Donny Ray's fright—not that I am, either. Experience has taught me that psychopaths are quick-change artists who can conform to any shape imaginable. I don't yet know if that's what we're dealing with here, but I'm mindful of the possibility.

Adam and I step forward, and Donny Ray lurches back against the bed, hands clenching the guardrails, biceps flexing, breaths speeding. His restraints clatter; perspiration slides from sodden bangs down the bridge of his nose.

"Why am I being restrained?" he shouts through pallid lips, and I hear his thick southern drawl.

"You've been deemed a danger to yourself and others," I explain.

Donny Ray releases an angry howl and tries to jerk himself free; the bed rattles, squeaks, and shimmies. Recognizing his efforts as futile, he lets out a tiny, helpless moan.

"You're the behavioral guy," Adam mutters to me. "Have at it."

"It's okay," I tell Donny Ray Smith, keeping my body still and my voice level. "Nobody's here to cause you any harm."

A low and inarticulate plea escapes through chattering teeth.

I wait in silence and watch him, my passivity allowing an opportunity for trust. A few moments later, his breath slows and his jaw relaxes, but he still refuses to look at us.

I study him for a few seconds longer, then move closer. Donny Ray reacts instantly, shooting his terrified gaze directly at me, and now I'm the one who's startled. But not by his reaction—it's his eyes, blue, bright, but nearly colorless, perhaps the palest I've ever seen.

Wait a minute.

Because . . .

I know those eyes.

Or do I? I'm not sure. For the life of me, I can't place them. I examine his other features, but . . . I've got nothing, and now I'm more unsettled because this isn't a face I'd soon forget.

And right now, that's not important.

So I try to banish my speculations; but my suspicions may not be unfounded because now Donny Ray Smith is also searching my eyes in a manner that suggests recognition mixed with curious confusion. I study his other features.

A former patient, maybe?

"I'm Dr. Kellan," I move on, still scrutinizing his face as I motion Adam forward, "and this is Dr. Wiley. We'll be working together. I'm a psychologist and he's a neurol—"

"You have to take me out of here!" Donny Ray blurts, those eyes now ablaze and begging.

"I need you to try and calm down," I say. "Do you think you can do that for me?"

A slow nod. A vulnerable expression.

Adam's phone rings, and Donny Ray immediately jerks back. I raise a hand of assurance.

He settles.

"Sorry," Adam says. He checks the screen, silences his phone, then with a nod, encourages me to continue.

Still mindful of my new patient's overall appearance, I say, "I need to ask you a few questions."

Donny Ray is compliant but fearful.

"Do you know where we are?"

"We're at Loveland."

"Do you understand why you're here?"

"Please!" he shouts. "Help me!"

"We're going to find the truth. Whether that helps you or not remains to be seen. Are you able to tell me your name?"

"But you already know all this! What does it have to do with—?"

"I need your name," I say, this time as a firm mandate.

"Yeah . . ." he surrenders. "Okay. It's Donny Ray Smith."

"What's your date of birth?"

"December fourteenth, nineteen ninety-two."

"Can you tell me where you were born?"

"Real, Texas. Why are you doing this to me?"

I circle back to the question he failed to answer. "Do you understand why you're here?"

Donny Ray looks down at his bound hands, looks up, and his expression is markedly changed—something like nervous confusion diluted by distress. "I think . . . I mean . . . I just don't know anymore. They said . . ." His voice falters. "They say I killed that little girl."

Careful to keep my manner nonreactive, I ask, "And did you?"

"They told me they found evidence, you know? Things you can't fake. Like DNA and all that stuff, but as many times as I've turned things around in my head, I can't make sense of them. And then I keep forgetting things, and everything around me doesn't fit, and that just makes it worse . . ."

"Forgetting things," I repeat, because what he describes could hint at some kind of dissociative disorder.

Donny Ray closes his eyes for a moment, opens them. "Like I don't know where I've been for a while."

Tears start as he shakes his head. "Sir, I swear to you—on the Holy Bible—on my own life, even—I never saw that girl before. I mean . . . how do you kill someone you've never met? How can that happen?"

I offer no answer, because I've got none, and because I'm intrigued. Everything I've seen and heard so far rings genuine: his facial expressions, his response times, his vocal intonations and speech pattern. No cues of duplicity. Even his pupils, a clear and clinically proven indicator of tension and concentration, remain dilated.

But a psychopath can achieve all of this, so as a rechecking strategy, I relax my stance, then wait to see whether his presentation changes.

It does not. No loosening of muscles to indicate relief, no altered breathing pattern, no verifiable sign whatsoever of malingering.

There's only about a fifty percent accuracy rate in the study of micro-expressions and body language as indicators of deception, and if I'm indeed dealing with a pathological liar, that would reduce the reliability quotient to zero. It appears as though authorities have compelling enough evidence to prove that Donny Ray killed the girl. If they are right, the only question remaining is whether he remembers doing it. At least one person from Miller seems to think he does. As for me, I'm not yet sure. I can usually reach some level of intuitive deduction after meeting a patient for the first time, but this one has my needle stuck at the midway point. I'm not necessarily convinced he's being truthful—I'm not able to say he isn't, either.

But I don't need definitive answers right now. This is only a preliminary data mining effort, and there will be more opportunities to dig deeper.

Adam's cell vibrates in his pocket. He pulls it out, checks the screen again, then says to me, "I'm really sorry, but I've got to take this one. Go ahead and finish here. We'll catch up later?"

I nod, and he exits the room.

I turn back to Donny Ray. He looks at me with a begging expression, and I still can't shake the feeling we've met somewhere.

But for now, my work here is done, so I tell him, "I'll be back to see you tomorrow."

He's still staring at me. It feels awkward and strange.

Halfway to the door, I hear, "Christopher?"

I reel around, lock onto those eyes.

Where the hell have I seen those eyes?

"Do you think you can help me?" he asks.

"We're going to find the truth," I remind him.

"Maybe we can both find it."

I linger, appraising him from head to toe, and then, "I'm just curious. When I introduced myself earlier, I only gave my last name. How do you know my first?"

"I heard Dr. Wiley call you that."

I nod, then leave.

But as I move down the corridor, a sudden and jarring realization pulls me to a halt, a chill spiking up my spine.

I can't recall Adam saying my first name. We're best friends and colleagues, but he would never address me that way in front of a patient.

And he never calls me Christopher.

This patient knows me.

ABOUT THE AUTHOR

Photo by Thomas Photography, 2012

Andrew E. Kaufman lives in Southern California, along with his Labrador Retrievers, two horses, and a very bossy Jack Russell Terrier who thinks she owns the place.

His debut novel, *While the Savage Sleeps*, a forensic paranormal thriller, broke out on four of Amazon's bestsellers lists, taking the #1 spot on two of them and third place on the much-coveted. Movers and Shakers list. It also dominated six of their Top-Rated lists. His next novel, *The Lion, the Lamb, the Hunted* was on Amazon's Top 100 for more than one hundred days becoming their seventh bestselling title out of more than one million e-books available nationwide and number one in its genre. Andrew was also a writer for, *Chicken Soup for the Soul: The Cancer Book* (Simon & Schuster/2009), where he chronicled his battle with the disease.

His newest novel, *Darkness and Shadows*, is due out in 2013.

After receiving his journalism and political science degrees at San Diego State University, Andrew began his writing career as an Emmy-nominated writer/producer, working at the CBS affiliate in San Diego, then in Los Angeles. For more than ten years, he produced special series and covered many nationally known cases, including the O.J. Simpson Trial.

For more on Andrew and his work, please visit his website at: http://www.andrewekaufman.com